"Flannery runs in the same fast, high-tech track as Clancy and his gung-ho colleagues, with lots of war games, fancy weapons, and much male bonding."
—*New York Daily News*

"Clancy and Cussler need to look over their shoulders."
—*Library Journal*

"Flannery weaves an ever more striking tapestry . . . authoritative . . . taut and well constructed."
—*Publishers Weekly* on *Without Honor*

"*High Flight* ends the twentieth century with a bang, Russia versus Japan, with the U.S. caught in the middle. Perhaps it's time. There's a lot of techno and a lot of thrills in *High Flight*. Better strap in and hang on when you go for this ride."
—Stephen Coonts

"A maven of mach speed mayhem, intricately moves [the] pieces around his global chessboard, until many bodies, plane crashes, and a running sea battle later, action hero McGarvey wipes out the bad guys."
—*Booklist*

EAGLES FLY

Sean Flannery

A TOM DOHERTY ASSOCIATES BOOK
NEW YORK

This is a work of fiction. All the characters and events portrayed in this book are fictitious, and any resemblance to real people or events is purely coincidental.

EAGLES FLY

Copyright © 1980 by David Hagberg

A Forge Book
Published by Tom Doherty Associates, Inc.
175 Fifth Avenue
New York, NY 10010

Forge® is a registered trademark of Tom Doherty Associates, Inc.

ISBN: 0-812-53889-7

First Forge edition: September 1998

Printed in the United States of America

0 9 8 7 6 5 4 3 2 1

This book is for Todd and Tammy Kraus with the hope that all of their sunrises are as happy as mine.

PREFACE

The *Organisation der ehemaligen SS Angehörigen,* the organization of former members of the SS—Odessa for short—exists, and do not let anyone tell you differently.

Its avowed purpose is twofold: first to protect its own from prosecution, especially by Zionists; and second to somehow bring about the second dawning of the Third Reich.

Its membership is composed of former officers and enlisted men of the SS, as well as the children of those people.

Almost every country in the world has a few citizens who are Odessa members.

For the most part they seem ordinary people. Your next-door neighbor, perhaps. But no matter their circumstances, all of them subscribe to a higher belief: racial purity, unity, stability, and world peace administered by the German people.

To those ends, and for their avowed purposes, the Odessa will stop at nothing . . . literally nothing.

The Beginning
1979

Buenos Aires smelled of the summer sea. It was night, and a heavy fog rolled in from the Rio de la Plata Estuary over the municipal airport, blanketing the Third of February Park, covering Villa Crespo, and like some malevolent beast, oozed across the Federal District as far as Ezezia International Airport.

Many of the four million inhabitants of the great city slept. Some worked the night shift in factories, some were late party revelers, and a few were insomniacs. It was a Friday.

In other places in the city sleepy policemen in patrol cars crawled along the wide boulevards deserted not only because of the hour, but because of the heavy fog.

The shops were closed; the government house, Casa Rosado, on the Plaza del Congreso faced the national capital, Palacio del Congreso, in mute beauty, the buildings lit by spotlights dulled in the fog.

There was no one to see the short, dark, intense little man

park his Opel Rekord sedan one block away from the German Hospital in the Missiones Province just outside the Federal District. No one saw him peering through the fog to make sure he had not been followed, and no one noticed him hunch up his coat collar against the mist, and with hands stuffed deeply into his pockets, walk silently on rubber-soled shoes toward the hospital.

Since the late 1800s there had been a slow but steadily increasing exodus of Germans to the city. Before World War I and again during the depression that followed, the population of the Missiones Province increased sharply. These people who came to Argentina from the old country were mostly ordinary souls. Watchmakers, carpenters, bricklayers, farmers, merchants. Men with families who wanted a future in a new country. People for whom Germany no longer offered what they wanted.

Beginning as early as 1944, and lasting until as late as 1950, German immigrants of a different sort came to Buenos Aires. For the most part they were men who were wealthy, men who wanted to escape their Nazi past, especially the war trials and witch-hunt at Nuremberg. For them Argentina, which had been a pro-Axis country, was a safe haven.

It was these men who made the Missiones Province a wealthy district, almost exclusively German. And it was these men who had constructed the Missiones Hospital, whose patients and staff were almost exclusively German.

The dark man stopped in the shadows of a gift shop across a narrow street from the hospital, the hairs on the nape of his neck rising, his skin prickling. His fists clenched and unclenched in his coat pockets, but he held himself in check against the anger that threatened to blot out all reason and sanity.

He hated Buenos Aires and its people, although he and his wife and two children had lived here for eighteen months, operating a travel bureau downtown. He could not get used to the reversed seasons, he disliked the strange customs, and most of all he hated the Argentinians because of their pro-Axis stand during the war and their continued love affair with the Germans.

But the little man hated Germans more than anything. He hated what they had been, what they still were, and what they could become if they were left alone.

He slipped around the corner of the gift shop and hurried down the side street, keeping to the shadows as much as possible. At a point opposite the rear of the hospital building he crossed the narrow street and, making sure no one was coming, quickly climbed over a low stone fence. Crouching low, his heart pounding he worked his way along a line of shrubbery to the nurses' entrance, where he hesitated just outside the circle of illumination from a light over the door.

It was shortly after two in the morning, so all the shift changes had been completed, and the staff would be busy on its rounds. He had been assured there would be no one in the staff lounge or in the lower corridor. The thought of what he was about to do sickened him, but he knew it was necessary. Too much had gone on during the past three months to let this opportunity pass.

He patted his breast pocket, assuring himself that he still had the miniature tape recorder and the hypodermic syringe loaded with sodium Pentothal, took a deep breath, and silently entered the hospital.

A wide corridor ran to the front of the building. To the right was the staff lounge, to the left the rear stairwell. Soft music came from speakers set flush in the ceiling. The smell of disinfectant permeated the air. No one was in sight. The hospital seemed deserted.

The dark man started up the stairs, sweat forming on his upper lip.

He had been nothing but a watcher these past eighteen months. Because of his travel bureau, he had made contacts with all the major airlines at Ezezia and so knew the comings and goings of most foreigners to Buenos Aires.

Three months ago a man by the name of Ronald de Hoef, who was president of the All-America Insurance Corporation in Miami, Florida, arrived in Buenos Aires. He was identified as a possible former SS officer and probable member of Odessa.

There was no proof of that, of course; there never was. Which was why the American Department of Immigration had never made a move against him.

The dark man stopped at the third-floor landing, cautiously approached the steel door that led to the ward, and peered through the small glass window. Two nurses, their backs to the door, stood at the ward station talking. The dark man backed away from the window and leaned against the wall.

The day after de Hoef arrived in Buenos Aires, a man identified as Thomas Heinzman showed up. He was the assistant administrative director of the Georgetown University Hospital in Washington, D.C. He too was a probable former SS officer.

Over the next week seven more men who were thought to be SS officers and Odessa leaders showed up, and the dark man had made his reports. In each case the men were met at the airport by a chauffeur-driven limousine, and in each case none of them were seen until one week ago when all of them but one left Argentina the same way they had come: by commercial airliner, each accompanied by several husky men who were in all likelihood personal bodyguards.

The dark man peered through the window again. The ward station was deserted. His heart hammered. He'd not been trained for this sort of thing. At home he had been a minor government clerk. He had done his stint in the Army, as had his wife, and he wanted only to settle down and raise his family.

He hesitated a moment longer at the door and once again

nervously checked to make sure he still had the hypodermic syringe and tape recorder in his breast pocket.

Two days ago the man who had remained in Argentina had been admitted to this hospital. He was Albert Spanndig. Seventy-two years old. Retired in Lisbon, Portugal, from a highly successful fertilizer manufacturing company. He was probably an SS *Oberst* by the name of Albert Spannau who had worked in the Abwehr directly under Admiral Canaris during the war.

This afternoon a package had been delivered by messenger to the travel bureau containing the miniature tape recorder and the hypodermic syringe with instructions for its use. There were orders to enter the hospital, inject Spanndig, and question the old man about why the Odessa's top leadership had come to Buenos Aires.

The dark man had discussed his orders with his wife. Neither of them could understand why they were not getting help on this.

"The Odessa meeting was important," he said. "So why didn't they send a professional to break it up—or find out what was going on?"

But orders were orders. In six months he could return home and bring some semblance of order and sanity back into his life.

He checked the window again, and carefully opened the door. Making no noise, he hurried past the ward station and at the last door he stopped to listen. There were no noises from within, so he gently pushed open the door and slipped into the room.

The emaciated figure of a frail old man lay huddled beneath a sheet on the bed. He was surrounded by several pieces of equipment connected by wires and tubes to his nose, arms, and chest. The only light in the room came from the bulbs on the equipment, and from an oscilloscope screen over the bed across which a green trace monitored Spanndig's feeble heart.

For a brief moment the dark man's anger was replaced by pity for the dying man. But he thought of what Spanndig had done with his life, and what he represented, and the anger returned.

He went to the bedside, took the tape recorder out of his pocket, switched it to record, and laid it on the pillow next to Spanndig's head. The old man's breath came in ragged gasps. There was a powerful odor of age and death from him.

Next, the dark man withdrew the hypodermic syringe from its case, checked to make sure there was no air in the needle, then pulled the intravenous tube from the needle in the old man's arm.

Spanndig jerked on the bed, and his eyes opened as the dark man plunged the hypodermic directly into the intravenous needle taped to the old man's arm, and pushed the plunger.

Spanndig tried to cry out, but his head fell back on the pillow, and his eyes glazed over.

"Spannau," the man whispered. "I need your help, Spannau. The Fuehrer needs your help, Spannau."

The old man mumbled something indistinct.

"Where did you meet, Spannau?"

Again the old man mumbled something.

The man and his wife were the only ones stationed in Buenos Aires, so despite the fact that nine suspected Odessa members had shown up, he had not been able to follow them.

He pushed harder on the plunger, sending even more sodium Pentothal into Spanndig's bloodstream.

"The Fuehrer sends his greetings, Spannau, but he must know where you held your meeting."

"Aerie," Spanndig mumbled.

The dark man leaned closer. "Where is that?"

"Aerie," Spanndig mumbled again, spittle drooling from the corners of his mouth.

"What is the plan, Spannau? The Fuehrer must know what you have planned."

"We have found the man," Spanndig mumbled with obvious difficulty. "At long last . . . two more years . . . the man . . ." The old man suddenly went rigid, his mouth opened wide as if to scream, but then he slumped back on the bed. Above his head the heart monitor showed a straight line. He was dead.

The dark man's eyes jerked up to the monitor and then to the door. Someone would be coming. There was no time left.

He withdrew the syringe and with shaking hands replaced the intravenous tube, grabbed the tape recorder, and went to the door just as it slammed open.

Framed in the light from the corridors, one of the nurses stood in the doorway. She started to cry out, but the man slammed his fist into her face and she went down, her head bouncing off the floor.

He jumped over her body and raced down the corridor toward the stairwell door as the other nurse came in a run from the opposite direction.

"Stop!" the nurse screamed, but the man flung open the door and took the stairs down three at a time, his heart hammering.

Spanndig had talked. He had not said much, but it was something. The tape would have to be saved at all costs.

Six steps from the ground floor the man lost his footing and pitched forward. A metal-edged tread smashed into his forehead, and in the next instant his left arm was beneath him, breaking with a sharp snap. Pain raged through his body like nothing he had ever felt.

He was conscious of someone shouting and of footsteps on the stairs above him as he dragged himself to his feet. Everything swam before him, and blood running into his eyes from a large gash in his head made it nearly impossible to see.

He somehow made his way to the rear door. Outside he half ran, half stumbled into the line of thick bushes that led to the low stone fence.

Someone shouted from behind him, and from the front of the hospital he could hear a car start and race off with squealing tires.

He was making too much noise. He knew it. Very soon they would have him, unless he could make it over the stone wall and somehow get back to his car.

A vision of Spanndig's emaciated body and cadaverous face swam before his eyes, and the bile rose from his stomach, gagging him. He had not wanted to do it. He had not wanted the assignment, but it had been given to him in such a way that he could not refuse.

And now what?

A light swept the bushes behind him, and he dropped to his knees, the sudden jar sending waves of pain from his arm throughout his entire body.

The tape. His mind locked on that one thing. At all costs it would have to be saved.

With his right hand he fumbled with the tiny front cover of the miniature recorder until he managed to get it open. When he pushed the eject button, the tape spool, no larger than a small sewing thimble, popped up. He ripped it out of the machine and put it in his mouth. He clawed at the dirt beneath one of the bushes, managing to dig a small hole. He pushed the tape recorder and the hypodermic syringe into the hole, covered them with dirt, then crawled as fast as he could to the stone wall.

A man shouted to his left, and a moment later the beam of a flashlight swept the stone wall over his head.

He leaped up and, using his right arm as a lever, managed to slip over the wall.

There were more shouts from behind him now. The dark man picked himself up and stumbled out into the narrow street in time to hear the engine of a large car. Headlights bore down on him.

He tried to make it out of the way, but at the last moment he knew he was a dead man, and he swallowed involuntarily, forcing the tape down his throat.

PART ONE

1

As Albert Spannau, alias Albert Spanndig, lay dying in Buenos Aires, a Boeing 747 from New York City touched down at Frankfurt's Rhein-Main Airport with a sharp bark of its tires, followed by the roar of reversing jets. At the end of the long runway the giant plane slowed, turned, and majestically taxied to the Pan Am gate at the modern steel and glass terminal building.

Among the jumbo jet's 348 passengers was a man who appeared to be in his late thirties or early forties: huskily built with fashionably long hair, a thick drooping mustache, pale blue eyes, and a modish suit with an open shirt collar. A thin gold chain encircled his neck.

He had purposely joked and kidded with the stewardesses during the long flight over the Atlantic so that they would clearly remember him if anyone should ask about the man in 12B first class.

Upstairs in the cocktail lounge he had insisted on leaving a large tip with the black bartender, and on the way back down the stairs he had stumbled, grabbing for two young men who saved him from a nasty fall.

For that same reason he had spoken at length with the businessman seated next to him, introducing himself as Werner Hempel from Minneapolis.

No one had questioned his behavior or even stopped to wonder exactly who he was. He had learned by long experience that the more obvious you were, the more likely people were to accept who you appeared to be.

"It was nice talking to you, Wernher," the businessman next to him said. "If you're ever in St. Louis, look me up."

Hempel smiled. "I'll do that."

The businessman removed his single piece of carry-on luggage from beneath his seat and made his way with the other departing passengers down the aisle as Hempel retrieved his attaché case and jacket from the overhead compartment.

All of the first-class and most of the tourist-class passengers had already deplaned by the time Hempel had gathered his things and made his way past the first-class galley to the open door.

The stewardess who had waited on him was the only one left at the door.

"It's been a pleasure, Margory," he said. His accent was American Midwest.

She smiled. "The pleasure was all mine, Mr. Hempel."

Hempel guessed the girl was in her early or mid-twenties, and probably from somewhere on the east coast. She was slender, with a well-rounded face and pleasant, soft green eyes. He regretted for a moment that he did not have the time for her. She was obviously interested in him.

He smiled again, left the plane, went downstairs, retrieved his single leather suitcase from incoming luggage, and went through the swinging doors into customs. As he came into the large room that was rapidly filling with passengers from the plane, he stiffened imperceptibly at the sight of several uniformed customs officers. But outwardly he seemed relaxed if somewhat fatigued from the flight as he approached one of the officers and laid his suitcase and matching attaché case on the counter.

"Good afternoon, sir, Welcome to Germany. May I see your passport?"

Hempel smiled as he handed over his American passport. The officer opened it, studied the photograph, then looked up at Hempel's face before he stamped it and handed it back.

"The purpose of your visit to Germany, Mr. Hempel?"

"I'm a magazine writer, and I'm here to do a series of tourist stories."

The customs officer smiled. "Have you anything to declare?"

Hempel shook his head.

"If you will just open your suitcase, please."

Hempel complied, and the officer efficiently went through his things: a couple of suits, underwear, shirts, a pair of shoes, a toiletries kit, and a large, all-band portable radio-cassette tape recorder.

The customs officer looked through the toiletries kit and then picked the radio-recorder out of the suitcase and turned it upside down. "How does this open, sir?"

"Let me," Hempel said. He could feel a slight trace of sweat in his armpits, and it annoyed him. He laid the radio on the counter, undid the four snaps holding the back cover in place, and opened it. Inside was a maze of electronic circuit boards and components.

"Japanese?" the customs officer asked pleasantly.

Hempel nodded. "Sony."

"I have a Sony," the man said. He turned to the attaché case. "Would you open that, please?"

Hempel buttoned up his radio and then opened his attaché case. As the customs man looked through the magazines, two paperback tourist guides, and a few files on German sights of interest, Hempel returned the radio to his suitcase.

"Thank you, sir," the customs officer said, making a small chalk mark on both pieces of luggage. "Have a pleasant stay in Germany."

"I will, thank you," Hempel said, and he left the airport, taking a cab into the city.

All her life the Pan Am stewardess Margory Cummins had a recurring dream that one day she would become a stew for an international airline and would meet the man of her dreams who would marry her. They would settle down in her hometown of Palmer, Massachusetts, or perhaps Cape Cod with a couple of children, a dog, a station wagon, and a white picket fence.

At twenty-eight she was grown-up. She had a job with a major international airline, and she had met plenty of men. Tall men, short men, skinny men, fat men, but mostly men who either had wives or who were too old for her.

Margory had become impatient over the past couple of years. According to the timetable she had carefully worked out for herself, she was already three years overdue for her marriage, two years overdue for her first child, and at this moment she should be pregnant with the second.

And yet, she mused as she lay back in the hot bubble bath in her room, she had not met a likely candidate in all these years. Had not, she smiled, until today.

It was shortly before two in the afternoon, and the two other girls with whom Margory was sharing this room on their twenty-four-hour layover had left earlier to go shopping.

Margory had begged off, claiming tiredness. But it was not tiredness that kept her from going with her friends. It was Wernher Hempel, 12B first class.

She finally got out of the tub, let the water run out, and began drying herself as she thought about Mr. Hempel. Actually, she knew quite a bit about him. His customs declaration form, which he had filled out before they landed, had listed his age as thirty-eight and his occupation as travel editor for a magazine in Minneapolis. He was good-looking, had a nice body, a pleasant smile, a deep masculine voice, and best of all, he had money. You could tell it not only by the way he dressed but by the way he acted.

Jimmy in the cocktail lounge had told her in operations after the flight that Hempel had left him a fifty-dollar tip.

And Franz in local reservations had informed her that Hempel was staying for three days at the Hotel Frankfurt Intercontinental, the best hotel in town.

Only two things could spoil it for her, she thought. The first would be if he was married. He did not wear a gold band, nor did he act like any of the married men she had ever met, so at this moment she felt that possibility was the least of her worries.

The second consideration, however, did cause her some concern.

She let the towel drop to the floor and looked critically at the reflection of her nude body in the full-length mirror on the back of the bathroom door.

She did not look twenty-eight; she looked more like twenty-two or twenty-three, which could either be an asset or a liability, depending upon how mature Hempel liked his women. Her face was pleasant, her eyes expressive, and her mouth was directly out of a fashion magazine courtesy of more than two thousand dollars worth of dental work over the past eight years.

Her breasts were too small, in her opinion, and her tummy was slightly rounded, but her derriere and long legs were perfectly formed.

She smiled at her reflection. Her major concern was time, she told herself. In order to make a man interested enough to pursue her, she would have to spend time with him.

And she would be damned if Mr. Wernher Hempel of

12B first class was going to spend the remainder of today
and tonight alone. With any luck, when she got back on the
plane tomorrow afternoon for New York, he would never
forget her.

In twenty minutes Margory had put on her makeup, had
dressed in a skirt and low-cut, ruffled blouse, and had gone
downstairs where she climbed into a cab.

"The Frankfurt Intercontinental," she told the driver, and
she sat back to plan the finer details of the conquest of Mr.
Wernher Hempel.

Hempel was not a normal man when it came to sleep. In
fact, he could not remember ever having slept eight hours
at one stretch like normal people. For him, fifteen-or twenty-
minute catnaps several times during a twenty-four-hour pe-
riod were sufficient.

He had read once that the American inventor Thomas
Edison had been the same, and it was one of the reasons
that the man had been able to accomplish so much.

Now Hempel rose from one of these catnaps completely
refreshed, ready to begin the assignment he had been sent
here for.

In the bathroom he peeled off his wig, revealing cropped
steel gray hair. He took out the contact lenses that made his
eyes blue and pulled off the mustache.

After a quick shower he returned to his suitcase at the
foot of his bed and pried the lining loose from its Velcro
fasteners. Taped to the lid were two sets of papers; one set
identified him as Walter Handel, an agricultural consultant
from the University of Nebraska, the other as Walter Holvig,
a professor of engineering from the University of Heidelberg. He pulled the German papers out and refastened the
lining.

Working quickly but efficiently, as he had been trained,
Hempel took his toiletries kit into the bathroom, where he
laid out the aftershave lotion bottle and an electric razor. He

opened the back of the razor and took out a set of contact lenses, which he placed in his eyes, making them a dark brown. Next he patted a few drops of liquid from the after-shave lotion bottle on his cheeks and nose, which instantly stung like fire. Within a few seconds his face took on a definite reddish hue, the thin capillaries along his cheeks and nose suddenly appearing as the blue tracks of a man in his fifties or perhaps early sixties. The effect would only last for a couple of hours, but it was long enough.

Returning to the bedroom, he replaced the kit in his suit-case and dressed in a dark suit that was baggy and un-pressed. He knotted his tie crookedly.

He stuffed his identity papers into his breast pocket, then laid the radio-recorder on the bed and unsnapped the back cover. Four fasteners held the main circuit board in place, and Hempel undid them and lifted the electronic assembly out of its holders. Beneath it was a 9mm Beretta silenced automatic with a full magazine of ammunition. He withdrew the gun and placed it in his belt and put the radio back together.

All of this took less than ten minutes, and before Hempel left his room, he checked his appearance in the bathroom mirror.

Walter Holvig, sixty-two, Heidelberg, looked at him. He smiled, turned, and shuffled like an old man to the door, his mind split into two functions.

A part of him was thinking engineering formulae, stu-dents, faculty, research projects. The other, that most secret part of his mind where the real person lived, was going over this assignment and his escape.

No one saw him leave his room, nor did he run into any-one as he went down the back stairs and out the rear en-trance of the hotel. Once he was on the street, he merged with the Frankfurt crowds.

Two blocks from the hotel he got into a cab and ordered

the driver to take him to the Telecomm, GmbH, building on Theodor-Heuss Allee.

"Sigmund Lascher," his contact had told him two days ago as they walked along the Boston Commons. The man had come to the bookstore where Hempel worked as a clerk and asked for a copy of a limited edition of the *Rise and Fall of the Third Reich*. Hempel had told the man they did not have such a book, but the man had insisted, claiming a friend had told him that at least a dozen of the 300-series of the book were to be had at this store.

Hempel suggested he try some of the shops around the Commons, and the man had left. One hour later Hempel was free for his lunch break and he met the man on the Commons.

"There is a file with Lascher's photograph and other details, along with identity papers for you, at your apartment. Lascher works for Telecomm in Frankfurt. His office is on the seventh floor. Research."

"What has he done to us?" Hempel asked.

His contact, a well-dressed man in his fifties, stopped and looked across at the State House. "Nothing as yet," he said. His voice was soft, cultured, but he did not sound as if he came from Boston. His accent was more New York.

Hempel waited for the man to continue.

"Three of our people in Hamburg have been arrested as suspected former members of the SS Enlisted men. It was a foolish move on the part of the State's Attorney's office in Hamburg because they have no proof."

The man looked directly at Hempel. "Our people at Telecomm informed us this morning that Lascher has been commenting on the case, which goes to trial next week. Lascher has been telling anyone who will listen that he knows two of the men from the war, and knows for certain that they were in the SS."

"What is Lascher's connection?"

"Beyond the fact he worked for Farben as a research engineer during the war, we don't know. There hasn't been enough time to put it together."

"But he may be telling the truth?"

The man nodded, a grim expression in his eyes. "It is important for us to protect our people. They themselves are not important, but they are comrades. If we let this go, it could get out of hand."

"I see."

"Are you willing to accept the assignment?"

"Of course. I'll be on a plane the day after tomorrow."

"When will you do it?"

"Immediately," Hempel said. "Have a suitcase and alternate identity papers waiting for me at Orly in Paris that same night."

The man nodded. Hempel turned on his heel and headed back to work at the bookstore.

The cab pulled up at the curb; Hempel paid the driver, got out, and entered the Telecomm building, shuffling past the information booth in the lobby.

His shabby appearance elicited some attention, and Hempel made it a point to joke with the elevator operator on the way up. The man would later remember him and would give the police a very accurate description.

On the seventh floor Hempel stepped off the elevator and hesitated only long enough to note the position of the door to the stairwell before he shuffled down the corridor and entered Lascher's outer office.

The room was large and contained a dozen desks, all occupied. Hempel stepped up to the first desk and bowed slightly.

"Herr Doktor Lascher, bitte," he said politely.

The woman looked up at him and smiled. "May I say who is calling, *mein Herr*?"

"Professor Doktor Walter Holvig, Heidelberg." He

leaned slightly forward. "I have something of importance to discuss with the great man," he said, patting his breast pocket.

The secretary picked up the telephone. "Herr Lascher, there is a Professor Doktor Walter Holvig from the University of Heidelberg here to see you. He says it is a matter of importance." She nodded a moment later. "Yes, sir," she said, then replaced the receiver. "You may go in, Herr Professor."

"Danke," Hempel said, and he shuffled past her desk, knocked once on Lascher's door, and entered his office.

Lascher was a barrel-chested old man with a thick shock of white hair and gold-rimmed glasses. He looked up, curiosity on his face as Hempel closed the door behind him, reached beneath his coat, and withdrew the Beretta.

"Odessa sends its regards, Herr Lascher," Hempel said, and as Lascher held out his hand and opened his mouth to cry out for help, Hempel fired two shots, the first hitting the man in the forehead and the second in his chest.

The silenced Beretta made only a slight plopping sound, but Lascher was flung backward, his head striking the edge of the bookcase behind his desk with a dull thud. He slumped sideways out of his chair.

Hempel replaced the gun in his belt, took a deep breath, turned, and went back out into the office, closing the door behind him.

The secretary looked up.

"Forgive me," Hempel said apologetically. "Herr Doktor Lascher is looking at some papers I brought him and wishes not to be disturbed. Meanwhile, like the old fool I am, I have forgotten my briefcase in my car. I will return in a moment."

"Certainly," the secretary said, but Hempel was already in the corridor, shuffling toward the stairwell door.

Ten minutes at the most, he thought, as he opened the door and headed down the seven flights of stairs.

The secretary would not become curious until Hempel failed to return, unless Lascher received a phone call or another visitor. She would remember him, as would the elevator operator and cab drivers. But they would remember Walter Holvig, who would cease to exist as soon as he returned to his hotel room.

If anyone happened to see the old man going into the young American Wernher Hempel's room, they might put two and two together and would get an accurate description of Hempel from the stewardess on the airplane. But Hempel did not exist either.

A taxi was just passing when Hempel emerged from the Telecomm building. He waved it down and got in, giving the driver an address a few doors away from his hotel.

As they drove across town he kept looking out the rear window, each time making sure the driver was not watching him, but all the way across town there was no sign of pursuit.

When the cabby left him off, Hempel waited until the taxi was out of sight before he walked to the hotel and entered the busy lobby. No one paid him any attention as he took the elevator up one floor beyond his own.

He hurried down the corridor and, making sure no one was there to see him, took the stairs down one flight and hurried along the corridor to his room, where he unlocked the door and entered, again making sure no one had seen him.

"Who are you?" It was a woman's voice.

Hempel turned around as Margory Cummins emerged from the bathroom, and for an instant they just looked at each other until recognition dawned in the young woman's eyes.

"I know you," she started to say, but Hempel was across the room to her in a few quick strides.

He grabbed her by the throat and pushed her back into the bathroom, closing the door behind them with his free hand. "How did you get in here?" he snapped.

The girl was frightened, her eyes wide, her mouth open. He relaxed the pressure on her throat.

"I asked how you got in here," he said.

"You're Mr. Hempel . . ." she started to say, but again Hempel clamped down on her throat, cutting off her wind.

"Who are you working for? Who sent you?"

The girl's face was beginning to turn a deep red, and she struggled against his powerful grip.

"I want answers! Now!" Hempel said. Once again he loosened his grip.

"The floor maid . . . she let me in . . . I told her we were lovers . . ." Margory gasped.

"Who sent you?"

She shook her head. "No one sent me. I came here to . . . see you."

Hempel tried to think. He had covered every step. There was no way anyone could have known what he was here for.

He looked at the girl. She had recognized him despite his disguise. She knew too much. It was a shame, but it had been his own fault. He should have anticipated such a possibility when he saw how she had looked at him on the airplane.

There was a strong probability that she had told someone that she was coming here to see him. In addition the stupid floor maid who had let her in knew that she was here.

Soon there would be a manhunt for Walter Holvig, the professor from Heidelberg who had murdered Doktor Lascher. And soon, he thought grimly, there would be a manhunt for Wernher Hempel, the murderer of Margory Cummins.

"What are you going to do to me. . . . ?" the girl stammered as Hempel opened the bathroom door and dragged her back into the bedroom.

He could not leave her alive, and yet he could not kill her without a clear motive for the police.

"If you make a sound, I will kill you," he said softly.

She whimpered.

He shoved her down on the bed and jammed a knee between her legs. She started to cry out, but he clamped his left hand over her mouth, and with his other hand ripped the front of her blouse open and tore off her bra.

Margory struggled wildly against him as he pawed savagely at her breasts, leaving bright red finger marks, but he was too strong for her, and she could do nothing against him.

It was a shame, he told himself. But it was his own fault.

He forced her skirt up over her hips and ripped her panty hose open, then unzipped his trousers, releasing his erection. He entered her quickly and pounded hard against her, coming almost immediately.

Still on top of her, he suddenly twisted her head around with both hands until her neck snapped with a sickening sound of grinding bone and tearing muscle. She stiffened in his grasp, her body convulsing, then she went limp beneath him.

Hempel got to his feet and looked down at the young woman's body with little or no emotion other than professional interest and a slight feeling of pity that it had to end this way for her.

There would be no doubt why the man from the airplane had killed her.

Working very carefully so that he would make no further mistakes, Hempel changed his clothes and his appearance, flushing the identity papers, contact lenses, and facial solution he had used as Professor Holvig down the toilet.

When he was finished Holvig had disappeared, and the room belonged exclusively and obviously to Wernher Hempel, from 12B first class.

Walter Handel, from Nebraska, paused at the door before he left to catch a train to Paris and looked back at the ruined remains of Margory Cummins.

It was a shame, he told himself. But he would never make that same mistake again.

2

The day was hot. The wind that blew up from the desert was like the breath from a blast furnace in the man's face, but he did not seem to notice. He used a pair of powerful binoculars to study the Syrian outpost that had come into being this morning a thousand yards below him just across the border. All day half-tracks hauling men, supplies, and two short-range missile launchers had come across the desert from the east. Latrines had been dug, tents had been set up, and at this moment several dozen Syrian troops were eating their noon meal.

For the past ten days similar outposts had sprung up along the area bordering the Israeli-occupied Golan Heights, and Major Levi Asheim supposed it would not be long before the fighting began. Once again he would be asked to take a field command.

He lowered his binoculars and turned to look down at Kibbutz Rafid, which consisted of little more than a dozen prefab buildings and less than an acre of irrigated garden, in time to see two men starting up the long hill toward him.

He raised his binoculars and looked down at them. One of the men was Colonel Yizhak Gurion, a cousin of David Ben-Gurion and assistant chief of Aman, the Israeli Military Intelligence Service. Asheim had worked for him for five years. The other man wore civilian clothes and looked familiar, although he could not place him.

Asheim squatted down on his haunches, letting the binoculars hang loose from the strap around his neck. Neither of the men was in his prime; it was obvious from their difficulty in climbing, and by the time they reached the top of the hill they would be fatigued.

He lit a filter-tipped Time and waited, the Syrian outpost below him at his back, the tiny kibbutz below him to the west.

They were coming to offer him troops who would be moved up to defend the kibbutz, but he was not going to accept it. He would recommend that the tiny settlement be moved out of the way. The Golan Heights was a no-man's-land. A land in which they had no business. If these two coming now were here to present that proposal, he would make them work for it.

At fifty-five, Asheim was a hard man, tough of body as well as of mind. Back in Tel Aviv his nickname had been "tough old bird." And his people here at the kibbutz said of him that he was one man who could outdesert an Arab nomad, could outfight a Syrian legion, and who could outshoot the finest marksman.

But Asheim was also a practical man, and although the defense of the kibbutz and others like it was possible, the Golan Heights was simply not worth the loss of life it would take to hold it. Especially if the Syrians mounted an all-out attack along the entire border.

He had expressed his views at length in Tel Aviv to little or no avail other than to earn him the increasing irritation of his superiors. And when he had been offered the job as kibbutz commander six months ago, he had accepted in disgust.

In 1948 he had fought the British and the Arabs for Israel's independence, and since that time it seemed like he had fought on every battlefield. He had been wounded seven times, had been one of the team members who kidnapped Adolph Eichmann from South America, and was one of the planners of the raid on the Entebbe Airport.

For almost thirty years he had fought and nearly died for his adopted country, and now they were going to ask him to go into battle again. But he was sick of fighting. Of the killing. Of the dying. He wanted to settle down and enjoy his life with his two married daughters, their husbands, and his five grandchildren. Perhaps he would even find another wife to replace the woman who had left him and returned to the United States in 1953.

Colonel Gurion and the civilian, who carried a briefcase, finally reached the top of the hill, and as they approached, Asheim flipped the cigarette away and stood up. Both of them were winded and were sweating heavily. Both of them seemed grim.

"They said we'd find you up here," Colonel Gurion said, puffing. He was short and fat. He'd been born in New York City and would have continued in his father's garment business had he not been caught up with the idea of an independent Jewish state in 1950.

"I've been watching our friends setting up their missile launchers. Russian, I think."

Colonel Gurion did not bother looking that way. "I know," he said, still trying to catch his breath. "We had a fly-over early this morning and picked them up on infrared."

"Is that what you've come all this way to tell me?" Asheim asked. There was something in Gurion's eyes that he did not like. It was bothersome.

The colonial shook his head. "I have some rather bad news, I'm afraid. Lev."

"What is it?" Asheim asked, steeling himself. He had often been the recipient of bad news: when his wife left him; when his father, who had come from San Diego to Israel with him, was killed in a bombing raid; and when his mother died eight years ago of a heart attack.

"Is there someplace we can talk?" Colonel Gurion asked, looking around.

"This is as good a place as any," Asheim said. "What has happened?"

Colonel Gurion had been a good man to work for. Although he was somewhat soft at times, and often saw things through rose-colored glasses, he was a dedicated man. And he had always defended Asheim, who had the habit of butting heads with the wrong people.

"It's Benjamin," Colonel Gurion said gently. "He was hit by a car in Buenos Aires three days ago and killed."

Asheim's heart skipped a beat. "What about Deborah and the children?"

"They're safe. They'll be coming home in a couple of days."

Several large troop transport trucks bumped along the dirt road from the town of Rafid three miles away. Asheim watched the dust rise. "I didn't know my son-in-law was working for you, Yizhak. They never told me a thing."

He turned to look again at Colonel Gurion. "Was it an accident, or was he murdered?"

"We think he was assassinated."

"What was he doing for you?" Asheim's voice turned harsh.

The civilian, a tall, well-dressed man in his early sixties who until this moment had said nothing, spoke up. "Major Asheim, may we go down to your office? There is much we need to discuss with you."

Asheim glanced at the civilian. "Who is this man?"

"Excuse me," Colonel Gurion apologized. "I'd like you to meet David Goldmann—"

Asheim interrupted him, suddenly remembering the man. "Mossad. You were the brains behind the Eichmann thing."

Goldmann nodded. "Your son-in-law was murdered, and we need your help, Major Asheim."

"A revenge mission?" Asheim spat out the words. "I'm not interested."

"Not a revenge mission," Goldmann snapped.

"You're still fighting Nazis real or imagined?"

"The Nazis are not imagined. They killed your son-in-law."

"And I'm to replace Benjamin in Buenos Aires and spy on them?"

"I don't want you to do anything against your will, Major," Goldmann said, disgusted. "What I did expect, however, was that you would extend me the courtesy of listening to what I have to say. In the last twenty-four hours I've had to fight my superior officers all the way up to Dayan and Rabin, and I'm not about to stand on this hilltop arguing with someone who does not care. I will go elsewhere and find another man who will listen to me."

Conflicting emotions raged inside Asheim, but uppermost in his mind was a grudging respect for Goldmann, who obviously was a fighter. "I'll listen to you, but I won't promise any more than that."

Goldmann smiled. "That's all I want, Major. Believe me, that's all I want."

They started down the hill, Asheim falling into a loping stride that would not tire him out in twenty miles. He was a large man, over six feet, two hundred pounds, with a trim body that made him look and act more like a man of forty. His hair, however, was pure white.

In every way including thinking, he was opposite of what Benjamin had been. And yet over the years that the little man had been married to his daughter, Asheim had come to

admire him. Benjamin had been a man who was slow to
come to a decision, but once it had been made, nothing
could sway him. Deborah and the children had loved him
very much.

It had hurt when they left eighteen months ago to open
the travel bureau in Buenos Aires. But the hurt, Asheim had
to admit, came not so much from the fact they had left Israel
but more because they had not explained the real reason
behind the move. He had suspected something, but he had
never been a doting, meddlesome father, and had merely
made them promise to write frequently, which they did, still
saying nothing.

Now Benjamin was dead. Deborah and the children were
alone. Probably frightened. And certainly grief-stricken.

At the bottom of the hill they entered the kibbutz and
started across the central square as the first of the troop
transport trucks rolled in and pulled up in front of the administration building.

"Your replacement will be in later this afternoon," Colonel Gurion said.

Asheim glanced at him.

"If you decide to stay, of course, he will be your second-
in-command."

"You expect fighting soon?" Asheim asked, not breaking
stride.

Gurion shrugged. "Anything is possible."

The first of the troops jumped down from the trucks. Asheim stopped long enough to direct two of his lieutenants to
see to their billeting, and then he, Colonel Gurion, and Goldmann entered his office.

"Have a seat, gentlemen," Asheim said, going behind his
desk.

"Will we be disturbed, and can anyone overhear us in
here?" Goldmann asked.

Asheim looked at him. "Sit down, Mr. Goldmann. We
will not be disturbed."

Goldmann and Gurion sat down across the desk from Asheim, and for a long moment the three of them were silent. From outside they could hear the shouted commands to troops, and in the orderly room outside Asheim's office they could hear the sounds of many people coming and going, typewriters clattering, and telephones ringing. The effect was lulling, but Asheim broke the spell.

"What was my son-in-law doing for you in Buenos Aires?"

Goldmann placed his briefcase on his lap but made no move to open it. "Major, what do you know about the SS?"

"The usual," Asheim said. "But I asked you a question."

"Which I will answer in my own way."

Asheim's eyes narrowed. He was not going to put up with this. "I agreed to listen to you, but I don't want a sales pitch, Goldmann. Give it to me straight."

Gurion started to object, but Goldmann held him off. "He is right, Yizhak," he said, and turned back to Asheim. "Before I tell you what your son-in-law was doing for me, and what I am going to ask you to do for me, I must give you some background information. But I'll tell you from the start that the attitude about all this that you evidently have is shared by almost every government in the world, including our own."

"But not by you," Asheim said dryly.

"Not by me," Goldmann replied softly. "I've been working at it too long."

Gurion broke in. "David's wife, his parents, and several aunts and uncles all were murdered at Auschwitz. David managed to escape to fight with the Danish underground. In 1947 he came to Jerusalem."

"So you hate Germans and are still fighting the war," Asheim said. He had had enough of this, and he started to rise.

"I have no hate left," Goldmann said, his voice very soft. "Only fear."

The comment stopped Asheim, and he sat back down in his chair. Goldmann was no fanatic. He was more like a dedicated man. "I'll listen."

Goldmann nodded. "I'll be brief," he said, and he paused a moment to organize his thoughts.

Gurion sat back in his chair and lit a cigarette.

Asheim listened, intrigued despite himself, the sounds from outside his office fading as if they had stopped.

In 1925 Adolph Hitler created the SS *(Shutzstaffel)* as a corps of troops loyal to him personally. But they were nothing more than a ragtag band of thugs until 1929 when Heinrich Himmler, the chicken farmer from the Bavarian village of Waldtrudering, took over command. At that moment the SS had its real, and very terrible, beginning.

Its primary objective, of course, was the extermination of every Jew from the face of the earth. But every facet of Germany's military-industrial complex had its complement of SS liaison officers.

To a man they were loyal to no one but Hitler and to no belief other than world domination and racial purity.

"But they were not stupid men," Goldmann said. "As ruthless as they were; they were intelligent. Their ranks were composed of some of Germany's most brilliant minds."

As early as 1940, many officers in the SS High Command, however, realized that Hitler was engaging them in a world war that Germany could not possibly win. So they began to hedge their bets.

At first they shipped gold, art objects, and anything else of value that was portable to Switzerland. But as the war deepened, this wealth was shipped in increasing amounts to Argentina, to Portugal, to Egypt, to Mexico, and even to the United States and Canada.

When the war was over, these men reasoned, they would

not be able to remain in Germany, but wherever they went, they were determined not to live as poor men.

In 1943 the exodus began. Slowly at first. A colonel changing his identity and slipping into Switzerland. A major who spoke perfect English rowing ashore from a submarine off the coast of North Carolina. A captain abandoning his ship in the Buenos Aires harbor.

All over the world SS officers scattered to rejoin the fortunes they had shipped out of Germany, to escape charges as war criminals, to begin new lives.

"Most of those people were caught, returned to Germany, and hung or imprisoned, I thought," Asheim said.

"Several thousand of them, mostly enlisted men who were not being sought actively by the War Crimes Commission, did manage to remain free. In addition a number of high-ranking officers, the cream of the crop, eluded capture," Goldmann said, and he continued with his narrative.

In 1946 a number of those SS officers, all of them wealthy, organized the Odessa with the avowed purpose of protecting its own people, and somehow, someday, reactivating their Fuehrer's dream of the "Thousand-Year Reich."

For the next few years the Odessa was a tenuous organization at best. The Americans and British hunted them down, and for a time were quite successful, despite the Odessa's best efforts to protect its own.

But then something happened. In the United States, Senator McCarthy began hunting communists, and the Americans forgot about the SS. In England they were struggling to rebuild London and somehow pick up the pieces. In Germany itself reconstruction was going on, and everyone wanted to forget the war. And in Israel, the people—many of them survivors of the Holocaust—were again fighting for their survival. Odessa got its foothold. It grew strong. It grew even more wealthy. And even more ruthless in protecting its own people.

* * *

"But you have been fighting the Odessa all along," Asheim said.

"Yes I have, but with less and less support from my own superiors. I am considered a fanatic."

"It's been more than thirty years," Asheim said. "The officers who escaped during the war must be all old men by now."

"Old, very wealthy, still quite brilliant, and now more than ever because of their age, quite ruthless. When the last of them is dead and gone, the idea of Odessa will crumble and fall."

Asheim managed a grim smile. "You have these men identified?"

"We believe we've identified most of the High Command."

"Why not just assassinate them and be done with it?"

Goldmann shook his head. "Assassinate a multimillionaire whose factories are the backbone of Portugal? Assassinate the leading citizen of Buenos Aires? Assassinate the largest individual landholder in Mexico?"

"I see," Asheim said.

Goldmann sat forward in his chair. "When we kidnaped Eichmann, tried him, and executed him, the entire world came crashing down on our heads. At that time I was informed in no uncertain terms that nothing like that would ever be allowed to happen again. And it has not."

"So your hands are tied."

"Nearly, but not quite," Goldmann said. He sat back. "I have a small staff and an even smaller budget, but we do get results. There have been a number of deportations and subsequent prosecutions in Germany."

"But more failures," Asheim said softly, and he could see that he had hit a nerve.

"A man who was to be a star witness in a trial against three suspected former SS enlisted men was murdered three days ago in Frankfurt. We are sure it was an Odessa job."

"I'm to go after the murderer?"

Goldmann shook his head. "It's more complicated than that."

Asheim glanced at Gurion, but the man refused to meet his eyes. "It has to do with why my son-in-law was sent to Buenos Aires?"

"Yes," Goldmann said. He seemed even more grim than before. "The Odessa organization, although pervasive, is very loose. Until three days ago it consisted of twelve old men—former high-ranking SS officers who are outstanding citizens of a half-dozen countries. Each of these men has at his command anywhere from a few dozen men to as many as five hundred or one thousand loyal troops. Some of the troops are themselves former SS members, but many are the sons and daughters of former SS people.

"Since the war, the major concentration of Germans, among them former SS people, has been Argentina, more specifically Buenos Aires. The top man in Odessa, we believe, is a man who now calls himself Kurt Stoeffel, seventy, and all but retired from the International Bank of Buenos Aires—which he founded with SS money."

"Benjamin went to Buenos Aires to watch Stoeffel?" Asheim asked.

"Not quite," Goldmann corrected. "Stoeffel lives in a mansion at the center of two hundred acres of jungle, fenced and guarded, which he rarely leaves. There is no way for us to get close to him without all hell breaking loose. We sent your son-in-law to Buenos Aires to watch the airport. To report back to us the comings and goings of Odessa's top leadership. Nothing more."

"What was that supposed to have accomplished?" Asheim asked. He wondered if he had overestimated Goldmann's abilities.

"Within the limitations I have to live with, as much as can be expected. At least we had advance warnings of any project by who came to confer with Stoeffel.''

''Who did Benjamin report coming to Buenos Aires?''

Goldmann opened his briefcase and withdrew twelve file folders, which he placed on Asheim's desk. ''These twelve men represent the known Odessa leadership. All of them are former SS officers of the rank of lieutenant colonel or colonel. Three of them, Stoeffel included, live in or around Buenos Aires. The other nine, arrived in Buenos Aires within a week of each other, where they remained for nearly three months before departing the same way they had come: one at a time and under heavy personal guard.''

Asheim flipped through the files. Each folder contained photographs and brief dossiers on the man's work during the war and his life since. One of the files was marked with a green stripe. Asheim held that one up. ''What about this man?''

''Albert Spannau, alias Albert Spanndig. The man from Lisbon. He died at the Missiones German Hospital in Buenos Aires three days ago.''

Asheim stared at the photographs of Spannau, the most recent showing a frail old man in a business suit that looked three sizes too large. ''Benjamin was alone down there?''

''We have a few people who report to us and offer some help from time to time, but they are Argentinians, and we cannot involve them too heavily. Certainly in nothing covert.''

Asheim looked up. Anger was beginning to build inside of him. ''So you sent Benjamin after this man.'' He tapped Spannau's file folder with a blunt finger.

''The entire Odessa leadership had met in Buenos Aires, probably at Stoeffel's mansion, for three months. It was unprecedented. We couldn't and wouldn't send Benjamin to try and penetrate the meeting, but when we learned that Spannau had become sick and was probably dying, we saw it as a chance to find out what went on at the meeting.''

A sick feeling rose up inside of Asheim as he envisioned

his son-in-law, frightened and uncertain, but committed to do a job.

"We sent Benjamin to the hospital in the middle of the night with a hypodermic syringe of sodium Pentothal and a miniature tape recorder. One of our Argentinian friendlies works as an orderly at the hospital. He left the rear door open, arranged for the drug and to have Spannau's guards absent when Benjamin arrived."

Goldmann had begun to sweat, and Asheim felt on the verge of hitting something, anything.

"Major, you must understand something. It was never my intention to—"

Asheim cut him off. "What happened at the hospital?"

Goldmann did not look away; his eyes were locked into Asheim's. "Your son-in-law managed to get into the hospital and into Spannau's room. He administered the drug and questioned the man. But Spannau died before he could get very much information.

"On the way out of the hospital he was discovered. He did manage to make it to the street, off hospital grounds; but that's as far as he got. He was hit by a car and left to die. A passing motorist discovered his body and reported it to the police as a hit-and-run."

Asheim could say nothing for the moment. It had all been a waste. A terrible waste.

"Tell him the rest of it," Gurion said softly.

Goldmann took a deep breath. "Your daughter managed to pull some strings and have her husband's body transferred to La Plata Hospital, where their family physician is a resident. He is a friendly and managed to obtain permission to conduct the police-ordered autopsy."

"The tape recorder and hypo were not found on him?"

"No. Whoever hit him may have removed them. We hope not, but we have no way of knowing for certain," Goldmann said. He reached into his jacket pocket and withdrew a tiny tape spool. "During the autopsy this was found lodged in Benjamin's throat. He evidently tried to swallow it before he was struck by the car.''

A blackness seemed to envelop Asheim. ''My God, he suffocated.''

Goldmann nodded. ''The doctor gave the tape spool to Deborah, who recognized it for what it was, and she sent it here by courier. It arrived this morning. She had to remain in Buenos Aires until the police investigation was completed.''

Asheim could not take his eyes off the tape spool as Goldmann took a miniature tape recorder out of his briefcase, inserted the spool in the machine, and punched the play button.

At first they could hear nothing, but then there were sounds of mumbling and ragged breathing. Benjamin's voice was the first on the tape.

''Spannau . . . I need your help, Spannau . . . the Fuehrer needs your help, Spannau . . .'' There was more mumbling. ''Where did you meet, Spannau?'' Again mumbling. ''The Fuehrer sends his greetings, Spannau, but he must know where you held your meeting.'' Another voice, much older, barely distinguishable from the background noise, mumbled the single word ''Aerie.'' Goldmann stopped the tape.

''We believe Aerie is the name Stoeffel has given to his compound northwest of the city.''

Asheim said nothing, but his mind was reeling. He hoped that Deborah had not heard this tape, that she never would.

Goldmann punched the play button again.

''Where is that?'' Benjamin's voice came from the tiny speaker. ''Aerie,'' the old man mumbled again. ''What is the plan, Spannau? The Fuehrer must know what you have planned.''

Asheim leaned forward, closer to the tape machine.

''We have found the man . . . at long last . . . two more years . . . the man . . .'' There was a gurgling sound, then nothing for a long moment.

Goldmann reached out to shut off the machine, but Asheim's massive right hand shot out and grabbed his wrist, pinning it to the desk, and the tape continued for nearly two minutes with the confused sounds of Benjamin's flight from the hospital, then it went blank. Asheim released his grip, and Goldmann shut off the machine.

"Your son-in-law evidently removed the tape from the machine at that point, and we can only hope that he hid the recorder and the hypo somewhere. If that is the case, they do not know that we were successful."

"What do you want of me?" Asheim said. All he could think about were his daughter and her children.

"We have two years to discover Odessa's plan, find out who the man Spannau talked about is, and stop them. Will you take the job?"

Asheim looked at him but said nothing.

"I can offer you no help or support other than funds with which to travel, false identity papers, and the names of a few friendlies in a half-dozen countries. If you are caught operating illegally in any country, or if you are forced to kill, you will be publicly denounced here at home."

Asheim nodded "Why me?" He was thinking about his daughter and how she had loved her husband.

"Frankly," Goldmann said, "there is a fight brewing with Syria, we'll need all the officers we can get, but you have made it clear you do not want a field commission. Plus you are very good. Or at least you used to be."

Asheim looked into Goldmann's eyes. "Yes," he said. "I suppose I will do it."

3

Two days later and halfway across the world, the wind that blew was cold despite the fact it was mid-June. Dr. Richard Kelsey shivered where he stood at the open grave just outside Minneapolis, Minnesota, as the minister finished the brief funeral ceremony.

Part of Kelsey's chill was because of the raw wind, but much of the coldness he felt was in his soul because it was his wife's body that lay encased in the copper-tone casket resting on its skids over the open hole.

A sense of unreality surrounded him. This could not be, should not be, happening to him. Only last week he and Colleen had had a furious argument. They had never really made up, and at this moment, God help him, he could not even remember what they had argued about. Now there would never be a chance for him to tell her he was sorry. Tell her how much he loved her. There had been no parting words. It was over suddenly, completely . . . so terribly final.

Kelsey shook himself. His father, who stood next to him,

tears streaming down his cheeks, put his arm around his son protectively.

They had been married only two years, and during that time they had made plans, they had loved, and most of all they had enjoyed each other and the life they had at the University of Minnesota Hospital.

Colleen was an R.N. in the cancer research center, and he was doing advanced specialty training in reconstructive plastic surgery across the quadrangle.

Six months ago they had wrangled the same shift, so for the first time in their brief marriage, they had been able to spend some time together.

"Dust to dust . . . ashes to ashes . . ." the minister intoned.

Two dozen people, including Colleen's parents from New York, were huddled around the grave. Kelsey looked across at them, but they did not look up.

They had never liked him, not from the beginning.

"My parents are stuffy old-money New York, and your background is questionable," Colleen had explained one evening.

"Questionable?" Kelsey laughed.

"You're a foreigner. A war baby from the wrong side of the lines. Daddy fought the Germans during the war, and now he'll be damned if his only child is going to marry one of them."

Kelsey laughed again, but the comment had hurt. "What about you?" he asked.

"Immigrant—as my father calls you—or not, Dr. Kelsey, I love you."

It was true, Kelsey reflected as he watched her parents in their grief. He had been born in 1940 in Berlin, and when he was four his mother had been killed in one of the Allied bombing raids of the city.

Two months before the war ended, his father escaped with him to Switzerland, where they lived until six months later

when the Americans recalled his father to help with reconstruction.

They lived for nearly a year and a half in Berlin, helping
the Americans until they were allowed to emigrate to the
United States, where they settled in Chicago.

Kelsey's father put his son in the best private schools as
he built up an electronics firm from a small beginning in a
rented garage to its present level just behind Texas Instruments with assembly plants in four cities and the home office and research center in Chicago.

During the bombing of Berlin the sight of the ruined and
maimed bodies had made its impression on the young boy,
planting in his mind the seed of a desire to help people.
When he graduated from prep school in 1958, he told his
father he was going to study to become a doctor. The elder
Kelsey had offered no real objections beyond the vague desire that his son should study business to take over the company one day, and Kelsey enrolled at Harvard.

"... and we commend this soul to His kingdom for life
everlasting. Amen."

Kelsey looked up as the cleric came around from the head
of the coffin toward him. Sixteen years he had studied and
worked, first receiving his medical degree from Harvard, his
primary specialty training in plastic surgery at UCLA, and
then his residency at Boston Memorial Hospital's Burn
Treatment Center. Finally two years ago he had come here
to take advanced training in reconstructive plastic surgery,
and his colleagues and teachers all told him he was the best
they had ever seen.

"Yours is a rare skill, Dick," the head of the department
told him last month. "You've combined the skill of the
practiced surgeon with the artistry of the sculptor. You'll do
great work in your lifetime."

But now he was alone.

"Dr. Kelsey, please accept my deepest sympathy for your
loss," the minister said, placing a gentle hand on his shoul-

der. Kelsey looked into his kindly eyes. "But take comfort from the knowledge, my son, that your wife was a good woman who is now enjoying the fruits of Heaven with our Almighty Lord."

Kelsey's throat constricted and he could not talk. His knees felt weak; only his father's supportive arm held him up.

The minister left, and others came over to offer their condolences. Many of them were Colleen's friends, some of them were colleagues of his. Others he did not recognize, and he supposed they were people from New York. Colleen's parents did not come over, and everyone else was a blur to him. Nothing seemed to make any sense until he was in the backseat of the limousine with his father and they were driving back into the city.

"A terrible blow," his father was saying. "I am sorry for you, Richard."

Kelsey looked into his father's eyes. "It doesn't make any sense, Father," he said.

His father squeezed his arm. "It was an accident. Nothing more. She lost control of the car. It was no one's fault."

Since his mother died years ago, Kelsey had taken all of his strength from his father, who was always there for him when he needed a strong hand. It had only been since he had met Colleen and they were married that he had ever turned to anyone other than his father for advice. And now, looking into the old man's eyes, Kelsey drew some measure of comfort. His father had lost a wife and understood how his son felt. He was the only other person in the world who really understood, and Kelsey cried as he had not cried since he was a child.

"You must leave Minneapolis now," the elder Kelsey said.

"I can't, Father. Not yet."

It was early evening and they were finally alone in his father's hotel suite near the airport. They had talked for more than an hour.

"Your work at the university is done, you said so yourself. And now everywhere you go, everyone you see, is going to remind you of Colleen.''

"Please, Father, not now . . .'' Kelsey protested, but his father overrode him.

"Listen to me, son, I know what I'm talking about. You'll accomplish nothing if you remain here. You'll just wallow in your own grief.''

His father's words hurt deeply, and Kelsey wanted him to stop. And yet a part of his mind knew that the old man was correct.

After the funeral he had not been able to return to his apartment and had come instead with his father to the hotel. Tomorrow would be no better, he knew. And beyond that was a dark void.

"I thought about a trip for you. Perhaps to Europe, maybe even South America. But that would do no good either. You'd be alone.''

Kelsey looked at his father seated across the room from him.

"So I came up with another idea which will make use of your talent and at the same time keep you busy.''

Again pain washed over Kelsey. He and Colleen had planned on applying to a number of research institutes. He as the researcher and she as his assistant.

"I know it hurts, son,'' his father was saying. "God, I know how you must feel. But you have to live. You must continue. I can't believe that Colleen would have wanted you to shrivel up and die.''

"So soon, Father . . .'' Kelsey said, trailing off. He turned away.

"No,'' his father said sternly. "We are leaving for Chicago in the morning. I'll arrange to have your things picked up and shipped down to you.''

"No,'' Kelsey said halfheartedly. He could feel his resistance slipping. It would be so easy to let go. To let his father, who had always been there for him, take charge now. So easy. So comforting.

"Then on Monday we are going to drive up to Lake Geneva in southern Wisconsin. I own forty acres outside of town on the lake itself."

Kelsey looked at his father, but said nothing.

"We're going to open a clinic there. The Kelsey Clinic, specializing in reconstructive plastic surgery. You can assemble a staff, and you will work and direct the place."

Kelsey shook his head. "I'm a researcher, not a clinician."

"A researcher who by his own admission a few weeks ago did not have a long-range project in mind. A researcher who was still looking for something to do."

"But a clinic wouldn't be the answer. Not now."

"On the contrary. You can take charge of the clinic for a couple of years or for however long it takes you to come up with a project. Something worthwhile, something viable."

"And then?" Despite himself, Kelsey found himself becoming interested. It seemed somehow immoral to him coming just hours after he had buried his wife.

"When you have your project I will open a small research institute in Chicago for you, and someone else can take over the Lake Geneva clinic."

"No," Kelsey said flatly.

"Yes," his father said, standing up. "First of all, I need the tax write-off, and second of all, you are simply too good a doctor to be buried as a little cog in some big research institute wheel."

"I can't," Kelsey said weakly. He could feel that he was nearly at the point of collapse, and he could not understand why his father was persisting.

"You not only can, but you will," his father said, and Kelsey suddenly knew that the old man was correct . . . both logically and compassionately right. But he was not quite ready to concede. Not tonight.

"I love you, Father," he said softly.

"I love you too, son," the old man replied.

4

They stood in Goldmann's office, a small, plain, windowless room. On one wall was pinned a faded world map, and along the opposite wall was a row of eight file cabinets, all locked, steel rods running down the faces of the drawers. Outside a dimly lit corridor led to the front of the basement of Government House, where the offices of the other Mossad departments were located.

"Welcome to C-Seven," Goldmann said, indicating a chair for Asheim to sit down.

"I spoke with my daughter last night," Asheim said, his voice controlled.

Goldmann had a pained expression on his face. "I was hoping to avoid that."

"I didn't tell her I was working for you. I just told her I was going to have to go away for a while."

Goldmann said nothing.

"She's taking it badly. But the worst part for her was that her husband had to do it alone. He had no help."

Goldmann wore a dark suit with a vest. He adjusted his tie and sat down, then looked slowly around the room at the map and the file cabinets as if he were cataloging the contents of his office. "Except for another room down the hall about the same size as this one that houses my two assistants, this is all of C-Seven. It's never been any bigger, and it never will be." He looked up at Asheim. "We have a budget to match, if you can call it that, and everyone works alone. Everyone."

Asheim could see the expression of hurt and bewilderment on his daughter's face when he had picked her up at the airport. But she had not let go until they got back to his apartment and put the children to bed.

"Benjamin was nothing more than a fucking government clerk, in federal travel records. He had no business working for you."

"Your son-in-law was suited for the job. I explained to him and Deborah exactly what was expected of them, and they both accepted. With their eyes open, Major. They did not have to go down there."

Asheim's other daughter, Sandra, was driving up from Kibbutz Ze'Elim in the south to pick up her sister and the two children, who would return with her. "Is it that important?" he asked, the harshness suddenly gone from his voice. He sat down in his chair.

"I think so," Goldmann said softly. "But you don't have to do this, you know. You can back out."

"I'll do it."

"Because you're sick of fighting Arabs?"

Asheim shook his head.

"Because of your son-in-law?"

"Partly."

Goldmann looked away. "Travel section has your papers ready, at least your initial identification. As and when you need others, they will be gotten to you."

"When do I leave?"

"In the morning. We have an apartment for you in Buenos Aires, and Israeli Press Service is expecting you, although you won't have to do much for them."

"I can penetrate Stoeffel's stronghold. I've studied the photos you gave me, and I know I can get in there," Asheim said.

Goldmann shook his head. "It wouldn't accomplish a thing. This isn't a cops-and-robbers game. The people we're dealing with are all wealthy, all respected, and all very shrewd men, each with his own private army. Even if you did manage to get into Aerie, let's say even hold Stoeffel at gunpoint to get the story out of him, you'd never live to get the information back here. Not now. It's too early."

Asheim started to protest, but Goldmann cut him off.

"Listen to me, Asheim. We're not dealing with ordinary men. We're dealing with sophisticated networks of men and women all over the world, in all walks of life. If you managed to take out even one or two of them, it would be nothing more than taking a couple of legs off a centipede. Nothing more than a minor irritation."

"I could take out the eleven leaders, one by one."

Goldmann waved that off, obviously irritated. "We've already gone over that, Major. You either are going to cooperate with me or not. Which is it to be?"

Asheim lit a cigarette, inhaled deeply, and then sat back in his chair. Deborah and the children would be all right at Ze'Elim. There was a good school there and plenty of work for her to do. Beyond that he had no ties here.

"What am I to do?" he asked.

Goldmann looked relieved. "At first nothing more than watch."

"And then?"

Goldmann shrugged. "We play it by ear. We improvise. Which is exactly why I came to you. You're known as a man who is able to think on his feet."

Asheim noticed a framed photograph on the desk facing

Goldmann, and he nodded toward it. "Your family?"

"I have no family," Goldmann said, and he turned the photo around. It was a picture of Adolf Hitler. "He is the reason for this office and my job."

There was so little to go on, Asheim thought as he stared at the photograph. Yet what little they had was the cause of his son-in-law's death.

He looked up at Goldmann. "The Odessa has planned some unknown scheme, which will involve some unknown man, whom they have finally found apparently after a long search, and in two years this scheme is to be pulled off. Not much to go on."

"No, there's not," Goldmann admitted. "But somewhere among Stoeffel and the other ten Odessa leaders there will be a clue. It is up to you to find it. And find it within the two-year time limit."

"After that?"

"Stop whatever it is they are up to, any way you can."

"With little or no help, and with nearly everyone outside this room against me."

Goldmann nodded. "Welcome to C-Seven."

5

It was one week to the day from Colleen's funeral when the chauffeur-driven limousine pulled off Highway 50 outside the town of Lake Geneva, onto the property of the old Mac-Arthur summer residence. Kelsey had consented to look at the place, and this morning he had driven up from Chicago with his father.

The last week was a blur in Kelsey's mind. He had not returned to Chicago with his father immediately but instead had remained in Minneapolis to close down his apartment and make his good-byes at the university.

He had toyed with the idea of heading for California for the summer but then had dismissed it. He and Colleen had wanted to go to San Francisco during their summer break, and he could not stomach the idea of going out there without her.

Instead he had gone to Chicago, where he had stayed with his father in the large house in Evanston for a couple of days. The old man, persuasive as ever, had finally convinced him to take a look at the place on the lake.

"Old man MacArthur gave this place to his kids, but none of them wanted it, so I bought it a couple of years ago," Kelsey's father said.

A narrow blacktop road led off the highway through a tall, wrought-iron gate and down a steep, wooded hill toward the lake. The day was bright and warm, and yet in the thick woods it seemed like twilight of a cool day.

"Did the MacArthurs ever live here?" Kelsey found himself asking for want of anything better to say. He was really not interested.

"A few summers, from what I understand. But the house has spent most of its fifty years empty except for the caretaking staff. I kept them on after I bought the place."

Kelsey turned to his father. "Why'd you buy it? Were you planning on moving up here?"

The old man smiled wistfully and patted his son's arm. "I thought about it. I thought it would be a nice place for my grandchildren to visit."

Pain stabbed at Kelsey's heart. He turned away as the car came around a bend at the bottom of the hill, and the Mac-Arthur summer place came into view.

It was a mansion in the grand tradition: row upon row of windows like soldiers stacked three stories high; chimneys bristling above the tree line; cornices, and balconies, and a balustrade at the main entrance.

"Stop here a moment," his father told the chauffeur. They stopped across a football-field-sized lawn from the house.

"It's grand, isn't it?" the old man said.

"My God, it's huge," Kelsey said. "There must be twenty-five or thirty rooms in it."

"Thirty-two rooms to be exact. Sixteen of which are upstairs bedrooms, not counting the servants' quarters."

"And this was a summer house?"

The old man smiled again. "MacArthur loved to entertain. It is a bit ostentatious . . . as a house, that is. But as a clinic . . ."

Kelsey looked sharply at his father. "Don't start with that again, Father. I told you I was coming up here with you for the drive. Nothing more."

The elder Kelsey was a small man, his face lined with age, and his hair thin and white, but his eyes were clear and very penetrating. "Now that I've got you this far, would you like to take a look inside?"

"As a tourist, nothing more," Kelsey said, and the chauffeur drove them the rest of the way, parking in the wide drive at the front entrance.

"Around back are the garages and maintenance building, which includes a generator powerful enough to run the entire household in case of electrical failure," the old man said as they climbed out of the backseat of the Mark V limousine. "Below, on the lake is a boathouse, a patio, and a sauna big enough to hold two dozen people. We passed the groundskeeper's quarters, and stables by the highway."

"All it needs is an airstrip," Kelsey said as they started up the steps.

"The workmen are coming next week to install a helipad on the roof."

"For what?" Kelsey asked sharply, stopping at the massive, hand-carved front door. "Are you planning on moving here and commuting to your office in Chicago?"

"No," the old man said, and Kelsey was about to protest what he knew was about to come, but his father opened the door and went inside. Kelsey followed.

The entry hall was huge. A massive staircase curved to a second-floor balcony, on one side of which could be seen another staircase leading to the third floor. A man in white coveralls was polishing the deep walnut woodwork at one end of the entry hall while another similarly clad man was installing a new light fixture from the ceiling high above them. From other parts of the mansion Kelsey could hear the sounds of work going on; hammering, sawing, drills buzzing.

"You're going ahead with this, aren't you?" he said, following his father across the entry hall toward a set of double doors to one side of the stairway.

"If you mean am I opening a clinic here, yes, you're right. But what part you play in it, or don't, is up to you." The old man opened the double doors with a flourish. Kelsey followed him into a huge room that had apparently once been used as a library or study. Now it was completely refurbished into a large, elegant, and very comfortable office, furnished with everything including books, a massive desk, a leather couch and chairs, modern drapes at the French doors that led to a small private balcony, and plush carpeting.

"This is to be the medical director's office," the old man said, crossing the room to a bar set up on a sideboard. He poured a drink and offered one to his son.

Kelsey waved it off, but remained where he stood by the open doors. "I told you I was not interested."

"Fine," the old man said. "This office connects with another, slightly smaller office for the administrative director. The remainder of the staff will have their offices and workrooms across the entry hall. The east wing will contain consultation rooms, a small laboratory and supply, as well as the kitchen. The west wing will house an operating theater, recovery rooms, another complete laboratory, and a small intensive care facility for burn victims who come here for reconstructive surgery."

"Goddammit, father . . ." Kelsey sputtered, but the old man slammed his whiskey glass down on the sideboard, slopping some of the liquor on the hardwood cabinet. He was angry.

"Don't you goddamn me, Richard. If you want to wallow

in self-pity, that is your business. Meanwhile I've decided to open the Kelsey Clinic with or without you. I've hired the administrative director and all the nonmedical staff. What remains is the selection of the medical director–chief surgeon and his staff, who will supervise the design and installation of the medical facilities."

He took a step forward. "I'm an old man, Richard, and I've accumulated more wealth than I ever dreamed of having. I can use my money for evil or for good, or when I die, let the government take most of it. I choose to do good with my money in my lifetime. I've set up a trust fund, the principal recipient of which will be the clinic. Later, in a couple of years, I'll divert a substantial portion of the fund into building and operating a research institute in Chicago."

Kelsey could think of nothing to say, although he wanted to go to his father and calm him down.

"I'm just vain enough to want to call this place the Kelsey Clinic, and the research facility, the Kelsey Institute," the old man said sadly. "And it was pride that made me believe you would open this place, run it for a couple of years, and then take over the research institute."

Kelsey turned away and walked slowly out into the entry hall. The workmen were still busy at their jobs, but the one polishing the woodwork looked his way and nodded. Kelsey nodded back.

"You Doc Kelsey?" the man shouted across the hall.

"Yes, I am," Kelsey said.

"You're sure going to have a swell place here," the man said, and he went back to his work.

Kelsey shook his head and walked across the hall and down the wide corridor into the west wing of the mansion.

Here there were no workmen, but the rooms had been gutted and completely redone with spotlessly polished tiled floors, acoustical ceilings, recessed lighting, and extra-wide doors. In the largest of the rooms, at the center of the wing, there were already nonsparking safety electrical outlets, as

well as piping for oxygen, nitrous oxide, and hospital vac-
uum. Beyond that room were others, some with heavy electrical cables for X-ray and other equipment, some with
cabinets and laboratory shelving already installed, and others with overhead electrical connections for patient monitoring devices. At the end of the corridor was a large
elevator that could be used for transporting postop patients
to their rooms.

It was all here. Or at least the makings of a fine clinic
were already begun. All it needed now was a doctor to complete the design and installation of the proper equipment,
and then run the place.

"I had originally planned that Colleen would be head of
nursing," Kelsey's father said.

Kelsey turned. "I don't know if I can handle this."

"Perhaps you can't, but what's the alternative?" the old
man asked.

"Nothing is the same," Kelsey said. "I can't feel anything anymore."

"It was the same for me when I lost your mother. But
life is for the living. I can't believe that Colleen would have
wanted you to die with her."

The ache was so bad that Kelsey wanted to lie down in
the middle of the corridor, curl up, and drift away.

The old man pressed the elevator button and the door
opened immediately. "Let's go upstairs and look at the
rooms. There are sixteen of them for patients. The servants'
quarters will be used by the staff."

"What about quarters for the administrative and medical
directors?"

"I bought a condominium in town. It's only a five-minute
drive."

Kelsey shook his head. "I'd have to stay here."

"No," his father said firmly. "You need this place for
your work. To fill that part of your life. But you must include people. You'll live downtown."

6

It was his night to close the bookstore, and it was well after 9:00 P.M. by the time the last customer left and he locked the doors. He placed the evening's receipts in the safe, signing the cash register total slip with the name he was using for this cover. At other times he had been other men. Werner Hempel. Walter Holvig. Walter Handel. But here, he was Arthur Stornberg.

The weather in Boston was unseasonably cold and blustery. The rain came in sheets directly into his face as he headed on foot the two blocks to the parking ramp where he always kept his car.

Very few men knew his real identity, and the few outside the Odessa leadership who had made the mistake of recognizing him were dead.

But he had the facility of forgetting who he really was, sublimating his personality to whoever he was posing as at the moment. And at this moment, Stornberg was glad when he turned in to the nearly empty five-story parking ramp. He was cold.

He trudged up the stairs, but at the open door on the third level he stopped a moment in the shadows. Something was wrong. He could feel it.

This level was empty of cars except for his battered Fiat parked about fifty feet away from where he stood. There were no sounds except for the rain and the wind, and yet he sensed something. And then it struck him. He was smelling a man's cologne. Very faint. As if someone had passed this way a short while ago.

He edged away from the door, hurried down one flight of stairs, and then ran along the second-level ramp, turning left at the end to take the driveway up.

Someone was waiting for him near his car, he was almost certain of it. And he had survived this long by listening to his hunches.

As the ramp rose to meet the third-floor level Stornberg ran in a crouch, hiding behind the low wall that held the parking meters, until he came to the thick concrete post at the corner. He stood up and eased around the corner. There, in the shadows behind a similar concrete post about five feet from his car, a man was watching the stairwell door.

Stornberg stepped away from the post and walked directly to him, making no noise.

He stopped five feet from the man. "If you move, I'll kill you," he said softly.

The man stiffened but did not turn around.

"Why are you waiting for me?"

"Herr Stornberg," the man said. "I've come from a friend in Miami."

This was all wrong. Either the man was a government investigator who knew about Stornberg's Odessa connection, or he was who he claimed to be, a messenger boy. In either event he was an amateur.

"Move your hands away from your body and turn around very slowly," Stornberg said, and the man complied, a wide grin on his face.

"I didn't think you were coming at first," the man said, "I thought you were off work at six, so I was here at five forty-five, but when you didn't show up I got worried."

Stornberg said nothing. There was something strange about this. The man was about his height and general build, and appeared to be about the same age. But he was a fool. They would not send a fool to contact him. Yet they had.

"They told me not to go to the bookstore, so I had no other choice than to go to your apartment. I thought maybe you had left your car here for some reason and got a ride home."

"You were at my apartment?" Stornberg asked quietly.

"Yes . . . sir," the man said. "There was no answer at your door, but your landlord told me that you were probably working late at the bookstore."

A faint flicker of surprise played across Stornberg's features. The man was more than an amateur. He was a dangerous bungler.

"So you came back here to wait for me?"

"Yes." The man nodded. "I have a message for you, and instructions."

"Yes?"

"Number one: You are to destroy your identity here. Number two: I have a key for a public locker at Logan International which contains your new identity. Papers, clothes, money, and all that. Number three: You are to proceed as soon as possible to Aerie for a long-term assignment. And number four: I am at your disposal if you need help." The man said it all as if he had learned the words by rote.

Stornberg suddenly understood why this particular man had been sent to him. "I am going to need your help."

The man lowered his hands, his smile even more effusive.

"Anything, Herr Stornberg. Anything at all. Just ask."

For several moments Stornberg stood silent, his head cocked at a slight angle as if he were listening for something. But he was quickly going over each step he would have to take to make good his untraceable escape to Aerie. The groundwork had been laid for him; all he had to do was follow through with it.

"Where is your car parked?" he asked.

"It's a van, actually. Upstairs on the fifth level."

"Anyone else parked near by?"

"Not as of ten minutes ago."

"Fine," Stornberg said. "I'll drive you up. Get in."

They climbed in the car, and Stornberg drove up the two levels to where the man's Ford Econoline van was parked. He pulled up next to it.

"Do you have a spare can of gasoline by any chance?" Stornberg asked.

The man looked slightly puzzled. "As a matter of fact, I do. They said you might need it."

Stornberg smiled. "Not me. You're going to need it."

"Sir?" the man asked.

"It's simple," Stornberg said. "You and I are going to change clothes and IDs. I'll take your van out to the airport to pick up my alternate identity papers and then take a flight to New York. There I'll destroy your identity, and with my new papers I'll take the first flight to Buenos Aires."

"What about me?"

"Posing as Arnold Stornberg, you are going to take my Fiat and drive back to Miami tonight. You'll carry the extra gas so that you won't have to stop at a gas station until you're well out of Boston. In Miami you'll be given instructions for getting rid of the car and assuming a new identity."

The man seemed pleased. "I've been a loyal supporter of the organization for a long time, but this is the first assignment of any importance I've ever been given. It is an honor to work with you, sir."

Stornberg patted the man on the arm, and they got out of the car and went into the back of the van, where they quickly changed clothes, including everything in the pockets. As Stornberg suspected, the man's clothing fit well.

"It's been a pleasure working with you, sir," the man said, shaking Stornberg's hand.

"Sure," Stornberg said. They got out of the van and Stornberg walked back to the car with the man.

"I'm glad I could be a help to the cause," the man said, beaming.

Without warning Stornberg smashed his right fist into the side of the man's head, knocking him unconscious across the front seat of the Fiat.

He grabbed the gas can from the back and splashed the entire five gallons in and around the car, making sure the unconscious man was soaked.

He put the gas can in the rear of the van, then climbed in behind the wheel, started the engine, and backed out of the parking spot, swinging around so that he was behind the Fiat.

The man *had* served the cause well, he thought as he cranked down his window and lit a book of matches. And the man would continue to serve the cause well, he thought as he flipped the burning matchbook toward the Fiat, then slammed the van in gear and took off.

An intense ball of flame lit up the entire fifth floor. A moment later the van was around the corner and headed down toward the street.

Witnesses would tell police they saw a van leaving the parking ramp. It would be found at the airport. But by then Stornberg, under his new identity, would be on his way to Buenos Aires. The old Stornberg would be burned beyond recognition in the Fiat.

He emerged from the parking ramp and headed in the rain toward the airport, looking forward with pleasure to whatever the long-term assignment was that awaited him, completely putting out of his mind the man he had just murdered.

TWO YEARS LATER
1981

A crowd of people had gathered in front of the American embassy near downtown Buenos Aires, and the black Cadillac limousine had to slow down to avoid hitting the Argentinian soldiers ringing the area.

Many of the protesters carried posters, shaking them angrily over their heads. Inside the bulletproof limousine the chauffeur and the two old men seated in the back could hear the shouts and chants.

"Americans go home!"

"America the backstabber!"

Sigmund Dortmund turned to his friend seated next to him and smiled, his teeth yellowed from the cigars he smoked, his breath coming in a ragged wheeze. "We never allowed such things to happen. It was one of the secrets of our success."

Dieter Schey, a man equally as old as Dortmund and equally as frail, patted his friend's knee. "You are living in the past, my old comrade."

Dortmund looked beyond Schey at the crowd outside and nodded. "Perhaps," he said thoughtfully.

Behind them traffic began to back up, and several drivers honked their horns; a number of them leaned out their windows and shouted at the soldiers to clear the way for them.

Only a few white clouds scudded across the perfectly blue sky; the sun glinted off the windows and polished bits of exposed chrome and steel throughout the great city.

It was mid-December and summer had come to the southern hemisphere, a fact of nature that neither Dortmund nor

Schey had ever become accustomed to despite the fact that this had been their home since they had fled Germany early in 1945. Both men missed the dark German beer from small country towns, the knockwurst and other fat sausages from the East, the heady cheeses from the South, the rolling hills, the *Autobahns*, the Munich beer halls, the Schwartzwald, and most of all Nuremberg. Glorious Nuremberg.

There had been no response to the crowd from within the American embassy, and the several hundred angry students had begun to weary of their demonstration. The soldiers, who at first had been frightened that they would have to engage in a battle, had become bored with what had turned out to be nothing more than a stupid demonstration. Now the soldiers sensed the crowd's waning enthusiasm, and they began to clear a way for the traffic to move through.

"Just a moment now, *meine Herren*," the chauffeur said, glancing in the rearview mirror at the two old men in the backseat.

But Dortmund had not heard him. Instead his mind had turned inward to his memories. Nuremberg. One million troops assembled in precise orderliness for the greater glory of the Third Reich.

"*Sieg Heil!*" The cry had arisen simultaneously from a million pairs of lips. "*Sieg Heil!*" It rose up out of the stadium. It rolled across the countryside. It echoed and re-echoed around a world that their Fuehrer had nearly brought to its knees.

The limousine began to move finally, the driver working his way slowly and cautiously past the soldiers, through the remnants of the departing mob.

A rock struck the side of the car. Two soldiers pounced upon the student who had thrown it and clubbed the young man to the ground with the butts of their rifles. None of the other demonstrators came to the young man's rescue. The heart had gone out of the crowd. They wanted no trouble. Most of them wanted only to return to their homes and nap so that they would be refreshed for the dinner hour, which began at ten o'clock.

"Nuremberg?" Schey said softly.

Dortmund looked up out of his thoughts and smiled somewhat guiltily. His wife said that particular expression made him seem more like a little boy than an SS *Oberst*.

A few windows had been broken in the embassy building, and the iron fence had been splattered here and there with bright red spray paint. Other than that, little or no damage had been done.

By the time the limousine had made it to the end of the block, the last of the demonstrators had either scurried away or been dragged into two waiting military vans with flashing blue lights.

In Berlin in the early days such people would have been summarily shot, Dortmund thought. No. Actually such demonstrations had been impossible. Unthinkable. In those days there had been order. Purity of thought and deed. Stern purpose.

In 1937 Dortmund had been a schoolteacher in Hamburg. Schey had been the headmaster of the school. Together they had joined the *Schutzstaffel*. Together they had gone through officers school, had trained in intelligence together, and both of them had been transferred to the Abwher, working for Admiral Canaris.

It was not surprising this had happened, because both of them had been very good at what they did, both of them had ties, however slight, with Canaris' family, and both had been friends in school together.

"Opportunists under the same banner," Schey had once said.

Free of the traffic jam caused by the demonstrators, the limousine sped along the Libertador Highway to the northwest, the Rio de la Plata Estuary to their right. Dortmund put the window down a crack so that he could smell the ocean. He breathed deeply.

"It reminds me of Usedom Island when I was a boy."

Schey laughed, and Dortmund glanced sharply at him, somewhat irritated.

"It was a resort before Peenemünde was constructed as a rocket research station."

"You are too thin-skinned these days, Sigmund," Schey said in a conciliatory tone. "As a boy my parents took me to Usedom one summer, and I was merely remembering with you the loveliness of a summer's day."

Dortmund looked out the window at the azure ocean, and for a moment he could let himself believe that he was a little boy again with no worries instead of an old man whose life was nearing an end. There had been so many plans for the future.

"One race united under a common flag for a common purpose." Poland. Czechoslovakia. Romania. Yugoslavia. Greece. Italy. Norway. France. Libya.

The flags are high . . .

The ranks are tightly closed . . .

Bits and pieces of the Horst Wessel song ran through Dortmund's mind along with snatches of the melody of "*Deutschland Uber Alles.*"

To walk the streets of Paris as a conquering hero. To enter Rome a venerated ally.

Thirty-five miles north of the city, near the town of Campana, the limousine turned off the main highway onto a narrow dirt road without slowing down, and Dortmund came out of his thoughts. The thick jungle had closed in around them, and it was dark in the car.

"The Americans have gone too far with this Chinese thing," Schey said.

Dortmund shook his head. "There will be some unrest. But we missed our golden opportunity in the sixties."

"We made money," Schey countered.

"Yes, but what has it done for us? Made a few old men like you and me and the others a bit more comfortable?

Financed a few minor acts of retribution?'' Dortmund shook his head. *"Ach du lieber meiner alter Freund.* But did our money keep poor old Spannau alive? Has it advanced our cause significantly?''

Schey said nothing.

"What we need is a purpose. A direction."

"You forget the plan."

Dortmund waved Schey's comment away as if he were brushing an irritating insect from his face. "We have heard nothing for nearly two years. Stoeffel hides here in his fortress like some medieval king without a word to any of us until now."

"There is the Jew."

Dortmund laughed, the sound more like the crackle of dry branches in the wind. "Yes, our Jew watchdog. He has been to watch de Hoef in Miami, our poor little mouse Heinzman in Washington, D.C., you, Stoeffel, and me here in Buenos Aires, and everyone else. But he has accomplished nothing. He is no more than a puppy dog for Goldmann.''

Their conversation was cut short when the chauffeur stopped at a tall gate in the wire mesh fence surrounding Stoeffel's estate. A burly man in a security guard uniform approached the car. Dortmund lowered the window.

"Dortmund and Schey."

"Guten tag, meine Herren. Herr Stoeffel and the others are waiting for you in the house," The guard said.

Dortmund raised the window as the man stepped back and waved them through.

Half a mile later they came out of the jungle into a large clearing at the center of which was Stoeffel's twenty-seven-room baroque mansion built with SS funds shortly after the war.

Leaded windows, stone arches, parapets, and gargoyles along the roofline made the mansion seem like something out of a fairy tale. But both men knew, despite Dortmund's comments to the contrary, that the future of the Odessa, and therefore their hopes for a new Third Reich, lay here.

Stoeffel had been the organizer of the Odessa. He had been the most brilliant, the most wealthy, and the best connected of them. Even now, despite the occasional bickering between the old men, he held them together. In fact, the plan was his idea. And as insane as it had seemed to them, they had all gone along with it.

The limousine drew up to the mansion's main entrance, and the chauffeur helped Dortmund and Schey out of the car. They mounted the steps as the ornately carved wooden door opened. Stoeffel's personal secretary, a former low-ranking SS officer, took their coats and hats, and showed them to Stoeffel's study at the rear of the house.

Kurt Stoeffel was seated at the head of a long conference table in the center of the huge, high-ceilinged room. Eight other old men were seated around the table. When Dortmund and Schey came in, they looked up, and Stoeffel got to his feet.

"We were becoming concerned. What kept you?" he said. Stoeffel's voice was soft, but it held a note of genuine concern.

"There was a traffic tie-up near the American embassy," Dortmund said. In front of him on the table was a single sheet of paper upon which had been typed a timetable. "Am I to assume that you are ready to proceed with this scheme?"

"It is up to this gathering to decide that," Stoeffel said graciously. He was a tall man and very thin with intense blue eyes. He had aged better than any of them and always dressed exceedingly well. "I am merely ready to report that the first phase of the operation has been completed."

Dortmund's right eyebrow rose. He hadn't thought it would have gone this far. He looked at the others around the table but could find no hint of his own skepticism in their eyes. He shook his head.

"What's the matter, Sigmund?" Stoeffel said. "When we first began planning this operation it took three months to convince you. Have you changed your mind again?"

"On the contrary." Dortmund fingered the piece of paper in front of him. "But this is a desperate gamble. I've maintained that all along."

"There are no other alternatives."

"I cannot believe that," Dortmund said. He knew he was being arbitrary, but he could not help himself. "If this fails, we all may be exposed."

Stoeffel laughed. "The youngest man in this room is sixty-nine years old, Sigmund. We have come to the end."

"But the young men will take over from us," Dortmund said. It was the same argument as two years ago.

"No," Stoeffel said gently. "They have no direction. No sense of purpose."

"For a good reason," Thomas Heinzman said at Stoeffel's right. Dortmund looked his way.

"What might that be, Thomas?"

"We had our Fuehrer to lead us. The new ones only have us."

Dortmund looked around at the others, and despite himself, he had to smile. The mouse Heinzman had a point. Who would follow a group such as this for anything other than money, which was the worst of all loyalties?

"It comes down to one man, one rule, one philosophy," Stoeffel said. "We have the philosophy—and by association the mechanism for the rule. We have only needed the man."

"He is ready?" Dortmund asked.

"At long last yes," Stoeffel said. His eyes were bright, and the others looked his way in expectation. Even Schey seemed eager. Dortmund felt his own pulse quickening.

"You have actually accomplished this thing? The training took? It worked?" Dortmund asked.

Stoeffel nodded. "Besides the fact he is of the correct build and age, he has an exceedingly quick mind, and since he was raised in the Midwest of the United States, he has the correct accent.''

"He has agreed to do this? To try?"

"From what I am told by the team who has worked on him these two years, that is a meaningless question. His mind no longer is his own. He is subject to total control."

"How can he operate successfully?" Dortmund objected. "The thousands of day-to-day trivial details would be beyond any kind of control."

Stoeffel leaned forward. "You misunderstand, Sigmund. His mind is essentially the same as it has always been, with only two differences. Like a dog, he has been trained to respond to given situations in certain very carefully defined ways. It's as if he was in reality a German shepherd who has been thoroughly trained to act, and especially react, as a Saint Bernard."

"If he is dressed in a Saint Bernard's costume, he will appear to actually be a Saint Bernard," Schey interjected.

"Exactly," Stoeffel said.

"And the second difference?" Dortmund asked.

"The second difference is our control. Our Saint Bernard will be on a leash no matter where he is, what he is doing, or what is demanded of him; we will have absolute control."

"Who knows of this besides us?" Dortmund asked. There was a cold feeling in the pit of his stomach.

"I've compartmentalized the entire project so that only those in this room as well as my personal secretary know all the details. My house staff and officers know bits and pieces, but they are loyal." Stoeffel paused a moment. "Which leaves only the medical team who have worked on him for the past two years. There are seven of them. They will be flown out of Buenos Aires in two days. Their airplane will explode in midair over the ocean. There will be no survivors."

"Everything has been worked out," Dortmund said as a statement, not as a question.

"Very nearly, as you shall see for yourself," Stoeffel said. He stood up. "Within a little more than one year our project will begin to bear fruit, and we will be headed toward a new Third Reich. Something we all have dreamed about for more than thirty years. Each of you will have a specific part in accomplishing this goal, which you will be expected to complete within the year. Later today you will be briefed on the specific details."

Schey sat forward in his chair. "Before we proceed, Kurt, tell me about this Jew watchdog of ours."

A brief look of consternation passed across Stoeffel's face. "What about him?"

"Is he a threat to this?"

"No," Stoeffel said. "There is little doubt that he is an agent for Goldmann from Tel Aviv, sent to find out who murdered the little Jew who killed Spannau. The man has found nothing—and will find nothing."

"Does he constitute a possible threat to this plan?" Schey persisted.

"An obstacle hampering our free movement, nothing more."

"Why not eliminate him?"

"No," Stoeffel said sharply. "Not unless he gets in our way. If he is murdered, Goldmann will be certain something is going on. At the moment he can only guess."

Schey did not seem satisfied, but he sat back. A moment later Stoeffel crossed the room to a large painting hung low on the wall.

"Let us begin," he said dramatically, and he touched something on the edge of the picture frame. The painting slid silently upward, revealing a large window that looked into what appeared to be a medical examining room.

A man in a white laboratory coat stood with his back to the window. When he moved aside, the eleven old men saw a man whom they had known variously as Hempel, Holvig, Handel, Stornberg, and a dozen other names, seated calmly on the edge of an examining table.

"For the moment they can neither hear nor see us, although the doctor has been signaled it is time to begin," Stoeffel said. He turned toward the conference table. "Comrades, I give you James Locke, a mechanical engineer from London."

Dortmund was confused. The man looked no different from the last time he had seen him three years ago. "I don't understand," he said to Stoeffel.

"Bear with me a moment, Sigmund, and you will understand," Stoeffel said calmly. "Mentally he is ready. Physically the only thing we have done for him is alter his dental work to match the subject he is to impersonate. His face will be changed by the best plastic surgeon available."

"Why hasn't that already been done?" Dortmund asked.

"Because it would have been impossible to bring that particular man down here for various reasons which I won't explain at the moment."

"But our cover?"

"As I just explained, for the moment this man is James Locke, a mechanical engineer. Mr. Locke is about to have a nasty industrial accident which will require total surgical rebuilding of his face. When that is accomplished he will be ready to assume his new role."

"Where will he be kept for recovery? And how long will it take?"

Stoeffel smiled. "It will take six months to a year. And he will be kept in Fairbanks, Alaska."

Dortmund was about to object, but then he understood perfectly, and he, too, smiled, and for the first time since this meeting had been called, he began to relax. Perhaps it would all work out after all?

"The control words are *eagles fly*," Stoeffel said. "Whenever, wherever, he hears those words, he will be compelled to make contact for instructions. Furthermore, when he hears those words, he will be compelled to do exactly as he has been trained and exactly as he is instructed.''

"Magnificent," Dortmund said softly.

Stoeffel turned back to the picture frame and again touched something on the ornate pattern of wood. "Eagles fly," he said, and the man seated on the examination table looked up, his face contorting into a boyish grin that was slightly reminiscent of someone else.

Stoeffel came back to the conference table as the white-coated doctor in the examining room began his work.

"Locke has been given a shot of morphine to kill most of the pain, but he knows what is coming. He has been programmed to completely accept his fate without objection. Among other things, it will be a test of how well his programming has taken," Stoeffel explained.

The doctor donned a pair of rubber gloves, then wheeled a tall cart over to the table. "Your right hand," the doctor said, his voice audible in the study over a loudspeaker, Locke raised his hand.

The doctor dipped a swab into a shallow metal tray on the cart and swabbed something on Locke fingertips.

"Sulfuric acid," Stoeffel said.

Locke stiffened, strain evident on his face, but he made no move to withdraw his hand.

"It eliminates the fingerprints."

Dortmund watched, fascinated by the absolute control the two words had imposed on the man whom they had all known as a fiercely independent operative. Locke was in great pain despite the morphine but made no move to fight the doctor's ministrations.

When the doctor was finished with the fingerprints on both hands, he set aside the swab and rolled the cart away, pulling into its place some kind of mechanical device.

"Mr. Locke will have an accident that will disfigure him

so completely that his entire face will have to be rebuilt. To our specifications,'' Stoeffel said. ''This device was perfected at Saschenhausen with the help of a couple of thousand more or less cooperative patients.''

The doctor strapped Locke's head in the device, then stepped back and pushed a lever down. The machine came into a life of its own, slamming specially shaped battering rams into Locke's face, blood gushing everywhere, the sound of crunching cartilage and breaking bones sickening over the small loudspeaker.

Locke began shaking, his legs twitching uncontrollably, but still he did not turn away from the devastating machine.

''Mr. Locke will be flown out of here tonight directly to London, where he will be admitted to the hospital we have arranged for his primary recovery.''

''And then?'' Dortmund asked, not able to drag his eyes from the gruesome sight.

''Within a few days he will be placed on an air ambulance which will take him to the plastic surgeon who will perform the work.''

Dortmund looked at Stoeffel. ''Where is the doctor?'' he asked.

''Lake Geneva, Wisconsin. It is the Kelsey Clinic,'' he said, and everyone in the room smiled broadly.

PART TWO

7

It was 7:00 A.M. Dr. Kelsey stood at the sliding glass doors in his fifth-floor condominium looking across Lake Geneva as he talked with his secretary on the telephone.

"Say that again slowly," Kelsey said, the sleep leaving his brain.

"I said someone broke in here last night," the young woman repeated herself.

"Drugs?"

"No, sir, that's what's odd about it. Our medical records section was broken into."

"That doesn't make any sense," Kelsey said, trying to think. "What the hell would anyone want with medical records on our patients?" He stopped a moment. "Have you had a chance yet to inventory for what's missing?"

"Not a thing is missing. In fact, we never would have known there was a break-in except for Digman, who happened on the man."

"Man?" Kelsey asked. The lake was not yet frozen over

for the winter, and a small boat with an outboard motor headed away from the public dock with two men attired in old coats and fishing hats. Kelsey wished that he were going out with them for a day on the lake.

"Digman was making his rounds about six this morning when he saw a light from the records room. He went in to investigate in time to see a man going through the medical files. The man knocked Digman on the head and got away."

"Jesus Christ," Kelsey swore, running the long, delicately formed fingers of his right hand through his thick shock of dark brown hair.

Kelsey was not an unhandsome man, but at six feet he was just a little too thin, his face just a little too angular and his features a little too fine to be considered masculinely good-looking. Some women found him attractive, while most found him lacking.

"Digman is all right, and the police are on their way," his secretary was saying. "Meanwhile you have a busy day."

Kelsey turned away from the window and, trailing the telephone's long extension cord, went into his bedroom. "You're sure Digman is okay, and nothing is missing, Marion?"

"Absolutely."

"All right then, what's on the deck besides the police?"

"At nine you have Mrs. Gardner's rhinoplasty, after which you've got a couple of screening interviews. And then at noon there's the Kiwanis talk."

Kelsey cut her off with a groan. "Is there any way you can get me out of that one?"

"Sorry, boss, but you promised. You backed out the last time and now they're counting on you. They've even sent a reporter from one of the Chicago newspapers up to listen to you."

"Christ," Kelsey swore again under his breath. "Why the hell me?"

"Because you're the best there is. You're news."

"Bullshit," Kelsey said.

"You're right," his secretary said, laughing. "At two you've got the augmentation mammaplasty on Shelly Hope, which not only should brighten your day, but probably is the reason for the Chicago newspaper's interest."

Kelsey smiled. Miss Shelly Hope was MGM's up-and-coming answer to Marilyn Monroe and Dolly Parton all in one. The young woman could act, could sing, and could dance. Six weeks ago, however, she had been injured in a freak car accident in which her breasts had been badly damaged by flying glass.

"See what you can do for her," a studio executive had asked Kelsey last month.

At first he had refused. Although the Kelsey Clinic did take such cases, they were booked solid for at least six months for anything other than vital emergencies.

But the executive had been persuasive. "Two things I want you to think about before you say no, Doc," the man had argued. "The first is that without big boobs, Miss Hope is as good as dead in the entertainment world."

"There are other doctors . . ." Kelsey had tried to interrupt, but the man had been firm.

"You're the best. I don't want some hack fucking her up. She's too important."

"And the second thing?" Kelsey said dryly.

"I spoke with your father. He tells me that before long you'll be opening a research clinic. You're getting out of the cash-and-carry business."

Kelsey had been instantly angry. His father had promised him the research institute if he would operate the clinic for a couple of years, but the old man had also promised not to interfere, and until this moment he had not.

"At any rate," the studio executive was saying, "do a

good job for us on Shelly and you will find that MGM will be very helpful and generous when it comes time for research grants.''

Kelsey had wanted to tell the man no, but he had thought better of it, and had finally capitulated. The ''cash-and-carry business,'' as the man had called it, was lucrative. The research institute would not be.

''Anything else?'' Kelsey finally asked, bringing his mind back to his secretary.

''You're open tonight,'' she started to say, but then stopped herself. ''Oh . . . I almost forgot. Your father called about fifteen minutes ago. Said he wanted to talk to you as soon as you came in.''

''Is he here in town?''

''No. He said you were to call him at his office.''

''Right,'' Kelsey said. ''I'll be there in a half an hour. Have Mrs. Gardner prepped.''

''Yes, sir.''

A Lake Geneva police car was parked in front of the clinic when Kelsey arrived. He parked in the back and entered by a rear door going directly to his office. The clinic's administrative director, Stan Lowe, Kelsey's secretary, Marion Bloggs, the night watchman, Phil Digman, and two police officers were waiting for him.

Lowe, a short, fat, bald man whom Kelsey had not liked from the first day they met, was sweating profusely. When Kelsey entered the office, he jumped up.

''Someone broke in here last night,'' he said excitedly.

''I know. Marion called me half an hour ago,'' Kelsey said.

The police officers got to their feet. One of them extended his hand. ''I'm Leroy Wilson, and this is my partner, Ralph Granville.''

Kelsey shook their hands and then went around his desk and sat down. ''Have you found anything yet?''

"No, sir," Wilson said. "And I doubt if we ever will."

Kelsey glanced at Digman, whose head was bandaged. "Are you all right, Phil?"

Digman nodded but said nothing.

"This obviously was the work of a professional," Wilson said.

"A professional what?" Kelsey asked. "And why would he want to break in here? Nothing is missing."

"That's what we'd like to ask you," Granville said.

"I don't understand."

"Have you any enemies, Dr. Kelsey?" Wilson said. "Any competitors who might want to look at your medical records?"

"I'm not in that kind of business, if you're talking about industrial spying. I've developed no new techniques that I haven't already published. And the clinic is open to visiting doctors.

Wilson nodded as if Kelsey's answer was the one he had expected. "Blackmail?"

"I don't think so," Kelsey said. "Most of my patients are proud of the fact they've had plastic surgery and can hardly wait to heal so that they can show their friends their new nose, or face-lift, or whatever."

Wilson shrugged. "No one here is being worked on in secret?"

Kelsey smiled. "I'm afraid not."

"Then we'll probably never know who broke in here last night, or why," Granville said.

"I thought Phil got a look at the man."

"Only from the rear," Digman said. "And it happened in a dark room and so fast, the only thing I could see was that the man was large and had white hair. Not much to go to the cops on."

"I appreciate your help anyway," Kelsey said, standing. "But whoever it was probably came here looking for drugs. Perhaps he thought he would find inventory files or something there which would tell him what kind of drugs we stocked and where they were kept.''

"Perhaps,'' Wilson said, and he and the other officer got to their feet, shook hands again with Kelsey, and left.

Lowe seemed on the verge of collapse. "I don't understand this at all,'' he said, shaking his head.

"Neither do I, Stan, but I think we'd better get back to work,'' Kelsey said. He turned to his secretary. "Is Mrs. Gardner ready?''

"Yes, sir,'' the woman said. She was short and trim and fairly good-looking. From the beginning she had had a crush on Kelsey, but he had never responded.

"Have someone take Phil home, but first get my father on the phone. I'll talk to him before I do Mrs. Gardner.''

Lowe was just leaving, but he stopped at the door and turned back. "Are you going to tell your father?''

Kelsey looked at him. "What do you mean?''

"Are you going to tell your father about what happened here last night?'' Lowe said. He seemed worried.

"I suppose. I don't know,'' Kelsey said. "I'm sure the man was after drugs. Why do you ask?''

"No reason,'' Lowe said just a little too quickly, and he left the office, Marion and Digman right behind him.

When they were all gone, Kelsey sat back down in his chair and lit a cigarette. Marion had brought him a cup of coffee, and he sipped it as he waited for his call to his father to go through.

There was something the matter with Lowe, he thought. The man had seemed almost frightened not only of what had happened last night, but of the possibility that Kelsey would inform his father.

The telephone buzzed, interrupting his thoughts, and Kelsey picked it up.

"Your father is on the line, Dr. Kelsey,'' Marion said.

"Hello, Father,'' Kelsey said.

"Good morning, Richard. How are things at the clinic?"

"Just fine," Kelsey lied, not really knowing why he had decided not to tell his father about their trouble.

"I've got a medical problem I need your help with."

Something clutched at Kelsey's stomach. "Is it you? Are you all right?" Kelsey had been expecting something like this for a long time now. Although his father was, as far as he knew, in good health, he was seventy-one years old and still worked six days a week. Kelsey had tried to make his father understand that a man his age had to slow down.

"It's not me," the elder Kelsey said, laughing. "And even if it was, I certainly wouldn't need a plastic surgeon. I've lived with this face long enough without feeling the need to change it."

Kelsey breathed a sigh of relief. "What is it then?"

"A friend of mine in London who owns Farley Chemicals telephoned me last night. One of his best engineers, a man named James Locke, was injured in an accident. Completely disfigured the poor devil."

"And you just happened to mention that your son was a plastic surgeon."

Again the old man laughed. "Actually my friend knew of you, and he came to me to ask if he couldn't send his man over here."

"We're stacked up for the next six months," Kelsey said. "Besides, my two years are up, I've decided on a research program, and you promised to get started on the research institute."

"I hate to be the kind of man to dangle a carrot, son, and I wasn't going to tell you this until next month, but we broke ground for the building five days ago."

Kelsey was speechless.

"I acquired some property in Lake Bluff, and the building should be done within nine months, ready for you to move in."

Kelsey had to laugh. "Which gives me enough time to help your friend's engineer. Right?"

"Something like that," the old man said. "You must admit that except for Shelly Hope, I've never interfered."

"And I've also got to admit that I've never been able to say no to you."

"A son's duty to his father."

Kelsey pulled a pad of paper toward him and picked up a pen. "Give me the name of the hospital he's at, and I'll make the arrangements for his transfer here."

"Won't be necessary," the old man said. "At this moment he is on his way by air ambulance. I've made arrangements for an ambulance to pick him up at O'Hare this afternoon. He should be arriving at the clinic around four o'clock your time."

"Goddammit, Father," Kelsey laughed, throwing down his pen. "You'd better have a great pile of money in that research trust fund, because I'm going to bleed you dry."

"Do a good job on Locke. Farley and I have been friends for years."

"I don't do anything but good work," Kelsey said.

"I know," his father said. "I know."

8

It was snowing in Chicago when Lev Asheim entered the Israeli consulate building on Wacker Drive, stamped his boots on the floor in the entryway, and approached the receptionist.

A folk tune that he could not quite recognize played softly from speakers set in the ceiling. The girl behind the desk was young, dark, and beautiful. The atmosphere reminded him of home, and the feeling hurt.

The young woman looked up and smiled, her white teeth flashing. "Good morning, sir; welcome to the national Consulate of Israel. May I help you?"

Asheim returned the smile. He was tired. It seemed as if he had not slept in a week—and had not relaxed in a century or more. "I would like to speak with the consul general if he is in this morning."

"Mr. Bernstein is in a meeting at this moment. Do you have an appointment?"

"No, I don't," Asheim said. The girl reminded him of

his youngest daughter. "But if you will tell him that Major Levi Asheim is here, I am sure he will see me."

"I am sorry, Major, but unless your business is urgent, I really could not disturb him." Her voice was soft with a definite accent, and Asheim was suddenly very homesick.

He smiled again. "He will see me if you let him know I am here."

"Yes, sir," she said. She picked up the telephone and dialed three numbers. "This is the desk. Would you inform Mr. Bernstein that Major Levi Asheim is here to see him with an urgent matter?"

Asheim turned away from the desk and looked around the large entry hall. On the far wall were several posters depicting vacation spots in Israel, among them the Sea of Galilee, Jerusalem, and Tel Aviv. He shook his head, unable to see anything in the posters other than what was never shown: gun emplacements, snipers, terrorists, tanks, mobile missile launchers. Israel at times became nothing more than an armed camp. Certainly not a country to visit as a tourist unless you were perverse or had pride in an independent Jewish state.

He had pride, he had to admit to himself. But at what cost? Once he had taken inventory not only of his friends, but of everyone he knew, and there was no one among them who did not have at least one family member who had died violently.

At what price? And what was he doing now to advance the cause other than fight Goldmann's war?

He shook his head in irritation. Two long, stinking, miserable years, for what? Two years of second-rate hotels. Second-rate restaurants. Two years of racing around the world following old men and their associates. Two years of looking at old records that told him nothing.

Deborah had met a man at the kibbutz, and three months ago when he had spoken to her on the phone from New York, she had invited him to the wedding. It had made him even more bitter, and he had not talked to her since.

"Benjamin has been dead less than two years," he had blurted. "What about the children?"

"We can't live alone, Father," his daughter said, hurt. "We loved Benjamin—and still do. But we cannot live alone."

"I'm sorry, sweetheart."

His daughter was silent for a long time, the hiss and static of the transoceanic telephone line the only sounds over the receiver. Finally her voice was back on the line, seemingly at the end of a long tunnel.

"Can you come to the wedding, Father?"

"No . . . I can't."

"You are working on it, aren't you?"

"Yes," he said.

Again his daughter fell silent for several seconds. When she spoke again her voice sounded cold and distant. "Be careful, Father. They are ruthless, and I'm not sure it's worth the effort."

"I don't think it is, either," Asheim said emotionally.

"Come home, Dad . . . please?"

"I can't."

"I love you," she said, and she hung up.

Asheim was choked up by the remembrance, and he jumped as someone touched his arm.

"Major Asheim?"

He turned to face a young man in a light gray business suit, his hair short-cropped in the military style, his features set and grim beyond his years.

"Mr. Bernstein will see you now."

Asheim followed the young man to a large office on the fourth floor.

"May I get you anything, sir?"

Asheim shook his head.

"Mr. Bernstein will be with you momentarily, then, sir," the young man said, and he left the room.

The office overlooked Wacker Drive. Asheim went to the window and looked down at the traffic making its way through the snow. On his way from Lake Geneva this morning he had heard on the radio that the storm was expected to end by early afternoon. But it made no difference to him. His work here was done.

The door opened, and Asheim turned as a squat, bald man entered the office and closed the door.

"Major Asheim?" the man said, coming across the room and extending his hand. "I am Peter Bernstein, the consul general."

Asheim met the man halfway and shook his hand. "I need your help."

Bernstein made no move to offer Asheim a seat. "I'm afraid I can't offer much."

"You know who I am."

"Your name appeared on a diplomatic circular some time ago. But my explicit instructions, Major Asheim—explicit— were to offer you aid so long as it was nothing illegal as far as United States laws were concerned."

"I need a secure telephone line to David Goldmann in Tel Aviv."

Bernstein looked at him. "What have you done, Major?"

"I don't understand."

Bernstein nodded to the left. "Two doors down the hall from here there are two men from the Chicago office of the Federal Bureau of Investigation waiting for me to return. They showed up here about ten minutes ago asking about you."

"In what connection?"

"They claim you broke into a clinic in Lake Geneva sometime this morning and killed a security guard."

Asheim's heart accelerated. "Why did they come here, did they say?"

Bernstein's expression did not change. "They were informed that an Israeli national by the name of Levi Asheim was working here illegally. Some kind of a network operation for which you needed a supply of drugs."

Asheim's mind was racing. For two years he had done his snooping. Had done his watching with no reactions. But now suddenly all hell was breaking loose.

"What did you tell the men?"

"I told them I had never heard of you, but that I would check our records. Naturally I was quite surprised, and certainly disturbed, when my aide said you were here."

Asheim went to the desk, picked up the telephone, and held it out to Bernstein. "The secure line to Goldmann, please."

Bernstein made no move to accept the phone. "Did you do what they said?"

"I broke into the clinic in an attempt to get some information, but I did not kill the security guard." Asheim could see the old man. The fright on his face. He could feel the strength of his blow. No. He had not killed the man. He had merely stunned him. If the guard was dead, he had been murdered by someone else.

Still Bernstein made no move to accept the telephone.

"Would it make any difference if I had killed the man in the line of duty?" Asheim said a little more sharply than he had intended.

Bernstein flinched. "I abhor violence."

"Then never return home, Mr. Consul General."

Bernstein's mouth opened to speak, but no sounds came out, and obviously torn by indecision, he stepped forward and took the phone from Asheim, then dialed a number.

"I need a secure line to Tel Aviv," he said, his voice harsh. "No. I want it now." He turned to look at Asheim, but said nothing.

"Were you advised as to my mission here?" Asheim asked softly.

Bernstein shook his head. "I have lived in America for nine years this time. I was born in Miami, but I emigrated to Israel in 1949. I am a Jew, yet I have a great feeling for this country."

"You are a foreigner in your own birthplace."

"Yes," the little man said bitterly, and he turned back to the phone. "Tel Aviv military operator? I need David Goldmann on a secure line please."

Asheim had suspected for some time now that the men he had been watching knew he was there but tolerated him as long as he did not get in the way.

In reality he was no threat to any of them. Their birth records and other documents detailing their lives up to and including the war were all either lost or had been carefully doctored to present a picture, in each case, of a man who had opposed the Nazi rule.

And since 1946 all of them had lived exemplary lives in their adopted countries. Lives of bankers and doctors and industrialists. Outstanding men in their communities. Respected everywhere they went.

Goldmann's "proof" that these men were indeed former SS members began with eyewitnesses. Jews who had survived the war and recognized the old men for what they had been.

"Mr. Goldmann, this is Peter Bernstein, the consul general in Chicago, Illinois. I have Major Asheim in my office. He wishes to speak with you." Bernstein handed him the phone.

"Go back to the FBI agents and tell them there is no record of me here," Asheim said. "Try to find out how they knew the name."

Bernstein nodded, the expression on his face grim, and he left the room.

The encryption device on the telephone line gave Goldmann's voice a certain curious, high-pitched quality, but Asheim could hear the note of excitement.

"It has begun, and already the roof is starting to cave in," Goldmann said.

"What happened?"

"A lot in the last three days, Lev," Goldmann said, his voice fading for a moment. "Now, listen carefully."

Asheim perched on the edge of the desk and lit a cigarette as Goldmann talked.

"Three days ago a man was moved from Aerie and was loaded on board a plane to London."

"How do you know that?" Asheim asked sharply.

"Six months ago I managed to come up with funding to reman the travel bureau in Buenos Aires. Our people in London identified the man as James Locke, who supposedly is a mechanical engineer with Farley Chemicals. He spent the last two days in a hospital with extensive injuries to his face and hands."

Asheim's mind was racing. It was beginning to fit.

"Early this morning Locke was loaded aboard a plane with a flight plain filed to Chicago. I'm assuming his ultimate destination is the Kelsey Clinic."

"I just came from there," Asheim said.

"I know," Goldmann shouted, the connection fading again. "About an hour ago Dayan himself came down to see me. Said the American ambassador is making waves. Seems your name was mentioned in connection with the murder of an American citizen at the Kelsey Clinic."

"So Locke is coming here to have Kelsey work on him. Give him a new identity."

"That's the assumption, but we still don't know why," Goldmann said. "Did you find anything at the clinic?"

"Not a thing. And it's going to be difficult to get back up there."

"Impossible," Goldmann said. "You have to get out of the country immediately. We've come too far to risk it all now with your arrest. Someone else will watch the clinic. The FBI has got your photograph and has issued an APB on a charge of murder."

"Have Mr. Begin explain it to the ambassador," Asheim

said, but he knew what Goldmann's answer was going to be even before the man spoke.

"No way. I was told to recall you. The operation has ended. It is a direct order."

Asheim tried to think. On his deathbed Spannau had mentioned a two-year plan and a man to carry it out. Locke was the man, and at this moment, the plan—whatever it was— was about to begin. And yet Goldmann was calling him back.

"I'll leave the country today, but I am not coming back to Tel Aviv," Asheim said.

Goldmann was silent.

"If it has already started, we have to find out what they are planning to do with Locke once Kelsey finishes with him. If we can come up with that information, you can take it to the Americans."

"What are you planning?"

"I am going to the source."

"Be careful, Lev. I can't do a thing for you. If you're picked up in the United States, Dayan says you will be fed to the wolves. And that too was a direct order."

"I'll leave tonight."

"They're probably waiting for you in Buenos Aires. They tipped the Americans off, and if you aren't caught here, they'll be expecting you there."

"What do you want me to do?"

"Officially, return home. This file has been closed."

"Unofficially, wish me luck," Asheim said grimly.

"Did you kill the man at the clinic, Lev?"

"No."

"Then *shalom*," Goldmann said, and the connection was broken.

9

Shelly Hope's operation had lasted much longer than Kelsey had anticipated it would, and it was well after four in the afternoon by the time he had taken the last suture.

Part of the delay was because Miss Hope's breasts had been cut up worse in the accident than he had expected. There had been a lot of excretory duct and glandular tissue damage that had not been evident until the operation began.

Rebuilding the tissue under normal medical practices was time-consuming, but rebuilding tissue in such a way that the scars would be hidden *beneath* the breasts after healing made it even more difficult.

The operation had gone well, though, and within six months to a year, Miss Hope's breasts would be the pride of the studio, and she could resume her stunning career.

But another reason for the delay, Kelsey had to admit to himself, was his own preoccupation. He had done everything very slowly, careful at each step to make certain that he was paying total attention.

But all through the operation he could not shake from his mind the incredible fact that Digman was dead.

The night watchman had insisted on driving himself home, and Marion had finally let him go only after he promised to check in at the hospital in Lake Geneva for head X rays. He never made it.

The two police officers who had been there earlier had returned shortly before noon with the news.

"The man was dead before his car went off the road," Wilson said. "The autopsy is going to show that the blow on the head killed him. We're looking for a murderer."

The police officers had pressed for more details about the clinic, its staff and patients, and Stan Lowe had taken care of them while Kelsey went to the Kiwanis lunch in town.

He finished cleaning up, and when he had changed back into his street clothes, he went out into the corridor and headed for his office.

Elizabeth Norby, the *Chicago Tribune* reporter who had covered the Kiwanis lunch, was waiting for him in the reception hall, and when he emerged from the clinic wing, she jumped up from where she had been seated.

"How'd it go, Doc?" she said brightly. "Will Shelly Hope pose for a pinup picture again?"

Marion Bloggs came out of the office wing and stood at the entryway, a disapproving expression on her face.

"She'll be fine. Maybe even a bit better than she was before the accident."

"That good, huh?" the woman said, her right eyebrow rising.

Marion Bloggs came across the hall. "Mr. Locke has arrived, Doctor," she said. "He's waiting for you in your office."

"Excuse me, Ms. Norby, but I have a patient to attend to," Kelsey said graciously.

The woman shrugged. "I have a few more things to ask you, so if you don't mind, I'll stay awhile."

"I don't know how long I'll be."

"I can wait."

"After Mr. Locke, you *are* open, Doctor," Marion said sweetly, and Kelsey glanced sharply at her. She was being catty, and he didn't like it when it was at his expense. But there was nothing he could do short of denying the reporter the continuation of the interview.

"When I'm finished I'll talk with you."

"Take your time, Doc," the woman said, and Kelsey followed Marion back to his office.

Just outside his office door Marion stopped him a moment. "I've started an admission jacket on him, and they're set up to receive him upstairs, but I thought you'd better take a look at him first."

"I didn't know he was ambulatory."

"He shouldn't be. He seems to be in considerable pain, but he's stubborn. Said he wanted to talk to you personally."

"All right," Kelsey said. "Barbara should be about finished in postop, have her come down to the examining room right away. I'll take a quick look at him and then he can go upstairs."

"Yes, sir," Marion said, and turned to go, but Kelsey stopped her.

"Don't play games with me and Ms. Norby. I'm not in the mood."

"A brassy little broad, isn't she?"

"Almost as bad as you," Kelsey said, smiling, then he went into his office.

Locke was seated in front of the desk, and when Kelsey came through the door, he looked up. His face and both hands were completely swathed in bandages, and Kelsey could immediately see from the way the man held himself that he was in considerable pain.

"My father told me that you were an employee of a friend of his," Kelsey said, coming across the room, "He didn't mention that you were a stubborn man, Mr. Locke.''

Locke coughed, the sound muffled by the bandages. ''Before they give me any more happy pills, I wanted to talk to you, Doctor.'' His voice was slurred. He was having difficulty talking.

''We can talk tomorrow,'' Kelsey said. ''I'd like to take a quick look under those bandages before we put you in your room and settle you down for the night.''

Locke got to his feet, careful to hold his head at a certain angle. He clumsily pawed a thick manila folder from the desk with his bandaged hands and handed it to Kelsey. ''They sent my medical records with me,'' he said as Kelsey took the thick package.

''I can look at these in the morning—'' Kelsey started, but the man cut him off.

''Before you tuck me in for the night, Doctor, I want you to look in the envelope. I've brought some pictures of how I want my face to look.''

''It's a little early for that.''

''No,'' the man said insistently. ''I want you to look at those pictures so that when you examine me, you can tell me immediately if you can do the work.''

''Why is this so important to you?'' Kelsey asked.

Locke turned away a moment, and when he turned back, he held out his bandaged hands. ''All my life, Doctor, I have been an ugly man. I'm not married, never have been, because there isn't a woman alive who'd look at me.'' He rocked his shoulders back and forth. ''This . . . accident . . . it was a blessing in disguise.'' He came a step closer to Kelsey and peered at him through the eye slits in his bandages. ''I was pretty well banged up in the accident. My nose is crushed, my cheeks were broken, and my whole face is a mess.'' He touched Kelsey's arm with a bandaged hand. ''All I want to know is if you can give me a nice face. I know it sounds kind of foolish, but I picked out the nose, the eyes, the cheeks, and the chin I'd like to have.''

Kelsey felt a compassion for the man. It was a familiar story he had heard over and over again. "I'll see what I can do, Mr. Locke. I can't promise you anything more than that at the moment."

"Good enough, Doctor," Locke said, a note of relief in his voice.

The examining room across the hall from Kelsey's office was ready, and Barbara Courtland, the chief R.N., was waiting when he arrived with Locke.

They helped the man lie on the examining table, and as Kelsey washed his hands and donned a white coat, the nurse carefully cut away the bandages covering Locke's face.

The man was a mess. There was substantial bruising and massive swelling of muscle tissue, but most of the skin was fairly well intact, so there would be no problem involving skin grafting to conceal scar tissue.

The nurse prepared a local anesthetic, and when Locke's face was sufficiently numbed, Kelsey began probing with a delicate touch for damage to the bones and cartilage.

The nose was completely crushed, as was the left cheekbone just below the eye. The right cheekbone had been chipped, a large piece of it floating loose within the muscle. Massive swelling of the masseter and levator labii superior muscles on both sides of the face had occurred, giving some indication that the jaw, also heavily damaged, had been dislocated and reset. Miraculously, none of the teeth had been damaged. And yet it was a wonder to Kelsey that the man was able to talk at all, or in any way stand the pain.

"I want a full series of X rays first thing in the morning," Kelsey said to the nurse. "Also work up a complete measurement profile on all features, as well as blood type, EKG, and the rest. We'll have to go in for some preliminary work tomorrow afternoon. I want to relieve the nasal pressure, and it looks as if there might be a slight pressure on the nerves controlling the orbicularis oculi muscle, at least in the right eye."

Kelsey stepped away from the examining table, and Locke pushed himself up on one elbow.

He couldn't talk because of the anesthetic, but he pointed frantically with his right hand at the manila envelope Kelsey had laid on the counter.

"All right, I'll take a look at your pictures," Kelsey said, helping the man back down. "But first I want you to promise you won't move. Every time you do, you risk the chance of severing nerves that I can't do a whole lot with."

Locke lay still, but he watched as Kelsey went across the room and opened the envelope.

Inside were Locke's medical records from the hospital in London, which indicated that in addition to the facial injuries, the man's fingers had been burned. There also was a series of what appeared to be photographs cut from magazines. There were several from different angles of a well-formed, if somewhat angular, nose, and others of cheeks, a chin, and eyelids. They all seemed to have come from the same, or at least a similar, face, and from what Kelsey had been able to see of Locke's features, he could envision no difficulty in complying with the man's wishes.

One thing he was certain of, however, and that was that Locke was either a liar, or was a man with some kind of a psychological problem. He had never been an ugly man. Kelsey could see that even though Locke's face was now badly disfigured. In fact, the man had probably not looked too dissimilar to the photographs in the manila envelope. At least the basic features had been similar, so matching the photos would present little or no problem.

Kelsey went back to the table and smiled down at the man. "If these photos are what you want, what you really want, I can do it for you, although I'd prefer to see a photo of you as you were and match that."

With great effort Locke managed to shake his head.

"All right," Kelsey said. "We'll start the preliminaries tomorrow. But you must know that this isn't going to happen overnight. You'll be here a couple of months, and then it will take another six months or so for you to heal.''

Locke managed a slight, off-center smile, and Kelsey washed up and left the examining room as the nurse rebandaged the man's face.

Elizabeth Norby waited for him in the reception area, and he realized that again he had forgotten she was here. At this moment all he wanted to do was go home, take a hot shower, and go to bed. It had been a long, tiring day.

"You look fagged," the reporter said.

"I am. You don't suppose we can do this some other time?"

They were alone in the entry hall and the young woman smiled pleasantly. "Are you finished here for the day?"

"Finally," Kelsey said. "I don't mean to be rude, but I'd just like to go home, have a drink, and go to bed."

"If you switch the order around, and have a drink first, I'll buy. We can talk for a few minutes . . . I promise, only a few minutes . . . and then I'll leave you alone."

Kelsey looked at her. She was a good-looking woman, somewhat reminiscent of his wife.

"I'm from the old school," he said, smiling. "I'll have that drink with you, but I'm buying."

10

It was six o'clock and already dark when Asheim left the Israeli consulate by a back door. The two FBI agents who had spoken with Bernstein had remained in plain view parked in front of the building all afternoon, and were still there.

They told Bernstein that they had received an anonymous tip from someone in Chicago, and that the intruder at the Kelsey Clinic was Asheim, which told him three things.

Despite his snooping over the past two years, and despite his intrusion at the clinic, the Odessa was not very worried about him.

If he was arrested, it would naturally be expected that he would tell the FBI everything. Who he was, what he had been doing over the past twenty-four months, and why.

But they knew that he would never be believed, simply because there was no proof of any of his allegations.

The second was a confirmation of Goldmann's supposition that Locke was the man Spannau had talked about.

Locke was coming to the clinic to get a new face. The Odessa had murdered Digman in such a way that Asheim's arrest would be ordered, and with luck he would be taken out of the picture.

The third was that the Odessa not only knew his real name and who he worked for, but they had a fair idea of his movements. If that included his room in the shabby boardinghouse in Cicero, getting out of the United States would become difficult at best.

It was snowing lightly as Asheim slipped out the back door and jumped down into the alley from a loading dock. He had watched out a rear window for more than an hour, but as far as he could tell, no one was waiting. Evidently the FBI agents believed Bernstein when he told them that Asheim was not there. They were keeping a loose watch on the consulate on the off chance that Asheim might show up after all.

He hunched up his coat collar, pulled his hat low, and trudged through the snow to the end of the alley, where he turned right. Few people were on foot, but traffic was heavy, and at the corner one block away from the consulate, Asheim boarded a bus with three other people, paid his fare, and settled into one of the seats near the rear door.

Earlier today he had parked the rental car, leased under the name Forest Tanner, in a ramp just off State Street near sixtieth. Going to it now would be the first test of exactly how much the Odessa knew about his recent movements, and how much in turn the FBI had been informed.

He rode the bus for ten blocks, then got off, walked two blocks, and hailed a cab, ordering the driver to take him to Garfield and State, several blocks from the ramp.

Goldmann had done and said what he had to. From this moment on, Asheim would be on his own. The word would go out that he was a renegade. A criminal in his own country.

It was understandable, though. Begin was in the middle

of new peace talks with Sadat, and the new American president, Barnes, and wanted no waves made anywhere.

Twenty-four hours ago Asheim might have agreed with his orders and returned home. But not now. He did not like being pushed, and he knew that if he did return home, there was a likelihood he would be handed back to the Americans to face murder charges.

Goldmann had evidently been told that Asheim was to be fed to the wolves. If any of them thought it would indicate Israel's goodwill and cooperation, Asheim would be on the first plane back to the States to stand trial.

And yet, he asked himself as he settled back in the seat and lit a cigarette, what could he possibly hope to accomplish? He was going up against a powerful, well-financed worldwide organization who knew his name, his face, and his purpose, whereas he knew little about their plans.

He had one advantage, however, he told himself, a half smile forming on his face. Twenty-four hours ago he was playing by Goldmann's rules: Watch, look, listen, but don't touch. Now he was going to play this game by his own standards.

During the last two years he had done a lot of thinking about his son-in-law Benjamin, who in reality had been only one more death among millions directly the result of the Third Reich. Death was something they understood best of all.

Death, he told himself, was what they were going to get.

The cab pulled up at the curb; Asheim paid the driver, got out, and headed the remaining distance to the parking ramp on foot as he thought out his next moves.

Of the eleven surviving members of the Odessa leadership, three lived in Buenos Aires, including Kurt Stoeffel, who ran the Bank of Buenos Aires and maintained the jungle fortress Aerie; Dieter Schey, who owned the Missiones Province Hospital and twenty-five others across South America; and Sigmund Dortmund, who was a high-ranking member of the Argentine Ministry of Finance and Planning despite the power he had held in the early days as a Peronista. So that city was his first logical step.

In Mexico City it was Louis Stebenfeld, a landowner; in Bonn it was Herman Mueller, a member of the German State Department; in London it was Alois Hartmann, a legitimate armaments dealer; in Cairo it was Walter Deering, a military adviser to the government; and in Paris it was Otto Bergholtz, who owned an aircraft engine manufacturing firm.

Which left the three here in the States: Thomas Heinzman, the assistant director of the school of medicine at Georgetown University; Ronald de Hoef, president of the All-America Insurance Corporation in Miami; and in Chicago, August Kelsey, head of Kelsey Electronics, Ltd.

After he talked with Goldmann, he had done some thinking while waiting for the opportunity to slip unnoticed out of the consulate.

At first he had considered remaining in the States and working on the three Odessa leaders there.

But he had rejected that plan because if he made too many waves this close to the Lake Geneva clinic, the plan—whatever it was—might be called off, and he would never know what they had intended.

There were risks in that kind of thinking, he knew. At this moment he had a chance to end the plan by returning to Lake Geneva and killing both Locke and Dr. Kelsey. The Odessa had worked on this scheme for two years or more, and such a move would eliminate any plans they might have, or at least seriously set them back.

By opting to go directly to Buenos Aires, to Stoeffel, he ran the risk of his own death before the plan could be stopped.

Goldmann's hands were tied. If Asheim died, there would be no time for him to send another operative, and the Odessa would succeed.

Asheim paused a moment across from the parking ramp,

studying the cars parked along the street and the people hurrying through the snow along the sidewalks.

Buenos Aires, it had to be, he told himself, taking a deep breath and starting across the street. It was the one place he was certain he could find out exactly what the plan was. If he could make it that far.

11

Kelsey picked up the Chicago and Minneapolis newspapers at a newsstand in town, as he did many mornings, and then headed around the lake on Highway 50 toward the clinic. The morning was cold, but the sun from the clear sky reflected brightly off the snow that had fallen most of the evening.

For the first night in a long time, he mused as he drove, he had not dreamed about his wife. Since her death he had been having a number of weird dreams about her. In one he was trying to save her from drowning but was held back by his own fear. In another he was the commander of a troop of riflemen who had lined his wife against a brick wall. At the moment he gave the command to fire, he would awaken.

Last night was different. He had dreamed, but this time it was about Liz Norby. In great detail, and in color, he had dreamed about moving to Chicago, where he had wooed and courted the young woman, finally taking her to bed.

Dreams, he had learned from the psychology courses he

had taken in med school, were nothing more than the release of stifled or repressed thoughts and feelings.

In his dreams about his wife, it was his guilt feelings being released. If he had gone with her the night she'd had her automobile accident, he might have been able to prevent it.

And last night's dream had been nothing more than a simple sexual fantasy. He had spent less than an hour with the young woman at the cocktail lounge, and during that time they had spoken only about Shelly Hope and about the clinic in general. But when they said their good-byes, he'd had the urge to ask if he could call her again soon, but had not.

He was horny. Nothing more, he told himself, smiling, as he turned off the highway and started down the entrance road to the clinic. He was attracted to the woman, and perhaps he would telephone her after all.

The driveway had not been plowed and was drifted over in spots, so Kelsey parked his car at the front entrance, not wanting to get stuck at the rear of the main building, and he mounted the steps and entered by the main doors.

At seven Marion had telephoned as usual with his day's schedule. Locke was prepped and would be ready for the first of his preliminary operations. The problem was to relieve the nasal blockage and the pressure on the nerves in the right cheek that controlled eyelid muscles without doing anything that would impede the planned reconstructive work that would begin shortly after the first of the year.

Then at eleven o'clock, he had a blepharoplasty on the upper and lower eyelids of a fifty-year-old woman from New York who had such a great amount of herniated fat in both lids that she looked like a hooded cobra.

He was free for lunch, but at one o'clock he had to begin an operation that usually produced tremendous results, but which he hated to do.

A young woman of twenty-five who had suffered severe

acne as a teenager had come to him for a dermabrasion, in which the outer layers of her skin would be literally sanded away.

It was a messy operation and always involved acute pain for his patients for weeks afterward. This afternoon's operation would only be the first of four planned for the young woman, who had been advised fully of the painful aspects, but who had nevertheless agreed.

Marion was emerging from his office when Kelsey came into the entry hall. She hurried over, out of breath, white-faced, obviously disturbed.

"What is it?" he said, forcing himself to remain calm, but a cold feeling was growing in his gut.

"The radio . . ." she said. "Did you listen to the radio on the way in?"

Kelsey shook his head. "What happened, Marion?"

"The newspaper reporter who was here yesterday . . . She's dead."

For several seconds Kelsey was aware of nothing but his breathing and his dream last night about the young woman. But then he took Marion's arm and guided her across the entry hall into his office.

"Now, take it slow, and tell me everything you heard," he said.

"They said Elizabeth Norby's car was found in the woods at the bottom of a ravine where it had gone off the road, turned over, and burned. It happened about two this morning."

"Where?" Kelsey felt cold.

"Off Highway 50, a couple of miles from here."

It didn't make sense. He had left her at the cocktail lounge around six-thirty, and she said she would be heading back to Chicago. So what had she been doing near the clinic at two in the morning?

Marion looked at him with a strange expression on her face. He focused his attention back to her.

"What else?" he asked.

"The police . . ." she started. "They said she had been seen with a man earlier in the evening. The police are looking for him."

Kelsey nodded. "I had a couple of drinks with her. But I went home—alone—at six-thirty. She told me she was going back to Chicago right away."

Marion said nothing.

He looked at his watch. It was just past eight o'clock. "I have to get ready for Locke, and afterward Mrs. Hermitage, but I'll be free about noon. I want you to call those two cops who were here yesterday and have them in my office."

Marion reached out and touched Kelsey's arm. "What is it, Richard?" she asked, using his first name, which she rarely did. "What's happening? First poor Phil and now that woman."

Kelsey shook his head. "I don't know, Marion, but we're going to find out."

Locke's operation, although it presented some difficulties, was, for the most part, routine. Beginning with incisions inside the nasal passages, Kelsey was able to get his instruments past the blockage of the airway and clear out the debris that had been pushed inward and toward the center, impeding the man's breathing. He did little at this point to repair the extensive damage or reshape the structure of the nose itself. That would come later.

The hair on the right side of Locke's head had been shaved two inches above the ear, and Kelsey made a long, sweeping incision above the normal hairline near the temple, down around the ear, following the natural preauricular crease. It was the same incision used for face-lifts, and in Locke's case it would be reopened later when reconstruction of the cheek and chin on the right side was begun. Once it healed, the very thin scar would be invisible unless his head was shaved.

.

Kelsey worked the fingers of his left hand beneath the flap of skin, probing the muscle tissue just beneath the eye until he found the large bone chip that had shown up on the X rays and worked it loose toward the opening. With his right hand he inserted a large curved tweezers and gently removed the chip from the muscle.

Had it been left in place, it would have caused damage to the muscle controlling the right eyelid's movements. Damage that could have been permanent.

By ten forty-five he was finished with Locke, and had washed up and changed gowns for Mrs. Hermitage's blepharoplasty, another routine operation.

The lower eyelids were opened just at the eyelash line, the fibers of the muscles were separated, and the tiny globules of fat were forced out of the central, mesial, and lateral compartments. A similar procedure was used to remove the excess fatty tissue from the upper eyelids, except that the incision lines were along the superior palpebral fold, the entire procedure for both eyes taking slightly less than two hours.

It was twelve-thirty when Kelsey was cleaned up, back in his street clothes, and in his office. Wilson and Granville, the two police officers from Lake Geneva, were waiting for him.

"Thanks for coming," Kelsey said, going around behind his desk. "I'm sorry I kept you waiting."

The two cops exchanged glances. "When Mr. Lowe telephoned us about the discrepancy in your inventory, we thought we'd better come out and talk with you."

"What?" Kelsey said.

"You didn't know anything about it, Doctor?" Wilson asked, a strange expression in his eyes.

Kelsey punched the button on his intercom and Marion answered.

"Marion, have Stan Lowe come in here," he snapped.

"Yes, sir," she said. She sounded shook.

"When did Mr. Lowe telephone you?" Kelsey asked.

"About eight this morning," Wilson said. "He didn't tell you?"

"No," Kelsey said, tight-lipped, and a moment later Lowe came in the office.

"What the hell is happening around here, Stan?" Kelsey said harshly.

Lowe closed the door behind him and came across to the desk, nodding at the two cops. "I decided to check the inventory again this morning, and I found most of our morphine gone out of surgical supply."

"Who checked it yesterday?"

Lowe looked away from Kelsey's eyes. "I'm afraid I'm going to have to admit that I did. I just didn't catch it. I'm sorry. I guess I was just a little shook up."

"Why wasn't I told this morning?"

"I was tied up with some other work," Lowe said defensively. "By the time I was free, you were already in the operating theater. I had planned on telling you as soon as you were finished."

"I see," Kelsey said. "Is there anything else you've neglected to tell me?"

Lowe looked defiantly at Kelsey. "Nothing," he said. "Is there anything else, Doctor?"

Kelsey stared at the man for a long moment, but then he shook his head. "No, and I'm sorry I snapped at you, Stan."

"I understand," Lowe said, smiling.

When Lowe was gone, Kelsey sat down, his mind racing in a dozen different directions. Everywhere he turned there seemed to be some kind of mystery. And Kelsey did not like puzzles with no apparent solutions.

"I get the impression, Doctor, that there is something else on your mind," Wilson said.

"It's about Elizabeth Norby, the woman killed in the accident last night," Kelsey said. Neither cop's expression changed. "I had cocktails with her."

"Yes, we know," Wilson said. "You left her and returned to your condo about six-thirty."

Kelsey was startled. "How did you know that?"

"The bartender called us this morning and said you were with her until then. The night man in the garage at your place told us you came in alone about six thirty-five and didn't leave until a quarter to eight this morning."

"The news this morning indicated you were looking for a man who had been seen with her," Kelsey said.

"Yes," Wilson said. "She was seen leaving town around midnight with an unidentified man in her car. Not you."

Kelsey slumped back in his seat. Something was wrong, but he could not put his finger on it.

Wilson, who had been standing the entire time, leaned over Kelsey's desk. "What *is* disturbing you, Doctor?"

Kelsey looked up into his eyes. "Until yesterday this was a peaceful medical clinic. Yesterday someone broke in here, apparently to steal drugs, and killed my night security man. Later in the day a newspaper reporter came to talk to me, and a few hours later she was dead. What the hell is happening?"

Wilson shook his head. "Trouble comes in bunches, Doctor; believe me, it's nothing more than that. The FBI is working on the break in because we believe the man who was here is a foreign national. Your unfortunate Mr. Digman was an old man—the knock on his head was too much for him." He glanced at Granville. "And as for your reporter friend, we have it on a good authority that among other things, she has been working on a Mafia story. They finally got to her."

"That doesn't make sense," Kelsey said. "If she was that kind of a reporter, what the hell was she doing chasing a feature about a movie star's operation?"

"Her editor tells us that she was coming up here to meet a man who was going to give her information. She came to interview you only as a cover."

The feeling that something was not right was still strong in Kelsey, and it showed on his face.

Wilson smiled pleasantly. "From what I hear, Doctor, you're a hell of a plastic surgeon. But as a detective you're a washout."

Kelsey got slowly to his feet and shook the detectives' hands. "I suppose you're right," he said.

Wilson nodded. "We'll keep an eye on the place, but I doubt if you'll have any more trouble."

"Thanks," Kelsey said. "I hope you're right."

12

The lights of Buenos Aires lay like a million brilliant jewels on a black velvet backdrop as the 747 came in for a landing at Ezezia International Airport, but the splendor of the sight did little to ease Asheim's growing certainty that they were waiting for him. That they knew he was coming.

No one had been waiting for him when he retrieved his rental car in Chicago, nor had anyone been waiting for him at his room in Cicero. He had picked up his things, had driven up to Milwaukee, and had taken the first plane to New York. The next morning he had taken off for Buenos Aires, no one following him, no one stopping him.

He had expected trouble all along his route, and had planned on driving to Canada if need be. None of that had been necessary. But instead of giving him comfort that he had so easily managed to get out of the United States, it made him all the more leery.

The airliner bumped onto the runway, the jets screamed in reverse, and for a brief instant Asheim could see in his mind's eye every airport, every restaurant, every hotel, and every public records archive he had visited over the past two years. All of it to little or no avail until the Kelsey Clinic.

He had investigated the associates and families of the other Odessa leaders and had gone to Wisconsin only as a matter of routine, the last step in a long line of hundreds of others. He had not expected to find a thing at the clinic because in every case to that point, the children and families of the eleven Odessa leaders had been clean. The eleven old men had kept their families out of their business, much as the Mafia kept its families separate from its organization.

And, as he had expected, he had found nothing in Lake Geneva to connect Dr. Kelsey with his father's Odessa work.

But he had missed something. There was a connection. They had made it clear by murdering the night watchman and by informing the FBI that Asheim had done the killing.

It was as if they had lit up a neon sign for him, directing him to the fact that Dr. Kelsey was involved in his father's business.

And it had become even more obvious with Goldmann's information that the man called Locke was going to the clinic for plastic surgery.

Dr. Kelsey had to be deeply involved in the Odessa leadership, perhaps even being groomed as his father's successor.

And yet all of those conclusions set uneasily on Asheim's mind. After two years of poking around, the Odessa had finally moved against him, but unnecessarily. If they had left it alone, had allowed him to come and go in peace (he had found nothing at the clinic, a fact they must have known), he would have returned to Tel Aviv and dropped the investigation.

As the airliner taxied to the terminal, Asheim had another thought, however. It was possible that Dr. Kelsey did *not* know what was happening. It was possible that Dr. Kelsey's father was using him, presenting Locke as nothing more than an injured man who needed help.

In that case Asheim would have to be lured away from Lake Geneva so that he could be killed.

He looked out the window as the Jetway moved out from the building.

It was exactly what had happened. He *had* been lured away from Lake Geneva. He had come directly to Buenos Aires exactly as they had wanted him to.

If he had been killed in Wisconsin or in Chicago, questions might have been raised. Goldmann would have screamed his head off, of course, and although no one would have officially believed his unprovable allegations, they would have listened. It would have put authorities the world over on alert, thus hampering whatever plans the Odessa might have had for Locke.

But now he was like a fly coming to the spider's web. He only hoped that he had more cunning than the poor fly.

He left the plane with the other passengers, retrieved his single suitcase from incoming baggage, and went to customs, where he showed the Israeli News Service passport he had used when he had first come here.

The customs officer stiffened perceptibly, and his manner instantly changed from one of bored indifference to that of congeniality.

He handed the passport back, made a cursory check of the suitcase, wished Asheim a pleasant stay in Buenos Aires, and waved him on.

As Asheim passed through the doors from customs into the main terminal area, he had the uncanny feeling that he was being watched, that at this moment someone was sighting a gun on his back, finger on the trigger, squeezing. He resisted the urge to bolt, and instead walked steadily across the terminal and out the front doors where a crowd was jostling for a line of waiting cabs.

The night air was warm and humid, redolent with the odors of car exhaust and jet fumes.

A cab pulled up to the curb in front of Asheim, the rear door popped open, and a man in the backseat pointed a gun at him.

"Get in, Major Asheim," the man said with a German accent.

Asheim was about to roll to the left when two shots from a silenced pistol were fired from behind him, and the man in the backseat of the cab was flung backward, his face disintegrating into a pulpy mass of blood and bone. Someone grabbed Asheim's left arm and hustled him to a waiting car that had pulled up behind the cab.

Asheim started to resist, but the man whispered strongly in his ear, *"Guter fraynd,"* Yiddish for good friend, and Asheim let himself be shoved into the rear seat of the car, the man climbing in behind him.

"Move!" the man shouted to the driver, and they took off away from the growing crowd around the dead man in the cab.

"David Goldmann says to say hello," the man in the backseat with Asheim said when they were clear of the airport. He held out his hand. "Abraham Silverstein."

Asheim shook his hand. "You're running the travel bureau?"

Silverstein nodded. "And our friendly driver is Manuel Santini, my right-hand man, and one of the biggest crooks in all of South America."

The driver, a man in his fifties, turned and smiled, most of his front teeth missing, the others yellow.

Asheim nodded to the driver, then turned his attention back to Silverstein, who was a man in his mid-thirties, dark, with hooded eyes and sharp, angular features. "I'm going to need some help getting to Aerie, and I'll need a weapon. I had to get rid of mine before I left the States."

Silverstein shook his head. "Sorry, Major, but we have

our orders. The travel bureau is closed. Santini's brother has a boat, and we're going to take it across the La Plata to Montevideo, where a plane will be waiting for us."

"Goldmann ordered you to pull out?"

"No, it came in the diplomatic pouch from someone higher up, Goldmann asked if we would stay until you arrived."

Asheim sat back. There were two basic factors in any security operation that could cause its cancellation. The first was the lack of results, in which case funding would dry up. And the second was possible political embarrassment.

There had been no results in this operation for the two years since Benjamin's death, and Goldmann had hinted that his funding had been eliminated.

And now there was no doubt in Asheim's mind that the Odessa leaders had begun putting pressure on high government officials the world over to watch the Israelis closely in their peace negotiations with the Egyptians and the Iranians. Begin would be treading carefully, pulling back all possibly embarrassing operations.

"I'm staying," he said to Silverstein, and a slight smile crossed the man's features.

"Goldmann told me to expect as much."

Asheim looked at him. "Am I under arrest, is that it?"

Silverstein held up both hands. "Absolutely not, Major. My orders were simply to close down the bureau and get the hell out of here. What you do contrary to your orders is totally up to you. Like I said, Goldmann just asked me to stick around until you arrived. I've done that."

Asheim turned in his seat and looked out the rear window at the traffic behind them on the wide highway, and then once again looked at Silverstein. "Who was the man in the cab?"

Silverstein shrugged his shoulders. "A man who knew you were coming and wanted to kill you."

"You knew I was coming, but how did you know some-one would be waiting for me?"

"When Goldmann said you were coming, he mentioned that there might be trouble. I had Santini put his ear to the ground, and he found out that there's a contract on you. The police have been informed that you're a drug runner trying to bust in on a local operation. As far as they're concerned, you're better off dead. If the opposition doesn't kill you, the cops probably will."

They turned off the main highway onto a narrow dirt road and Santini floored the Peugeot.

"The boat is docked at the South Canal just below Puerto Madero, but we're going to first make sure that we're not being followed," Silverstein said. "They would have been content to let Manuel and me get out, but you're a different story. And now, by association, so are we."

"I'm sorry," Asheim said softly, and again Silverstein smiled, a touch of sadness in it.

"No need to be, Major. Your son-in-law Benjamin and I were friends, which is why I requested this assignment in the first place."

"I see," Asheim said, and for several minutes he fell silent as Santini drove them into the city, along back streets, down narrow alleys, and finally along another dirt road, the Rio de la Plata off to their left.

Silverstein finally broke the silence. "There is a paper bag with a gun in it on the floor. I have no idea how it came to be there, nor will it ever be said I gave it to you. He looked away as Asheim bent down and pulled the .38 Smith & Wesson out of the bag and stuck it in his belt.

Silverstein turned back. "If you are going to Aerie, to-night would be best. They would not be expecting you so soon."

"I'll take the car after you leave."

"I can do better than that," Silverstein said. "Campana lies just off the river Paraná, which empties into the La

Plata. Stoeffel's compound borders the river. It is the only way in for you.''

Asheim nodded and Silverstein held up one finger. ''But, Major, we will be able to wait for you only one hour. No longer. If you are not back by then, we will leave you.''

''Fair enough,'' Asheim said. If he could get to the house. If Stoeffel was there. If he could confront the man. And if he was not detected, he would get the answers he was coming for, or he would kill the old man and then somehow get back to Silverstein and the boat. After that his future course of action would depend on what he had learned or not learned. But at least they would know they had serious opposition who not only knew they were planning something big, but who was willing and able to do something to stop it.

13

On Saturday Kelsey went to the clinic around 8:00 A.M. to check on his patients. He had planned on taking the remainder of the day off for a much-needed rest.

Shelly Hope was awake and in good spirits, talking on the phone to her agent in New York when he came in. She flashed him a big smile and kissed him on the cheek.

Mrs. Hermitage, on whom he had done the blepharoplasty, was listening to the television, bitching about the fact it would be weeks before her eyelids healed enough to remove the bandages so she could see again.

And Locke was recovering nicely, although he was impatient for the real work on his face to begin.

"There are only a few days until Christmas, and sometime between then and New Year's Eve, I'll start on your nose," Kelsey said after examining the man. He had taken the surgery well.

"It can't be done any sooner?" Locke asked, still having

difficulties talking because of the injuries to the muscles, controlling his jaw.

Kelsey shook his head. "Your system wouldn't stand the shock. The human body can take just so much until it demands a rest."

"What about the photographs I brought, Doctor? Can you match them?"

Kelsey pulled a chair next to the bed and sat down. "Do you have any family, Mr. Locke? Any relatives we could telephone? Anyone you would like to visit you?"

Locke was silent for a moment, and when he finally spoke, his voice seemed to hold a great sadness. "There's no one. There never has been anyone."

"Parents? Sisters? Brothers?"

"No sisters or brothers, and my parents died years ago when I was a child. There is no one."

"A girlfriend?"

Locke somehow managed a bitter laugh. "I've visited whorehouses for my pleasure. And even there I have never been what you could call a welcome guest. I was an ugly man."

"That simply is not true," Kelsey said with feeling, leaning forward.

Locke stiffened in the bed, and he turned his bandaged face away so that he could look out the window. "Handsomeness or ugliness are more than something merely in the eye of the beholder, a phrase I've heard a million times. Ugliness is also in the mind's eye of the individual cursed with a face he is not happy with." He turned back to face Kelsey, and there was a passion in his voice. "All my life, Doctor, ever since I was a child, I have hated the way I looked." He shook his head sadly, although it was obvious to Kelsey that the motion caused him some pain. "Oh, I know that I have never been *really* ugly, not in the same sense as some poor deformed wretch. But my own feeling about myself, I am sure, has made itself clear on my face. It's like I've been making faces at the world all of my life. I have no friends, not one. I guess I'm counting on you to not only give me a new face but, because of it, a new personality in which I will like myself instead of despising my image in the mirror.''

Kelsey reached out and touched the man gently on the arm. ''Perhaps you need a psychologist. I think your problem is more inside your head than on your face.''

Locke half rose out of the bed. ''Promise me, Doctor, that you will do as I ask. That you will give me the face I have asked for. It can't hurt. The operations cannot be any different than restoring my face to what it used to be. And maybe it will help me.''

Kelsey got up and gently pushed the man back down on the bed. ''I'll do what you ask. I'm just suggesting that perhaps you need another kind of help as well.''

Locke seemed to relax. ''I'll promise you this much, Doctor, that if you do what I want you to do with my face, my entire life will change. For the better. If it doesn't, I'll go and have my head examined.''

Kelsey smiled. ''No more talking or you'll screw up my good work.''

''Right,'' Locke mumbled, and he reached over for a book from a pile of them on his night table as Kelsey got up and pushed the chair back into the corner.

As Kelsey turned to go, he happened to catch a glimpse of the titles of several of the books. Among them were *The Presidency: An Historical Survey, The American Political System,* and *Theory of Power in Government.*

Strange reading for an engineer. The fleeting thought passed through his mind and was gone as he left Locke's room and went downstairs. But then Locke was a strange man.

Two of the outside maintenance men had set up a huge Christmas tree in the entry hall, and Marion along with a couple of the nurses were unpacking several boxes of decorations. They had been too busy all week to do much more than string up a few lights around the hall, and this tree, Kelsey was sure, had been Marion's doing.

They stopped what they were doing and glanced his way, guilty looks on their faces.

Marion started toward him, a defensive glare in her eye, but he smiled.

"I was wondering if you people had forgotten about Christmas," he said.

"With the way things have been going around here lately, I thought we all needed a little cheering up. Even the patients are complaining about the long faces," Marion said.

"Don't blame it on me. I don't deserve the title of Scrooge," Kelsey said, holding up his hands in surrender.

"Oh, yes, you do," Marion chided. "But there is something in your office that will change that even faster than this tree."

He looked at her, but he could see no clue other than a twinkle in her eye.

"It's a present from your father. A messenger brought it a few minutes ago," Marion said, and she accompanied him to his office, where she made him close his eyes before she would open the door and lead him inside.

When the door was closed behind them and she had led him over by his desk, she said, "Now," and Kelsey opened his eyes.

Propped against the wall behind his desk was a large, framed architectural drawing of an ultramodern building perched on a cliff overlooking what appeared to be one of the Great Lakes. For a moment it made no sense to Kelsey until all at once it hit him.

"The research institute," he said softly, and he went forward to get a closer look.

"Your father told me about it a month ago," Marion said.

He tore his eyes away from the drawing and looked at

her. She was smiling, her eyes bright. "You didn't tell me."

"Nope," she said mischievously. "Your father swore me to secrecy. Said this was going to be your Christmas present."

Kelsey looked again at the drawing and noticed that a card was attached at the bottom corner. He went around his desk and pulled the card from where it was taped to the frame and opened it.

In his father's handwriting, the message was short and, to Kelsey's mind, very sweet.

Merry Christmas, Richard,
As soon as your work is cleared up at Lake Geneva, I'll expect you down here to begin equipping and staffing your research institute.

Love, Father

Kelsey looked again at the drawing, and for a moment his thoughts went back to his wife, but he could not conjure up a clear picture of her face in his mind.

Marion came around the desk to him, and he turned to look down at her.

"Merry Christmas, Doctor," she said, and stood up on tiptoes and kissed him lightly on the lips.

He let the card fall to the floor and took her in his arms and kissed her deeply, something one part of his mind told him he should have done a long time ago.

14

Santini's brother Eugenio turned out to be even older and more decrepit than Manuel, but the boat was a sleek forty-foot pleasure craft that Silverstein explained was rented on weekends to the Santini brothers' friends.

"I never ask where they go on their weekend cruises, and they never volunteer the information," Silverstein said as he and Asheim clambered aboard. "But she's seaworthy, very fast, and her hold is big enough for them to haul half of Buenos Aires in one trip."

Manuel and Eugenio hugged and slapped each other on the back as if they had not seen each other for years, and Manuel quickly explained to his brother Asheim's presence and what was requested of them this night before they crossed to Montevideo.

Eugenio, a concerned expression on his deeply lined face, parted from his brother and gravely shook Asheim's hand.

"Señor Stoeffel is a dangerous man," he said, his English heavily accented.

Asheim nodded. "He was responsible for my son-in-law's murder."

The old man looked even sadder. "Although I did not know Benjamin, Manuel and Abraham tell me he was a good man."

"Can you take me up the Paraná?"

"Would you kill Señor Stoeffel?"

"Only if I am required to," Asheim said. "But first I need information from him."

"Yes." Eugenio was nodding. "I will take you to Campana. But we will not be able to wait very long. And if we are discovered, we will have to leave you. Stoeffel is a powerful man in Buenos Aires. He has many friends. Many soldiers."

The boat was tied up at a wharf among hundreds of other similar craft. Asheim and Silverstein went below as the Santini brothers cast off and headed down the South Canal out into the Rio de la Plata Estuary, the twin diesels throbbing powerfully.

On deck the boat was spotlessly clean, and it came as no surprise to Asheim when they entered the main cabin to see that it too was in the same state of gleaming cleanliness.

"Unusual men, the Santinis," he said as he sat down. Silverstein poured him a brandy.

"What you are really thinking, Major, is that it is unusual for a man in my position to use the services of men like them." Silverstein was smiling, and he sat down across the highly polished wood table from Asheim. "Despite what our mutual friend David Goldmann probably told you about your son-in-law's assignment here, Benjamin was *not* the man for the job. He was in over his head."

Asheim looked away, focusing his gaze on a Picasso print hanging on the wall, and said nothing.

"He was an honest, honorable man. And this profession is not suitable for such men."

Asheim turned back to Silverstein. "What is your connection with Goldmann? Why were you sent down here?"

"I was born and raised in New York City. When the street wars became too tame for me, I went to Israel, where the real fighting was going on. From what Goldmann told me when I was recruited, he approached me the same way and for the same reasons he came to you."

"What was your connection with Benjamin?"

Silverstein took a sip of his brandy. "I don't imagine your daughter told you about me," he said. "Deborah and I had a thing for each other before she married Benjamin."

Asheim was surprised. He could not imagine his daughter seeing anything in this man. His feelings evidently showed on his face, because Silverstein laughed out loud.

"She finally saw through me, Major. Saw that I was not the man for her. I was too dangerous. 'Like a wild animal,' she said once. And I agreed with her. Told her Benjamin was the man for her."

"You said you were Benjamin's friend," Asheim said. He was tired and wanted to get the business with Stoeffel over with.

Silverstein put his glass down and leaned forward, an intense expression in his eyes. "I left your daughter because I thought Benjamin would be better for her than me. But I never stopped loving her. And when the babies came I was happy for her because I had been right—Benjamin was the correct man for her." He sat back. "When I heard Benjamin had been killed I put out the word that I would like to take his assignment. It took Goldmann nearly a year and a half to finally come to me, but he did."

Asheim could not decide if he liked or trusted the man, and yet he felt a compassion for him. "Deborah has remarried."

A startled expression crossed Silverstein's face, but then he smiled wanly. "Good. I am happy for her. With me she would have had no luck." He turned away. "It doesn't alter the fact that I want revenge for Benjamin's death. He was a good man.''

''If you were so concerned, why didn't you move against Stoeffel and the others here in Buenos Aires yourself?''

''A number of reasons,'' Silverstein said, turning back. ''Goldmann told me any such action would result in my immediate recall. I decided that when I made my move, it was not going to be in the dark. I don't enjoy batting my head against a brick wall.''

''And?'' Asheim asked.

''Goldmann told me about you and what you were doing, so I figured it would only be a matter of time before you showed up here.''

''You intend coming with me to Stoeffel?''

Silverstein nodded. ''I too have difficulty in following orders.''

''There's a good chance we'll just be beating our heads against your brick wall.''

Silverstein shrugged. ''They may be expecting you tomorrow, but I don't think they are expecting the both of us tonight. And not by water.'' He poured another drink. ''And now I think you'd better tell me what you have learned about this Odessa operation.''

''First you tell me how you met and recruited the Santinis,'' Asheim said.

Silverstein glanced up toward the closed hatchway, then shrugged again. ''When you are born and raised on the streets, you know such things. Manuel was easy, and he works cheap.''

Something was not quite right about any of this, but Asheim could not put his finger on it. ''Have you used this boat before?'' he asked to cover his momentary uncertainty.

''A number of times. Stoeffel's house is visible from the river. We've gone out there on a half-dozen occasions in the last few months.''

''Come up with anything?''

Silverstein shook his head. "Nothing," he said. "What's the matter?"

"How far do you trust them?"

"If you mean do I believe they might be working for Stoeffel, I think Manuel's actions at the airport covered that pretty well."

Still, it did not set right in Asheim's mind, and yet he told himself his feelings of uncertainty were probably the result of the events of the past two days, including jet lag—and someone trying to kill him at the airport. Goldmann could not have made that big a mistake in picking Silverstein for this job.

He took another sip of his brandy, lit a cigarette, and told Silverstein everything he had learned over the past two years up to the business three days ago at the clinic in Lake Geneva, and the FBI coming for him by name at the consulate the next day.

"Ingenious. They closed all avenues of escape for you except the one that led here to Buenos Aires."

Asheim nodded. "And here I am."

"You don't expect Stoeffel to tell you anything, do you?"

"Either that or I'll kill him."

"And then one by one kill the remaining ten Odessa leaders."

Asheim nodded again but said nothing.

"You'd never accomplish it all and you know it. But it won't stop you, will it?"

"No."

"I like that," Silverstein said, his feral grin returning. "I like that a lot."

The hatchway popped open and Manuel Santini was framed in the opening. "We've just entered the Paraná, so I suggest, Major, that you come on deck and get ready."

"I'm going with him, Manuel," Silverstein said as he and Asheim got to their feet.

Santini laughed. "I thought so. Your things are on deck, too."

"Enterprising," Asheim said.

"He knows me too well," Silverstein replied, and he and Asheim went up on deck.

Three men besides the Santini brothers were waiting on deck, each of them holding a lightweight Ingram submachine gun.

Silverstein dropped to one knee and reached for his pistol, but one of the men snapped the safety off on his gun and pointed it directly at Silverstein's head. "Don't," he snapped. His accent was German.

Asheim, who had reached for his Smith & Wesson tucked into his belt, slowly withdrew his hand from beneath his coat as Silverstein got to his feet.

The boat sliced almost noiselessly through the dark waters of the river. The farther upstream they traveled, the closer the jungle shores came together.

They came around a single bend in the river, and a hundred yards upstream was a well lighted dock. Beyond that, atop a slight rise in the jungle, Asheim could make out the lights of a large house in the distance. Stoeffel's Aerie.

One of the three guards followed Asheim's gaze, and then turned back. "Herr Stoeffel has been waiting for you all evening, Major Asheim."

Suddenly Silverstein leaped to the left as he reached inside his coat for his gun. One of the three guards nonchalantly fired a short burst from the Ingram, and Silverstein's body was flung violently backward, blood from a half-dozen wounds splattering the deck.

"It's all right," one of the guards shouted to several figures who had materialized on the wharf. He turned back to Asheim. "The firing pin has been removed from your weapon, Major, so you may keep it for now, or throw it away. It does not matter to me."

With a boat like this, and supposed weekend drug-running

trips, the Santinis were well-to-do. That was the flaw in Silverstein's thinking, Asheim realized bitterly. They would not work cheaply. They had no reason to work for Silverstein unless they had been ordered to do so.

They docked at the wharf. The three guards marched Asheim off the boat, and they climbed aboard a jeep and took off down a narrow dirt road through the jungle. The Santinis would dump Silverstein's body in the ocean halfway between here and Montevideo, clean up the boat, and then return to Buenos Aires as if nothing had happened.

Goldmann would fuss and fume for a time, but would be able to prove nothing, and would not even be able to go to the authorities in Buenos Aires. Even if they did believe him, and questioned the Santini brothers, the Israeli government would end up with egg on its face, not able to answer the simple questions: What was an Israeli agent doing working in Buenos Aires, and with, of all people, a couple of drug runners?

The two years of work had come to an end. Asheim had another bitter realization at this moment as well. Any time during the last two years the Odessa could have killed him, or simply picked him up and taken him away. It would have been child's play, as they had amply demonstrated this evening.

They wanted him out of the way. But they did not want to make a mess anywhere, so they had maneuvered him here, and had captured him.

The only question was, why hadn't they simply killed him as they had Silverstein?

As they drove up to the house, Asheim's thoughts went out briefly to his daughter Deborah and the children. He hoped they were happy with the new man in their lives. Deborah had explained that her new husband would not replace Benjamin, but Asheim knew better. Time did indeed heal all wounds.

The jeep pulled up at the side of the house and Asheim

was ordered out. One of the guards quickly and efficiently searched him, removing the Smith & Wesson and tossing it back in the jeep.

"If you will follow me, Herr Major," one of the guards said, clicking his heels.

They entered the house through a side door and marched down a wide back hallway and through a thick door into a large room. Persian carpets, heavily brocaded drapes at the French doors across the room, rich wood paneling, and book-lined walls surrounded a huge leather-topped desk; a grouping of leather chairs and a couch were in one corner near a sideboard.

Asheim was led to one of the chairs and ordered to sit down.

"There is nothing in this room that you can use as a weapon, Herr Major," his guard, a large man, said. "And once *Oberst* Stoeffel enters this room, you will be watched. Any sudden move on your part will result in your immediate death. Do I make myself clear?"

"Perfectly," Asheim said, nodding. "May I smoke?"

"As you wish," the guard said. As Asheim reached for his cigarettes and lighter, the three guards left the room.

A minute later an old, very tall and thin but distinguished-looking man whom Asheim recognized as Kurt Stoeffel entered the room.

Asheim started to rise, but Stoeffel waved him back. "It is not advisable, Major, that you move out of that chair. My captain of the guard would not understand."

"Why didn't you have me killed like Benjamin and Silverstein?"

"Heavens no, my good man," Stoeffel said, crossing the room to the sideboard. He poured two brandies and brought them back. He handed Asheim one, then took a seat in a chair a few feet away.

"Isn't it extraordinary that a high-ranking SS officer and a Jew are sitting talking?" He sipped his drink. "We are going to have a chat this evening before you are shown to your quarters. When we are finished you will understand the operation and the part you are going to play in it."

Asheim's eyes narrowed.

Stoeffel laughed. "Oh, yes, my dear Major Levi Asheim. You are going to be a part of this operation you have been watching these past two years. Not what you might call a significant part, but it certainly will be interesting."

ONE YEAR LATER
1982

It was Monday and despite the fact it was late fall, the snow had come only to the mountaintops, leaving the lower elevations still clear. But the large man with fashionably long, dark hair, thick beard, and intensely dark eyes stopped a moment outside his apartment building on Fairbanks's south side and took a deep breath. Snow would come soon, he thought. And if it did, he would have to remain here through the winter.

Although that prospect did not really matter to him, at least not in any ordinarily detectable way, something deep inside of his mind told him that he should be anxious about it. Something inside of his brain told him that he should be doing something soon.

What that something was, however, he could not quite put his finger on.

He shrugged finally and carried the bag of groceries from his jeep into the apartment building. His landlady, an elderly woman, came out of her first-floor apartment to get her mail from the boxes in the hall, and she smiled at the man.

"Mr. Wilcox," she said pleasantly.

The man nodded and returned her smile.

"Your telephone has been ringing off the hook all morning. Someone sure wants to get ahold of you.''

"I'm sorry if it disturbed you, Mrs. Saunders.''

"Oh, heavens, no,'' the woman exclaimed. "I just wanted you to know, that's all. Maybe it's your publisher calling.''

About a year ago the man had rented the apartment from the woman, presenting himself as a budding novelist who had come to Alaska to write the great American novel and recuperate. During the day he usually remained in his apartment typing, and during the night he read or watched television. Mrs. Saunders had only one wish . . . that all of her tenants were as thoughtful as Mr. Wilcox, and paid their rent as promptly as he did. A typewriter clattering, and today a telephone ringing, did not bother her in the least.

But what did bother her was that Mr. Wilcox was a loner. He had no friends she knew of, and although he had a telephone installed shortly after he had moved in, today's calls were the first he had ever received as far as she knew.

Mr. Wilcox was a mystery, as was the accident that he had come to recover from, but he was a pleasant mystery.

"Perhaps it is my publisher,'' the man said, and he trudged up the stairs to his one-bedroom efficiency apartment on the second floor, let himself in, and put the groceries away.

As he walked back into the tiny living room to put his coat away, the telephone on the table beside the room's one armchair rang, and he went to it and picked it up. "Hello,'' he said.

A man's voice, soft and cultured, came on the line. "Mr. Wilcox, are you alone in your apartment at this moment?''

The man was confused. "What?'' he said. "Who is this?''

"I am an old friend, and I have something to tell you, but I must know if you are alone at the moment.''

"Yes, I am. Now, what's this all about?''

"Listen to me, Mr. Wilcox. *Eagles fly.*''

Something snapped inside the man's brain, almost like a

pistol shot in a dark room, and suddenly a veil seemed to lift away from his eyes, making it seem to him as if he had been blind all of his life until this very moment.

"Yes?" he said. "What do you want?"

"You are going camping tomorrow in Mt. McKinley National Park. You will pack your gear and enough provisions for three days. You will tell your landlady that you expect to return home no later than Thursday."

"Yes," Wilcox said. Deep inside of him he knew that his name wasn't Wilcox, and that he was not a writer. He felt another personality beginning to rise. Yet he knew that second person inside of him, struggling at this moment to get out, was not him either. The one thing he did know for certain, however, was that the man he was speaking with on the telephone was to be obeyed without hesitation.

"By morning there will be a map and a small electronic device in the glove compartment of your jeep. Take those items with you. But no one must see them. Is that clear?"

"Yes," the man said, his Wilcox personality leaving faster and faster.

"Tomorrow night you will set up your camp at least ten miles away from the park entry point. You will remain at that camp until your job becomes clear to you."

"Yes, sir," the man said. Already the glimmerings of something that he would have to do began to come to him.

"Good luck," the voice on the phone said, and the connection was broken.

The fifteen-passenger Bell UH-1H helicopter with the seal of the vice president of the United States painted on its sides hovered for a moment over the green lawn behind the White House and then touched down.

A moment later the side door slid open and four of the vice president's six Secret Service agents jumped out. All of them were dressed in outdoors clothes and hiking boots.

Charles Anderson, head of this special detail, held a

walkie-talkie to his mouth and spoke briefly into it. A moment later he was answered.

"Eagle two will be with you in a moment," the tiny speaker rasped.

"Eagle two transport standing by," Anderson responded. He glanced at his people. "He'll be with us momentarily, gentlemen."

Anderson looked up toward the north side of the White House seventy-five yards away.

At forty-one he had been a Secret Service agent for six years, coming directly out of the Air Force Special Service program to work at first as a junior member of the detail guarding the President's family. Two years ago with Stewart Engstrom's election to the vice presidency, Anderson asked for and received a transfer to the detail guarding the VP, and two months later was promoted head of that detail, which was as far up that ladder as he wanted to climb.

Guarding the family of the President had been a pure pain in the ass, but guarding the Man himself would be even worse according to the stories he had heard.

Sorensen, head of the Service, had been on duty as a presidential agent in 1963 in Dallas, and he never let his people forget what had happened, and how it had happened.

But as Sorensen explained, "No one ever takes a pot shot at a vice president."

Which was fine with Anderson. He had had his fill of shooting and being shot at in Vietnam. Besides, he liked Engstrom better than he did President Philip P. Barnes, except for the one annoying habit Engstrom had.

While most Presidents and vice presidents took their relaxation on the golf courses like Jerry Ford, or sailing like Kennedy, or skiing like Barnes, Engstrom was the odd duck who wanted not only to hike and camp in the deep woods of Alaska, but who wanted to do it alone.

Since his wife died of cancer eighteen months ago, Engstrom had been spending time in Alaska with more and more regularity.

At first his trips had caused the Secret Service detail fits until Anderson had come up with the idea of equipping the VP with an electronic beeper and then following him at a discreet distance, monitoring his progress by radio.

If Engstrom got in trouble, any kind of trouble, he merely had to flip a switch on the beeper which would change its tone from a pulsating beep to a steady emergency signal, and a helicopter could be dispatched in a matter of minutes, homing in on wherever he was.

The system was fine to a point. Although they never had any troubles with it, he wondered what they would do if the vice president was unconscious and could not flip the beeper switch.

Engstrom radioed to his Secret Service detail every six hours, but if he was injured shortly after one of those broadcasts, he could spend six hours without aid.

The north door opened, and Engstrom along with two of his Secret Service detail, and a half-dozen reporters, headed toward the helicopter.

One did not argue with a vice president, however, Anderson thought as he watched the VP heading his way. Especially not a VP like Engstrom.

Engstrom and the reporters stopped at the edge of the lawn, and a few moments later, the VP waved, turned, and headed toward the helicopter.

He was a large man, husky, with rugged good looks, and he was dressed like Anderson in outdoor clothes with heavy hiking boots on his feet.

Where he went on these little wilderness trips was jokingly called the most loosely kept national secret in the history of the country. The Service tried its best to keep Engstrom's exact locations a secret, but it was impossible. Flight plans were easily obtainable, the helicopter service they used out of Fairbanks was an open book, and Engstrom himself liked to brag at Washington cocktail parties about his own exploits.

This trip was no different. Two days ago Anderson had read a column in the *Washington Post* about Engstrom's unusual method of relaxation, detailing this trip to Mt. Mc-Kinley National Park.

For sometimes as long as four days at a stretch, Stew Engstrom likes to be alone with God and nature in any stand of deep forest he can find.

Although much of Washington is a-titter about our "mountain man" vice president, and his Secret Service detail has its hands full, Engstrom seems to return from these jaunts strangely refreshed and ready to step back into the Washington grind.

This time the VP will be going back to the Alaskan wilds of Mt. McKinley National Park. America's second highest citizen will be tromping around America's first highest mountain.

Engstrom clapped Anderson on the back and beamed. "Don't look so glum, Charlie; the fresh air will do all of us some good." He had to shout over the noise of the helicopter rotors.

Anderson managed a slight smile. "Yes, sir," he shouted. "Your aircraft is ready and waiting on the ramp at Andrews."

"Let's get the hell out of here then," Engstrom said, and he climbed aboard the helicopter and strapped himself in one of the window seats.

"What's the schedule, Mr. Vice President?" Anderson asked as they passed over the Washington Navy Yard and crossed the Anacostia River.

Engstrom had been looking out the window. He turned to his Secret Service chief and grinned boyishly. "The governor is going to be in Fairbanks, and we're having dinner tonight. But it won't be late. I want to get an early start.''

Anderson sighed and Engstrom laughed out loud. ''I'm cutting this trip down to three days. Barnes wants me back in Washington on Friday when he leaves for the summit talks in Geneva. So this time it won't be so bad.''

''None of us mind, Mr. Vice President, honestly,'' Anderson said. ''It's just that when you're out there on your own, we can't offer you any real protection.''

Engstrom's expression darkened. ''Drop it, Charlie. I'm not taking these trips for your convenience. I'm taking them for my sanity.''

''Yes, sir,'' Anderson said, and he settled back in his seat.

The man who had most recently been known as Wilcox, before that Locke, and before that Hempel and a dozen other names, had spent thirty-six hours camped ten miles from the park entrance. Mt. McKinley was more than twenty-five miles to the southwest, yet the mountain towered over everything in the forest, and seemed to be only a couple of miles away.

Earlier this morning he had been awakened from one of his brief catnaps by a soft beeping from the small electronic device he had found in the glove compartment of his jeep the night before.

As the morning progressed, the beeping became louder. A small dial on the front of the device showed a relative heading toward the source of the signal, which was to the northeast.

Shortly before noon, the man laid out a campfire, put the coffee on, and set out his food and cooking utensils as if he were preparing for a meal. But instead of finishing his lunch preparations, he took one last relative-heading reading to the signal from his present location, marked it on his map, and then set out on a fast pace directly north, taking nothing but the map, the electronic device, and a small entrenching shovel.

Sooner or later the park rangers would come across his deserted camp and assume he had wandered off and gotten lost.

His two years of training in Buenos Aires had included a series of carefully constructed autosuggestions for this operation. The first trigger consisted of the words *Eagles fly.* From that moment the physical acts he was doing—the camping, the sounds of the beeper—all were additional triggers that when activated brought more and more of his specific training up from the depths of his subconscious.

Through the afternoon he had changed directions three times, each time stopping long enough to take a relative bearing from the receiver, each time marking the bearing on his map. By five o'clock the rough intersections of the readings on his map showed a small area to the southeast where the source of the signal was located. He headed directly that way now, following the needle in the darkness.

The long Alaskan night stretched ahead of him, and he made his way slowly and carefully through the forest toward the signal, taking great pains to make little or no noise.

At six o'clock the beeping from his receiver stopped, and a man's voice blared and crackled over the tiny speaker.

"Eagle two watchers, this is Eagle two settled down for the night."

"That's a roger, Eagle two. We're four miles behind you."

"Talk to you again at midnight. Good night."

"Roger, Eagle two."

The signal was strong. The man moved forward with extreme care until he could make out the faint flicker of a campfire below him about half a mile away, directly on the bearing the receiver showed.

The man got down on his hands and knees and crawled beneath some dense underbrush. With the small shovel he carried, he scraped away the thick layer of dead leaves and began digging a narrow trench about twelve inches long and a foot deep in the hard ground.

By the time he was finished he was sweating heavily so that the false beard and mustache came off easily. These he threw in the hole along with the colored contact lenses from his eyes, and the wig from his head.

Next he disassembled the receiver, smashed the parts beyond recognition, and threw them in the hole, the map following.

Finally he scraped the dirt back into the hole, smoothed it over, and then scattered the leaves and other forest debris over the disturbed ground until he was satisfied that the hiding place was undetectable. Especially so since soon the park would close for the winter, and this area would be covered with a deep blanket of snow.

By next summer someone might discover where he had hidden the items, but by then even that million-to-one long-shot chance would be too late. Far too late.

He crawled back out from the underbrush, got to his feet, and headed silently down toward the campfire, his new personality almost complete, his step jaunty, and the grin on his face almost boyish.

PART THREE

15

The Kelsey Institute was located near the Veteran's Hospital in Chicago's Lake Bluff suburb just off Sheridan Drive. Dr. Kelsey's office at the rear of the small, intensely modern building offered a dramatic view of Lake Michigan.

Although the Institute had only been in full operation for six months, the medical journals were already hailing it as the top research facility of its kind in the world.

"Directed by the capable Dr. Richard Kelsey, and financed by Kelsey Electronics, Ltd., and grants from MGM and other sources, the Kelsey Institute for Reconstructive Plastic Surgery Research wants for nothing," the *Journal of Plastic Surgery* reported.

> The staff is the best money and challenge can attract. The equipment rivals and exceeds anything even the largest of universities can provide. And the facility itself is bright, spacious, and functional.
>
> It is no wonder then that Dr. Kelsey and his staff

have undertaken such research projects as epidermal
regeneration by enzyme manipulation . . .

Marion came into Kelsey's office. He put down the journal he had been reading and looked up.

"They've found him," she said, excited.

Kelsey smiled. "Found who?"

"The vice president," she said, coming around the desk
and pecking him on the cheek.

Kelsey drew her down on his lap and kissed her. When
they parted she was radiant.

"Mrs. Marion Kelsey," she said, looking into his eyes.
"It has a nice ring."

"Don't let it go to your head, madam—you're still the
secretary around here."

"Have you always treated your secretaries this way?"

"Nope," Kelsey laughed. "You're the first one I've married." For an instant the words wanted to catch in his throat
as a feeling about his dead wife seemed to shudder through
his body. He could no longer bring up a clear picture of her
face in his mind, and he felt guilty about it.

Marion, who was a very sensitive woman, had forced a
discussion about her, and about Kelsey's feelings about her,
before they got married.

"I'm not a replacement for her, Richard," she told him
three nights before they were married. "I don't want you to
think of me in that way. You loved your first wife, and still
do. I don't want you to lose that."

She was correct, of course, and Kelsey loved her all the
more for her understanding. Yet he could not quite shake
his feelings of guilt because he could no longer visualize
what his first wife looked like, and because a part of him
still clung to the belief that had he gone with her the night
she was killed, she might not have died.

"What about the vice president?" he asked, coming out
of his thoughts.

"It was in the papers this morning; didn't you see it?"

Kelsey shook his head. "I've been snowed in all day thanks to your appointments book."

"He went camping again in Alaska. Early Thursday morning a storm came up, his Secret Service helicopter crashed, and he was alone out there for more than twenty-four hours. It's on the TV."

"Now?"

"They're running a special news show on it."

Kelsey followed his wife into her office, which adjoined his, where she had a small television near her desk. She often waited here, watching television, while he worked late, preferring to remain in her office instead of going back to their apartment alone.

A map depicting Mt. McKinley National Park filled the small screen, and as an announcer spoke, a series of dots marched across the map showing the route Engstrom had taken on foot from where the helicopter had set him down just inside the park entrance.

A small X appeared on the trail about eight miles from the entrance. "Early Wednesday evening the vice president camped here, radioing his Secret Service detail, which was camped four miles east, that everything was fine and he was settled down for the night," the announcer said.

The picture cut away to a pair of somber-faced newscasters seated at a desk behind which was a monitor screen still showing the map. One of them was holding a small electronic device.

"Engstrom carried this portable radio with him that emits a signal which his Secret Service detail can home in on in case of trouble," the one newsman said, holding up the device.

He flipped a switch and a high-pitched beeping began. "This is the signal the Secret Service was receiving. It meant that everything was fine, and Engstrom was in no trouble."

The announcer flipped the switch the other way, and the beeping changed to a steady tone. "This signal would mean the vice president was in trouble and needed help immediately."

"That's the signal his Secret Service detail received shortly after ten Wednesday night," the other announcer, a distinguished-looking gray-haired man, interjected.

"That's right, Howard," the first newsman said, turning to his coanchorman. "The Secret Service operational office in Fairbanks told us that at ten-oh-seven P.M. the beeper signal changed to a steady tone, which lasted for something under one minute. But it was a false alarm. Engstrom radioed a moment later that he had accidentally hit the switch."

Kelsey perched on the edge of Marion's desk as a meteorologist came on and explained the storm that had suddenly developed late Wednesday night and early Thursday morning. When he was finished the newsmen continued with their report.

"Charles Anderson, who is the head of Engstrom's Secret Service detail, radioed to the vice president that a storm seemed imminent, but Engstrom refused to be picked up, radioing that he would ride it out."

The map of the park area came back on the screen as the announcer continued.

"By six A.M. the storm was rapidly developing with rising winds and blinding snow, and at that point radio contact with the vice president was lost."

"Anderson made the decision then to go after the vice president," the other announcer said.

"That's right, Howard, but first he radioed to the Secret Service operational office in Fairbanks, assessing them of the situation. All aircraft in the Fairbanks area were grounded at that time."

A new series of dots moved up the trail toward where the

vice president was camped, and about one mile from his position a large red X appeared.

"The Secret Service helicopter went down one mile east of where Engstrom's last position was reported. Everyone on board except for Anderson was killed in the crash."

"Any word on Anderson's condition?" the second announcer asked.

"The last we heard was that he had been taken to the hospital at Fairbanks, where he is listed in serious condition with multiple internal injuries, and is—" The announcer broke off in midsentence, pressing the earphone plugged into his left ear a little closer.

He nodded once and then looked back at the camera. "The vice president's helicopter is just now approaching the Fairbanks Airport, where Air Force Two is standing by." He half turned in his chair to look behind him at the large monitor screen on the wall on which a signal from Fairbanks suddenly appeared.

"This is Roger Fleetwood, CBS News, at the airport in Fairbanks, Alaska. Behind me is Air Force Two, the vice president's plane, standing by to take Engstrom immediately back to Washington. In the distance to the west we can just see the helicopter bringing the vice president from the park. On board with him are two Secret Service agents from the Fairbanks operational office, along with two members of the Alaska Highway Patrol, and the chief resident from the Fairbanks Hospital."

"Roger, this is Howard in Washington," one of the studio newscasters interrupted.

Fleetwood held his left hand over his single earphone. "Yes, Howard, I can hear you."

"Has there been any word on the vice president's condition?"

"Mostly speculation at this point, Howard, but it seems he came through his ordeal relatively unscathed. From what we understand he refused to be transported on a stretcher, and his first concern was for Anderson and his Secret Service detail when he was informed their helicopter had crashed."

"We heard that Engstrom may have injured his hands in some way. What have you heard about that?"

"It's unclear at this point, but Engstrom may have frostbitten fingers, although we have learned that the burn treatment center at Bethesda Naval Hospital in Washington has been alerted."

The noise of the approaching helicopter rose up in volume, all but blotting out Fleetwood's comments. Several dozen police officers and Highway Patrolmen held back the crowd of several hundred newsmen and spectators pressing in toward Air Force Two.

The helicopter touched down about fifty yards from the vice president's plane, and the television camera zoomed in on the helicopter door, which slid open a moment later.

Two uniformed Highway Patrol officers jumped out and then assisted Engstrom down. The vice president remained standing by the helicopter for a moment, and then walked toward his waiting aircraft, waving his heavily bandaged hands toward the crowd.

His two Secret Service agents, the doctor, and several uniformed police officers as well as the two Highway Patrolmen who had ridden with him on the helicopter formed a protective barrier around Engstrom.

As he got to the boarding steps, he stopped, turned, and flashed the boyish Engstrom grin, again waving at the crowd, which responded with cheers.

The television screen showed a long close-up of Engstrom's face, which looked red and weather-beaten, and Kelsey slowly got up from Marion's desk and moved a little closer to the TV set.

Something in the man's face. The nose. The cheeks.

Something was familiar to him beyond the fact he knew and recognized the vice president.

Marion turned from the television set as Engstrom went up the boarding steps and entered the plane, and looked at her husband.

"What is it, Richard? What's the matter?"

Kelsey shook his head. "I don't know," he said half to himself. "I don't know. But there's something about Engstrom that's too familiar."

Marion shut off the television set and took her husband by the arm. "You've probably seen his picture in a hundred newspapers and magazines and on television."

"I don't mean it that way. I mean it feels like I know that face medically. I'm almost sure of it."

A vague, uneasy feeling was building inside of Kelsey, but he wanted to deny it, although he could not. He was getting the feeling that not only had he worked on that face before, but he knew who it belonged to.

16

The morning was cold and blustery. A low overcast scudded in from the northwest, threatening to bring a freezing rain or possibly the first snow of the season.

A wild-goose chase, Marion had called it. Kelsey glanced at her seated next to him. She stared out the window lost in thought as the woods and farmlands of southeastern Wisconsin rolled past.

Friday night after the vice president had been rescued and flown back to Washington, D.C., Kelsey and Marion had gone out for a late dinner and had not returned home until midnight.

The next morning Marion went shopping with a friend, one of the research assistants at the Institute. Kelsey had lain around their apartment watching the sporadic television news shows about Engstrom and his "latest adventure," as they all were calling it, and about the highly publicized summit meeting in Geneva that the president would be attending on Monday.

All through the morning and early afternoon the vague sense of uneasiness he had felt after Engstrom's rescue on Friday continued to grow despite Marion's insistence that he had an overworked imagination.

The final jolt, however, came on the six-o'clock news broadcast when Engstrom was leaving Bethesda Naval Hospital, his hands heavily bandaged.

"I've been given a clean bill of health, so there is no danger that I will be unable to cope with the rigors of the vice presidency," Engstrom joked, and the reporters laughed.

"What about your hands, Mr. Vice President?"

Engstrom held up his bandaged hands and managed a slight smile. "Certainly makes me glad I'm not a golfer. I'm afraid my swing would be a bit off for the next few weeks." He grinned, and again the newspeople gathered in front of the hospital laughed. They were loving it.

"Seriously," he said, lowering his hands to his sides. "I'll be bandaged up like this for a few weeks. During the storm my fingertips were frostbitten, and in an effort to keep warm I started a small campfire that got somewhat out of strict control in the high winds. As a result I burned my fingertips. Out of the freezer and directly into the oven, so to speak."

"How bad is it, Mr. Vice President?" another reporter asked.

Engstrom turned his way. "It hurts like hell, if that's what you mean," he quipped. "Second-degree burns, I'm told, that will heal with some scar tissue. The FBI will probably never be able to get a clear fingerprint from me again."

The television picture came in for a close-up of Engstrom's famous grin, his face still somewhat red from his ordeal. Kelsey's stomach flopped over.

Marion, who had finally come home shortly after four, laden with packages, was in the bathroom getting ready for the dinner party they had been invited to that evening.

Kelsey started to call her to come and look again at Engstrom but then decided against it. Instead he went into his study.

He could hear the reporters asking Engstrom about President Barnes's summit trip as he picked up his phone and dialed Sam Sharpenberg's home. Sharpenberg was the new medical director at the Lake Geneva clinic.

When the connection was made, it rang three times before Sharpenberg answered.

"Sharpenberg here," the man answered gruffly.

Kelsey liked the man the first time he had met him, and over a dozen other plastic surgeons he had interviewed for the position last year, Sharpenberg had come out on top. His father had concurred.

"Sam, this is Kelsey."

"Are you in town?"

"No," Kelsey said, looking up. Marion, with the back of her cocktail dress unzipped, had come into the study. "I'm calling from Chicago."

"This business or social?" Sharpenberg asked.

Marion came around the desk and presented her back to Kelsey for him to zipper her up. He held the phone in the crook of his neck and pulled the zipper up. "A little of both, Sam," he said.

Marion turned around and mouthed the words, "Sam Sharpenberg?" and Kelsey nodded.

"Okay," Sharpenberg boomed. "Loraine is fine, ornery as hell because I'm supposed to be getting ready for a hot night on the town tonight. She thinks I'm working too much. The grandkids are fine. And my back hasn't acted up on me in nearly a month, which is about how long it's been since you called last. How's Marion?"

Kelsey laughed. "She's standing right here menacing me. I'm supposed to be getting ready myself for a hot dinner party tonight."

"So make it brief and we'll both stay out of trouble," Sharpenberg said.

"I'm coming up to the clinic tomorrow morning."

"Shit," Sharpenberg swore. "I'll be out of town. I've promised to meet with some friends in L.A. Old university ties and all that." Sharpenberg had been hired from his position as chief of research at UCLAs Reconstructive Surgery Center.

"I'm sorry I'll miss you, Sam, but I'm just coming to look over some old patient records. I thought I'd let you know that I'd be poking around."

Sharpenberg laughed. "Hell, you own the joint, you didn't have to call me. But if you hadn't, I would have been pissed off. Anything I can help with?"

"No, it's just routine."

"All right, I'll tell them to expect you," Sharpenberg said.

"Don't mention this to Stan Lowe," Kelsey said impulsively.

"That fairy," Sharpenberg exploded, and then he lowered his voice. "What is it, Dick, are you being sued or something?"

"Nothing like that," Kelsey said. "I'm just toying with a wild idea. Talk to you about it later."

"You're the doctor," Sharpenberg said. "But if there's anything you need, give me a call."

"Thanks, Sam, I appreciate it. Have a nice trip."

"Yeah," Sharpenberg said, and clicked off. He never said good-bye on the telephone.

Kelsey hung up and looked at Marion.

"Engstrom?" she asked.

Kelsey nodded.

"I'm not going to ask anything else," she said. "But you're on a wild-goose chase."

"Maybe," Kelsey said.

* * *

It was 10:30 A.M. by the time they made it to Lake Geneva and drove slowly through the town toward Highway 50, which led around the lake to the clinic.

It was the off season, and the weather was so cold, there weren't many people walking around downtown. During the summer the streets and sidewalks were jammed, but now the town was peaceful.

Almost as if she were reading his thoughts, Marion turned to her husband. "I sort of miss this place."

"It's hell in the summer," Kelsey said, pulling away from the last traffic light in town.

"I always liked the fall and winter best of all. We had the place practically to ourselves. It was relaxed, not like Chicago."

Kelsey smiled. "Sorry you married me?"

"Only sorry that the Institute couldn't have been built here."

"Me too," Kelsey said, and he really felt it. But as they approached the turnoff to the clinic, his thoughts drifted back to the purpose for this trip.

He wanted to believe that Marion was correct, that this was a wild-goose chase. But he could not bring himself to accept that.

He turned onto the clinic road and drove slowly down the hill, parking in front of the large former mansion. He got out of the car, came around to Marion's side, and opened the door for her.

Together they went up the steps and entered the clinic. Pat Nelson, the chief R.N., was passing through the reception hall carrying a bundle of patient progress report clipboards, and when she saw them come in she hurried over.

"What a pleasant surprise," the nurse bubbled.

She hugged Kelsey, pecked him on the cheek, and then hugged Marion. "Marriage agrees with you two," she said, smiling.

"Nothing has changed, Patty—he's still a slave driver,

only now I can't complain about the low wages or long hours.''

Pat shook her head. "He's nothing like Sam Sharpenberg," she said. "Now, there's a man who will keep you running all day long and then have the guts to ask you why you're so slow."

They all laughed.

"Did Sam tell you we were coming up?" Kelsey asked.

The nurse nodded. "Said you wanted to look over some patient records." She nodded over her left shoulder. "I left the lights on, but if you need any help, you'll have to hang on for about half an hour or so. I'm late for my rounds, and the patients are already starting to complain."

"Go ahead," Kelsey said. "I'll let Marion dig out what I need. Is the primary lab open?"

"Sam is running a couple of cultures he wants me to keep an eye on while he's gone, so I left it open."

"Fine," Kelsey said. "We can manage."

"Are you two going to stay for lunch?"

"I don't think so. I've got to get back."

"Too bad," Pat said. "If I don't see you before you leave, don't make it so long between trips."

"Thanks," Kelsey said. The nurse turned and headed away. He turned to Marion. "I'm going to the lab. I want you to pull the records on James Locke. He was the man from London who was injured in the industrial accident a few months before we moved to the Institute."

The nurse had stopped short, and she came back to where Kelsey and Marion still stood. She had an odd expression on her face.

"Did you say James Locke?" she asked.

Kelsey looked at her, something stirring in his gut. "Yes. Why?"

"Stan Lowe called about ten minutes ago and asked me to pull Locke's jacket and lay it on his desk."

"Is his office open?"

Patricia nodded uncertainly. "He told me not to show those records to anyone until he came in later this morning. A patient request."

Kelsey forced himself to smile. "I'm sure that didn't include me, Pat. I'll just sneak in there and borrow them for a couple of minutes."

Patricia managed a slightly conspiratorial grin. "I'm sure it will be all right."

"Go ahead on your rounds," Kelsey said.

The nurse looked at him for a long moment, then turned and left the entry hall. When she was gone Kelsey and Marion hurried into Lowe's office, where James Locke's thick patient file was laying on his desk.

Kelsey picked it up and he and Marion went back out of the office, crossed the entry hall, and went into the primary lab in the west wing just off the operating theater.

At one end of the small but well-equipped room was an artist's light table on which the operating surgeon worked out the procedures he would use on a reconstructive operation.

Marion closed the door behind them and Kelsey took the file to the light table, where he pulled out the photographs Locke had brought with him, and the sketches Kelsey had made before each series of operations.

"Locke was the patient who paid his bill and checked himself out over your protests a couple of weeks before his bandages were due to come off," Marion said, coming up behind Kelsey.

"The same," he said, arranging the photos and sketches around the edge of the large table. "Do any of these look familiar to you?" he asked as he pulled out a large sketch pad and laid it on the table.

Marion looked over his shoulder at the photos for several long moments, but then shook her head. "Not especially so," she said.

Kelsey started to sketch rapidly, first the outline of a head, penciling in the chin, forehead, and then cheeks from the photos Locke had supplied, and from the sketches Kelsey had made previous to each operation. Then he started on the mouth, nose, and eyes, making changes here and there as he drew.

"I want to get this exactly as the photos depict so that when I finish we'll have a fairly accurate sketch of Mr. Locke," Kelsey said, finally penciling in the shadows around the nose and beneath the eyes.

Marion sucked in her breath suddenly as Kelsey put the finishing touches on the sketch, and he glanced over his shoulder at her.

"Do I need to draw in the hairstyle?" he asked softly.

Marion was staring at the drawing, and she shook her head. He turned and looked again at the sketch.

"Who would you say this man looks like?"

"Engstrom," she said, her voice hushed. "Vice President Stewart Engstrom."

17

The drive from Tel Aviv south to the kibbutz at Ze'Elim was eighty-five miles over dusty, narrow roads, but the distance seemed a million miles too short for David Goldmann.

He had not wanted to make this trip, and he had debated with himself for two days whether he should confront Levi Asheim's children in person, talk to them on the phone, or send them a long letter.

Last night he had made the only decent choice he could and this morning he had started out around 6:00 A.M., after a few sleepless hours.

Ze'Elim was one of the older "new" settlements in Israel and encompassed a large area of lush green cultivated fields irrigated from deep wells, trees, flowering plants, and a small patch of lawn in front of the kibbutz president's small bungalow.

It had been explained to Goldmann once that the lawn at Ze'Elim was a symbol not only of the progress the kibbutz had made against the relentless desert, but of Jewish freedom. Also, because of the grass, the kibbutz owned one of the first lawn mowers in the entire country.

Goldmann's jeep topped a rise below which, about two miles away, the kibbutz was a heady splash of green against the drab gray-yellow monotony of the desert.

He pulled over to the side of the road, parked the jeep, and got out to stretch his legs and have a cigarette. The morning was warm without being stifling, and the air smelled sweetly of growing things from the settlement.

He had rehearsed his lines a dozen different ways during the trip down, but now that he was almost there, nothing he planned on saying seemed correct. None of his lines had any compassion, any concern for the two women to whom he would have to speak them.

"The fact is, Deborah and Sandra, a body we believe was your father's was fished out of the La Plata Estuary just offshore from downtown Buenos Aires. What was left of it was sheathed in a large rubber bag and probably had been drifting around at sea for nearly twelve months." He spoke the words tonelessly into the soft breeze as he looked down at the kibbutz. "We can't be a hundred percent sure it was your father, however, because the body's head, hands, and feet had been cut off, and what remained was so badly decomposed that only the bones, the remnants of the clothing, and your father's watch and wallet were recognizable."

Goldmann suddenly ground out the half-finished cigarette in the dust at the side of the road, got back into the jeep, and started down the gentle hill toward the kibbutz.

"Also, I am sorry to say, although I know who killed your father, we will never catch him. My section, C-Seven, has been officially deactivated into nothing more than a records-keeping office. Read, clip, and file articles from newspapers and magazines. That's all we are allowed to do. So it is finished. They want to forget the war."

The kibbutz gates were open and unattended, and Goldmann drove into the settlement, parking in front of the long, low central building that served as the administration and planning center.

He was met by a young man in work clothes who checked his identification.

"I telephoned Mr. Ben Abel last night," Goldmann said. "He's expecting me."

"Yes, sir," the young man said. "He mentioned that you would be coming for a visit. At the moment, however, he is not here. He did say he would be back in a few minutes, so if you would like to wait for him in his office, you may."

"That would be fine, thank you."

"The young man led him across the orderly room to a small, pleasant office with two large windows that looked over the fields just outside the fence.

"Can I get you a glass of tea or something, sir?"

Goldmann shook his head. "Thank you, no."

"Yes, sir," the young man said, and left Goldmann alone in the office.

It had been one year since he had received the telephone call from Asheim in Chicago. And since that time he had heard nothing further despite his almost daily queries to Israeli field operatives in the United States and Argentina.

He sat wearily in the chair and stared out the windows, not really seeing anything. First Deborah's husband Benjamin had been killed. Then Elizabeth Norby, the operative who worked out of Chicago and who had been assigned to watch the Kelsey Clinic, had been found dead in her car. And now Asheim's body had been fished out of the ocean. In addition, Abraham Silverstein, who had reactivated the travel bureau in Buenos Aires, had disappeared about the same time Asheim had left the United States. He had never turned up, and Goldmann supposed his body would never be found.

He thumped his right fist on the arm of the chair. What had they gained by all those deaths? Nothing. Not one damned thing.

It had been three years since Benjamin had died tape-recording Spannau's final words. And Locke, the man they had traced from Buenos Aires to London and then to the clinic at Lake Geneva, had disappeared.

It did not make sense, Goldmann thought. He shook his head in irritation. Now that his department had been deactivated, he would never unravel it.

"I don't envy you your task, Colonel," a deep, rough voice came from the doorway.

Goldmann got to his feet as Jacob Ben Abel, the kibbutz president, came into the office.

He was a compact man who appeared to be in his late fifties or early sixties, and yet when he spoke, his voice seemed like it should be coming from a giant of a man.

Ben Abel stuck out his callused hand and Goldmann shook it.

"The Department of the Army phoned me yesterday a few hours before you called and told me the sad news about Major Asheim."

"I see," Goldmann said as Ben Abel went around his desk and sat down. "Have Deborah and Sandra been told?"

Ben Abel shook his head sadly. "No," he said, sighing deeply. "After your call I decided to wait until you arrived. I thought that together we might make it easier for them. Especially if you have any information. The Army could tell me nothing."

Goldmann again shook his head and sat down. "I have nothing that would make it easier for them. In fact, just the opposite is true."

"They are two good families," Ben Abel began, but Goldmann cut him off.

"I'm not here to recruit."

The older man seemed relieved. "I'll call them in."

Ben Abel's hand hovered over his phone for a moment. "Was it worth the sacrifice?"

Goldmann felt cold. "I hope they don't ask that question."

18

The home office of Kelsey Electronics, Ltd., was housed in a twenty-seven-story building a couple of blocks from the Sears Tower in Chicago's financial district. It had been built a few years ago at a cost of $80 million. All but the bottom four floors, which housed shops, a bookstore, a cocktail lounge, and some rental offices, were used by the company.

The top floor held the executive suite and August Kelsey's private dining room, used only by him, the board of directors, and the comptroller of the gigantic corporation.

Dr. Kelsey sat across the highly polished mahogany table from his father, the two of them the only ones in the room. The old man had seemed in a particularly ebullient mood, and Kelsey had wanted to wait until they were finished with their lunch to bring up the real reason for his visit.

Although the research institute was located only a few miles away from here, Kelsey and his father had both been extraordinarily busy over the past year and rarely managed to spend much time with each other. Kelsey had made the luncheon appointment with his father on the pretext that he merely wanted to see the old man, but his father saw through that.

"The chitchat is fine, and I'm glad that you managed to break free for lunch, Richard, but what's on your mind? More money for the Institute?"

Kelsey laughed and sat back in his chair, a wave of love for his father washing over him. "I never could keep anything a secret from you. Ever since I was a little boy and tried to hide the BB gun I swiped."

His father chuckled. "What's on your mind, Richard?"

Kelsey suddenly felt foolish being here. "Look, Father," he started, "if you're jammed up, I can come back another time. It's not all that important."

The old man tensed for a moment, almost as if he were a platoon sergeant making ready to bark an order at a subordinate, but then he relaxed, took a sip of cognac from the elegantly etched snifter, and smiled, the action deepening the lines around his eyes.

One part of Kelsey's mind was looking professionally at his father's face, which, with some minor surgery, could be fixed to make him look twenty years younger, and another part of his mind was seeing the man he loved and respected. A man who always had a smile for his son.

"I suppose I was being a little brusque," he said gently, and he took out his pocket watch and looked at it. "Are you going to be tied up at the Institute this afternoon?"

"Almost literally if Marion has her way. I have to be back by one-thirty. Carlson and some others from the AMA are coming to take a look at the setup. I'm supposed to be on my best behavior."

"How is Marion?"

"Just fine except for the fact she complains almost daily that you haven't been over to our apartment yet for dinner. She's a good cook."

"I thought perhaps that the three of us might sneak this

afternoon off. Take a drive up the lakeshore. Perhaps have dinner together somewhere. Before the snow flies.''

"I'd love to, and I know Marion would burn the Institute down if she figured it would help, but the AMA waits for no doctor.''

The elder Kelsey smiled, this time wistfully, and nodded. For a moment Kelsey caught a flash of his father as a very old man whose life was nearly over, and the feeling clutched at his heart. Until recently, Kelsey, like most children, had never thought of his father as mortal. The old man was an institution that was supposed to last forever.

"How about tonight?" Kelsey asked hopefully.

The old man shook his head. "Just wishful thinking on my part, Richard. I have a board meeting this afternoon at two, and I'm flying to Washington at six.''

At the mention of Washington, Kelsey's gut tightened. His father noticed the change.

"All right, we're both busy men, so out with it. When I mentioned Washington your back came up.''

"It's about Stewart Engstrom," Kelsey said, and this time it was his turn to notice a swift reaction in his father's expression.

"What about him?" the elder Kelsey asked.

Kelsey felt even more foolish, but his right hand went automatically to his breast pocket where he had the folded sketch he had made of Locke. He slowly withdrew it and passed it across the table.

His father opened the sketch and studied it for a brief moment, then he looked up. "A fair likeness of Stew Engstrom, I'd say, although it's hard to tell without the hairstyle.''

"It's a very good likeness of Vice President Engstrom.''

His father shrugged. "My son is an artist.''

"Who sculpts in human bone, cartilage, and flesh. That sketch represents the new face of James Locke, the mechanical engineer from London. I gave him that face a year ago.''

For a moment his father seemed puzzled, but then his eyes narrowed. He glanced again at the sketch and then back up at his son. ''You're saying that Jim Locke is going to try to impersonate Stew Engstrom?''

Kelsey shook his head. ''I think Locke has killed the vice president and is the man they pulled out of Mt. McKinley Park.''

For a moment the elder Kelsey held his breath, but then he laughed out loud, thumping his right fist lightly on the table.

Kelsey felt like a five-year-old boy caught with his hand in the cookie jar. Yet he could not shake the persistent feeling about Engstrom, or rather Locke, that nagged at his gut.

When his father had calmed himself sufficiently to speak, he leaned forward. ''You can't be serious, Richard.''

''I am, Father,'' Kelsey said. ''And it's not only the face. Locke's build is the same as Engstrom's, and when he came to us, his fingertips were burned with acid. Engstrom's fingertips were burned in a campfire. It's too much of a coincidence.''

''No, Richard, it's just too fantastic. Even if you fixed Locke so he looked exactly like Engstrom, he could never get away with the impersonation. The thousand and one trivial day-to-day details would be impossible to act out.''

''Since Engstrom's wife died a couple of years ago, there has been no one intimately close with him. It could be done.''

''How about his secretaries, the senators and congressmen he meets with every day, the journalists?'' the old man said. He shook his head. ''Locke is a mechanical engineer, not an expert in politics or government. He could not pull it off.''

Something Kelsey had been trying to remember suddenly popped into his mind. ''The day after Locke's first operation, I went to his room to see him. As I was leaving I noticed a few books he had been reading lying on the stand by his bed. They were about the presidency and American government. Strange reading, wouldn't you say, for a mechanical engineer from London?''

"I'll tell you what, Richard," his father said, pushing away from the table. "I'm going to Washington tonight, as a matter of fact, to attend a cocktail party at which Stew Engstrom is going to be the guest of honor."

Kelsey stood up, and the two of them went across the room to the door.

"I know Stew personally. I've known him for ten years. We've done some business together. I'll take a close look at him tonight. Ask him a couple of questions about business dealings we've had. If he is an imposter, there would be no way for him to know details such as those."

They stopped at the door and faced each other. Once again Kelsey felt a wave of love for his father. Once when he was a young boy, new in the neighborhood, he had shouted at the other children that his father could do anything. Now as an adult he could almost believe that was true.

"Thanks, Father. I'm being stupid about it, I know, but I just can't shake the feeling."

His father smiled. "I'll indulge your little fantasy, Doctor, but you're on a wild-goose chase."

"Marion said the same thing."

His father looked sharply at him. "You've dragged Marion into this nonsense?"

"Why not?"

The elder Kelsey smiled and shook his head. "When you were twenty I thought you had finally grown up. Then when you turned thirty and received your medical degree, I thought you had become a mature adult. But I can see that you're still in need of a firm hand."

Kelsey squeezed his father's shoulder affectionately. "My

dad can do anything," he said, and they both laughed and left the dining room.

At the elevator the expression on his father's face turned serious. "I wouldn't mention this to anyone else, Richard. They might lock you up in an asylum."

"I'll keep it to myself," Kelsey said. The elevator doors slid open. "Call me when you get back from Washington. I want to know what you think."

"I'll call you from Washington first thing in the morning," the old man said, and Kelsey got on the elevator.

It was a quarter after one when Kelsey got back to the Institute. Marion was waiting for him with a message from O'Hare Airport.

"Carlson's plane has been delayed by weather, and he may be a little late," she said.

"Good," Kelsey said over his shoulder as he went into his office with Marion right behind him.

He went behind his desk and sat down, then looked up at his wife waiting expectantly.

"Well?" she said. "What did he say?"

Kelsey smiled. "He called it a wild-goose chase, just like you did."

Marion came a little closer to the desk. "I don't know if I believe that any longer," she said. "You've almost got me believing in fairy tales."

"We'll know for sure tomorrow morning," he said.

"What do you mean?"

"Dad is leaving for Washington this afternoon to attend a cocktail party this evening at which Stewart Engstrom will be the guest of honor."

"Does your father know him?"

Kelsey nodded. "Said they had business dealings a few years ago. He's going to ask Engstrom a couple of questions about something only the real Engstrom knows. He'll telephone me first thing in the morning."

Marion seemed relieved. "Good," she said. "Then we can get back to normal."

"Have I been that bad?"

"I wouldn't call it an obsession. Yet. But unless you get some kind of a positive answer from somewhere, it could become a crusade."

Kelsey looked at his watch. "We still have a half hour or so before Carlson and his delegation gets here. There's something I want you to do for me."

"I've already done it," Marion said. "Do you want me to put the call through?"

Kelsey looked at his wife in open amazement. "Farley Chemicals, London?"

Marion nodded. "Robert Farley, president. I got the phone number this morning. He lives in London."

"I'll call him at his office."

"It's a little after seven in the evening there. I thought you might be phoning him when you got back from lunch, so I got his home number as well," Marion said. She came around the desk, picked up the phone, and a moment later the Institute's telephone receptionist was on the line. "Ruth, I want you to put through that call I spoke to you about earlier this morning."

She turned away from the phone and looked down at her husband. "Close your mouth, sweetheart," she said. "You look dumb with it hanging open."

It took several minutes for the overseas call to go through, and during that time Kelsey tried to organize his thoughts. One thing was certain, he told himself, and that was, he was not going to tell Farley anything other than the fact that as Locke's doctor, he wanted to talk with the man.

Marion was speaking into the phone again. "Mr. Robert Farley, president of Farley Chemicals?" she said. "I have Dr. Richard Kelsey calling from the United States. One moment please," she said, and handed the phone to her husband.

"Mr. Farley, I'm Dr. Richard Kelsey. I'm calling from Chicago."

"Yes, Dr. Kelsey, what can I do for you this evening?" the man said. His voice was rough with a heavy English accent. But there was something else in his speech that made Kelsey wonder if English was the man's native tongue.

"I'm trying to locate a Mr. James Locke, who was, or is, an engineer working for you. It was to my clinic in Lake Geneva that he came twelve months ago after his accident."

There was a silence on the line except for the occasional hiss and pop of the transatlantic connection.

"Mr. Farley?" Kelsey spoke into the phone.

"Yes, Doctor, I'm still here, but I'm afraid you've made some sort of mistake."

"Mistake?" Kelsey said. Marion was standing beside him, and he looked up at her.

"Yes. You see, we *did* have a fellow by the name of Jim Locke working here. Damned fine engineer, too. But he was killed in a motoring accident fourteen months ago."

"Are you certain?" Kelsey said, confused. "I mean about when it happened."

"One tends to be rather sure about details like that. So you see, Dr. Kelsey, you must have made a mistake. You could not have worked on our poor Jim Locke."

"I see," Kelsey mumbled. "You don't happen to know if there is another Farley Chemicals in or around the London area?"

"I don't believe so," the man said.

"Thank you for your help," Kelsey said, and he hung up the phone.

"What about a mistake?" Marion started to say when the telephone receptionist buzzed and Kelsey picked up the phone again.

"Yes," he said.

"Dr. Carlson has arrived, and your father is holding on line two."

"All right, Ruth. Tell Dr. Carlson I'll be right with him. I'll take my father's call first."

"Yes, sir," the woman said.

Kelsey's mind was still reeling from his talk with Farley when he punched the button for line two and his father came on.

"Our discussion this morning bothered me, Richard," the old man said without preamble. "So I phoned Stew Engstrom a few minutes after you left. We talked for half an hour or so, and I thought I'd better call you."

Kelsey sat forward. "Yes?"

"He's Stew Engstrom. There's no doubt in my mind. As a matter of fact, as we were talking he came up with a comment I had made five or six years ago that I had completely forgotten about. I promised that if he ever got elected as vice president, I'd donate five thousand dollars to his favorite charity. Well, he just reminded me. So your little flight of fancy has cost me plenty."

Kelsey had barely heard the last part. "Are you certain, Father? Absolutely certain that the man you spoke with is Stewart Engstrom?"

"Absolutely, Richard," the old man said. "Now you can stop your nonsense."

For an instant Kelsey debated whether or not he should tell his father about his conversation with Farley. But something made him hold back. "You're probably right," he mumbled.

"Of course I am," the old man said. "And now I've got my board meeting in a few minutes and you've got the AMA, so I'll let you go."

"Thanks, Father," Kelsey said, and hung up the phone. None of this made any sense, and for the moment he completely blocked the waiting AMA delegation out of his mind. He took the sketch of Locke out of his breast pocket and spread it out on the desk in front of him.

Marion was hovering over him, deep concern on her face.

"Do you mind telling me what's going on, Richard?"

He looked up at her. "Farley said the James Locke who worked for him was killed in a car accident fourteen months ago. That's the same time he was with us in Lake Geneva. And my father telephoned Stew Engstrom and said he's the real McCoy."

Marion said nothing, and Kelsey gazed again at the sketch. There was only one way to make absolutely certain that no mistake has been made, he told himself. Only one way.

He picked up the phone again and the receptionist came on.

"Dr. Carlson is getting a little impatient, sir," she said, flustered.

"I don't care," Kelsey said. "Call O'Hare and get me a seat on the next plane for Washington, D.C. Call me as soon as you've confirmed it."

"Yes, sir," the woman said, even more flustered.

Marion snatched the phone from her husband. "Make that two seats, Ruth, and tell Dr. Carlson that I'll be right out."

"You're not coming with me," Kelsey said as she hung up the phone.

"Oh yes I am, Doctor. Just try and stop me."

19

He had finally come to the decision he had been putting off for the past six months. It was a decision that he knew in his gut was his only choice. And yet he had avoided it all this time.

Like Asheim and so many others in Israel, Goldmann was a loner. His wife had been killed in Auschwitz, and he never had the time or the interest to remarry. Instead he had thrown himself body and soul into the creation of Israel and then Nazi hunting.

It was one of the reasons, he supposed, that he understood Asheim so well. The man had been very much like himself: a loner except for his children, who had thrown himself full tilt into his work.

He stopped his packing for a moment, went to the living room window, and looked out at the city of Tel Aviv, white, clean, and new in the bright fall sunlight.

They had come a long way since their war of independence in 1949. He had been a part of the tremendous changes sweeping the land. But then he had dropped out, creating the Nazi-hunting C-VII section, and plunging himself into his work.

From 1950 until 1960, Goldmann's chief target was Adolf Eichmann, the mastermind and architect of the Nazi's Final Solution.

He was traced to Argentina, where he was kidnapped and returned to Israel to stand trial. It was a triumph. But a short-lived one. Shortly after Eichmann's execution in 1962, the Israeli government's attitude toward escaped Nazi war criminals softened, and Goldmann's C-VII section suffered.

But he did not quit his work then, nor would he now.

He turned from the window and went back into his bedroom, where he resumed packing his one suitcase and small attaché case.

Today was his birthday. He was sixty-four, and he felt every year of it. Time was running out for him.

He was young by comparison to the Odessa leadership, men who were in their early and mid-seventies. Soon they would all be dead, and at long last it would be finished. And yet the man they had moved by air ambulance from Buenos Aires to London, and from there to the clinic in Wisconsin, had to be the key. There was no doubt in Goldmann's mind that the Odessa leadership was struggling to perpetuate itself.

It was the reason Benjamin had been murdered. It was the reason Asheim and the others had been killed. And it was one of the reasons Goldmann was going to Buenos Aires.

"We have decided to deactivate C-Seven, David," his superior Colonel Joseph Yesodat told him yesterday morning after he had returned from Ze'Elim.

"Why the sudden change?" he asked softly.

Yesodat shook his head sadly. "We've made peace with the Egyptians, but our troubles with the Arab world aren't over. No one cares these days about the Nazis. It's been too long."

"We struggled two thousand years against one oppressor. Are we going to give up against another after only thirty-five years?"

"It's no use, my old friend. Your job is finished."

"It will never be finished until all of them have been brought to justice," Goldmann said with much feeling.

"Bring to justice a small group of old men?" Yesodat shook his head again. "We weathered a storm of negative world opinion over Eichmann, the worst of the lot. What do you suppose would happen these days?"

"There is the other thing," Goldmann said. "This business about an Odessa-trained imposter?"

Goldmann nodded.

"First," Yesodat said, ticking off points on his fingers, "I'm not as certain as you that such an organization as Odessa even exists. Second, we know nothing about the man the Odessa supposedly trained. Third, we know nothing except the ramblings of a dying old man about the supposed mission the Odessa is mounting. And fourth, even if Odessa did train this man to be an imposter, who could he impersonate to do us any harm?"

"I can understand your skepticism, but answer one question for me. Why have four of our people been murdered?"

"I don't know. Perhaps there is some validity to the idea of an Odessa. Perhaps Major Asheim and the others were murdered for no other reason than the Germans are still fighting the war; they still hate the Jews; they don't like us poking around in their business."

"An interesting view," Goldmann said. "But not quite consistent with your policy of hands off."

Yesodat slammed his open palm on the desktop. "They say a Jew can argue the spots off a leopard, but until this moment I never believed it! David, for God's sake, leave it alone! I didn't make this policy. I am merely following orders. This came from the top."

"Perhaps we should check a little more closely into Begin's and Dayan's war records."

Yesodat turned white. "I know you don't mean that, and I'll pretend you didn't say it."

Goldmann hung his head. "Of course I didn't mean it." He looked up, anguish on his face. "What am I supposed to do after Auschwitz, and then thirty-five years of my life devoted to this project?"

"Retire."

The single word was like a slap in the face to Goldmann. "What?" he said incredulously.

"Retire from the secret service. Ben Abel was favorably impressed with you yesterday. 'A compassionate man,' he called you. He wants to step down. You would be a logical choice to run the kibbutz," Yesodat said, and his voice softened. "Asheim's daughters and grandchildren are there. I know you could become close. They need a father, and you need a family."

Goldmann finished packing, and he snapped the suitcase and attaché case shut, then set them by the front door. He went to the window and looked again out over the city he loved so well.

He had asked for thirty days leave to think over his decision. And Yesodat had been glad to give it to him, Goldmann supposed, for no other reason than to get the former C-VII chief out of the way.

His two assistants had been transferred to other duties, his offices were closed, and the records of thirty-five years of work were already in archives storage, where they would gather dust.

"No matter what your decision," Yesodat had said yesterday in parting, "C-Seven is no more. We are done hunting Nazis."

Almost the same words, he thought, that Deborah had spoken to him the day before at Ze'Elim.

"Our father is dead, so it is over now," she had said, her voice maddeningly calm and devoid of emotion.

He had not known exactly how she would take the news of her father's death, but the reaction, or rather lack of reaction, she showed had completely stunned him.

"Let it rest, Colonel Goldmann," Asheim's other daughter, Sandra, said, barely in control of her voice. "Deborah and I both agree that there has been enough death."

"I don't know what to say," Goldmann said softly, truly at a loss for words. "Your father was a good man."

"We know," Deborah said. "And thank you for taking the time to tell us the news in person. We appreciate it."

She and her sister left Ben Abel's office, and for a long time Goldmann sat staring out the window at the green fields outside the perimeter fence, until the kibbutz president broke the silence.

"They are two good and very strong women. True sabras."

Goldmann nodded. "Yes."

"Are you that strong, Colonel?"

Goldmann looked deeply into Ben Abel's kindly, understanding eyes. "I don't know. I don't think so."

Asheim's death would not remain in vain, Goldmann thought as he picked up his luggage, went out of his apartment, and locked the door behind him. Nor would the deaths of Benjamin, Elizabeth Norby, and Silverstein go unchallenged.

Downstairs on the street, the cab he had called for pulled up and he climbed in the backseat. "The airport, please," he said.

20

The newspapers were filled with Stewart Engstrom's apology to the American public and the promise that he would not go on any more of his backwoods jaunts after the *New York Times* had labeled his latest trip an "irresponsible escapade."

"So long as I hold public office I'll content myself to the golf course or the ski slopes," Engstrom told a news conference.

And the *Washington Post*, which all along had maintained the position that Engstrom's backpacking trips had "invigorated" the vice president, reported that since his latest adventure, he seemed a changed man. "Somehow younger and more vital."

Kelsey had pored over the newspapers during their flight east with a rising conviction that he was correct; the man pretending to be Stewart Engstrom was in reality a man he had known as James Locke.

Farley's stunning revelation from London that the real

Locke had died in a car accident fourteen months ago was not so surprising on reflection. The man Kelsey had operated on evidently had been aware of the real Locke's death and had merely assumed his identity for the few months he was at the clinic.

But what was disturbing, deeply disturbing to Kelsey, was his father.

He looked up as their cab pulled off the George Washington Memorial Parkway and headed toward the Marriott, where they had reservations. Normally he would have stayed in town, but he was only planning on staying overnight, and the Marriott was conveniently close to the airport. To the west, the Pentagon loomed like a vast dark cloud across the highway. Across the Potomac the city of Washington was spread out in the early evening.

"Now that we're actually here, I'm a little frightened," Marion said.

He looked at his wife. "I wished you'd remained home, but now I'm glad you came."

She smiled and patted his hand. "Your father is going to be surprised when we show up at the party."

" 'Irritated' would be a more apt word," he said.

"A son checking on his father's judgment?" Marion asked, but then she had a second thought, and the astonishment showed on her face. "You don't believe him."

Kelsey turned away from her, not able to hide the sudden emotion in his eyes.

She reached out and gently turned him back. "You think your father lied to you," she said, but he did not answer her. "Why? What possible reason could he have for lying to you?"

"I don't know," Kelsey said after a long silence, and they said nothing more to each other.

The cab pulled into the Marriott's driveway and stopped at the front entrance. Kelsey paid the driver and he and Marion got out, went into the motel, and checked in.

Upstairs in their room Kelsey took off his coat and loosened his tie, but Marion made no move to unpack their two overnight bags.

"If Stewart Engstrom is an imposter, maybe he is good enough to fool your father," she said. She stood in the middle of the room looking at her husband, who had pulled open the curtains and stared across the river at the city.

That same thought had raced through his mind a dozen times since this afternoon, and each time he had been forced to reject it. If there had been doubt, even a tiny doubt, in his father's mind about the authenticity of Engstrom, it would have been all right. But the old man had been so damned sure. Even to the point of mentioning the supposedly obscure five-thousand-dollar campaign pledge he had made several years ago. That was something an imposter could not know.

It all boiled down to two possibilities, however. Either the man who had returned from Alaska was in reality Stewart Engstrom, the vice president, in which case Kelsey was a fool. Or the man *was* an imposter, in which case Kelsey's father was a part of some insane plot.

He turned to face his wife. "My father was too certain that the man is Stewart Engstrom."

"Let's return home, Richard," she said in a small voice.

"I can't do that."

She absently brushed a loose strand of hair away from her forehead. "You can't be having doubts about your own father."

He started to speak, but he could not form the words even though that thought was foremost in his mind. Instead he went to the phone, got an outside line, and dialed his father's house in College Park.

On the second ring his father's Washington secretary, Rupert Livermore, answered the phone. "The August Kelsey residence."

"Rupert, this is Richard. Has my father arrived there yet?"

"Richard, it's so nice to hear from you," the man said. He sounded genuinely pleased. "We're expecting him within the hour. Are you in Washington?"

"No, I'm calling from Chicago."

"Is there some trouble?"

"Nothing serious," Kelsey said. "I'd like to talk to my father sometime this evening."

"He'll be here only briefly, and then he's going to a cocktail party for Vice President Engstrom."

"I see," Kelsey said. His heart was hammering. "If I miss him at the house, perhaps I can phone him at the party."

"Certainly," the man said. "It's being held at Senator Teller's home."

"Georgetown?"

"That's correct."

"Thanks, Rupert."

"I'll tell your father you called," the man said. "And by the way, say hello to your lovely wife for me."

"I'll do that," Kelsey said, and he hung up the phone. He looked at his watch, which showed it was shortly after seven, then took off his tie and began unbuttoning his shirt as he headed for the bathroom. "The first comers usually arrive at these things around eight," he said over his shoulder. "If we get there by nine, Engstrom should be on hand."

Marion opened the overnight bags and began unpacking. "Will you be able to tell just by looking at him?" she asked from the bedroom.

"If I get close enough," Kelsey said. He finished undressing and stepped into the shower, adjusting the spray as hot as he could stand it.

Locke's rhinoplastic operation that repaired and reshaped his damaged nose was all done within the nasal passages, so nothing short of a detailed physical examination would reveal the work for certain.

The postoperative scars from the repairs done to his cheeks were hidden in the hairline of the scalp as well as in the folds of tissue adjacent to his ears.

And the mentoplastic operation that reshaped his chin was done from inside his mouth, so no scars would be visible.

Which left no real clues for the untrained eye to detect the man was an imposter. But Kelsey was not untrained. And furthermore, he had come to intimately know Locke's face.

The shape and exact coloration of the eyes, for instance, Kelsey remembered vividly. And if the man was wearing tinted contact lenses to hide such details, that fact alone would be at least a partial indictment.

The man's skin texture was another of the factors Kelsey would pay close attention to, along with the coloration and quality of his hair, his eyebrow and eyelash lines, and dozens of other subtle little indicators that only a plastic surgeon would see.

If the man at the cocktail party tonight was James Locke, he would see it.

The home of Leonard Teller, junior senator from Alaska, was located in Washington's fashionable Georgetown district. It was an elegant two-story brownstone. The house had been in the Teller family for sixty years. Teller's father, Ronald, had spent five consecutive terms in the Senate from Oregon, and his father before him had been the representative from that state.

It was not clear in Kelsey's mind what his father's connection was with the Tellers, but the man had come to his graduation from medical school, and Kelsey had briefly met him then. Senator Teller had also sent a wedding gift when he and Colleen were married and again when he and Marion were wed.

By nine o'clock the house was ablaze in lights. Limousines were parked on either side of the street to the corner, and two uniformed doormen were checking invitations when the cab dropped Kelsey and Marion off.

The doorman holding a clipboard looked up, a pleasant expression on his face, as they approached. "Good evening," he said. "May I have your names?"

"Dr. and Mrs. Richard Kelsey. We're friends of the Teller family, but I don't believe we're on your list."

The doorman ignored the last part as he flipped through the invitation list. "Yes, here we are, sir," he said. "Mr. Livermore telephoned a short time ago and advised us you might be arriving. Go right in, please."

Marion clutched her husband's arm more tightly, and Kelsey felt a little light-headed. Livermore had known he was in Washington, and yet on the phone he had not let on that he knew. Every move they had made had probably been watched. It was frightening.

"Has my father arrived yet?" he asked, trying to keep his voice calm.

"No, sir," the doorman said.

Several other people had arrived and were approaching the entrance. Kelsey and Marion went up the stairs and entered the house, where a liveried butler took their coats.

They went through the vestibule, which opened to the left into a huge dining room and to the right into the living room. There were at least four dozen people there already. Some of them were gathered in small groups speaking intently to each other, while a dozen or more elegantly dressed men and women were seated or stood around Engstrom, who was leaning nonchalantly against the fireplace mantel, Senator Teller at his side.

Kelsey stopped just under the archway into the living room and stared across at Engstrom, his stomach flipping over several times.

promised to pay five thousand dollars into my favorite charity if ever I made it. When I talked to him on the phone this afternoon, I reminded him of the bet.''

Teller chuckled at the story, but Kelsey had been listening less to the words and more to Engstrom's tone of voice.

"Have you got a cold, Mr. Vice President?'' he asked.

Engstrom turned back to him. "Yes, as a matter of fact, I do," he said. "Another of the things I unintentionally brought back from Alaska with me.''

The voice was Locke's. Kelsey was one hundred percent certain of it. And for the briefest of moments he had to resist the almost overpowering urge to reach out, grab the man, and make him admit the truth. But the feeling passed as a heavyset woman in a tightly fitting cocktail dress came up to them.

"Mr. Vice President, there are some people you absolutely have to meet this instant," the woman boomed in a Wagnerian voice.

Engstrom nodded his apologies and asked Kelsey to say hello to his father, and then he was gone.

A little while later Teller drifted off, and Kelsey and Marion found themselves alone near the front vestibule.

"It wasn't Engstrom, was it?" Marion said in a half whisper.

Kelsey shook his head. "The vice president is the same man I operated on at the clinic. I'd bet my life on it."

Marion looked pale. "What do we do now?"

"I don't know," he said. "I just don't know."

21

Kelsey and Marion left about an hour after they had met the man posing as the vice president, and climbed into a taxi that pulled up out front. More people were arriving at the party.

"The airport Marriott," Kelsey absently told the driver, and the cab pulled away from the curb as he settled back in the seat, his right hand resting on Marion's hand in her lap.

For several minutes they rode in silence, Kelsey deep in his thoughts. Locke did look and act amazingly like Engstrom, and so far he had evidently fooled the people he had come in contact with. The cocktail party tonight was probably some kind of a test of just how good the masquerade would hold up in a group of people who knew the real vice president. From what Kelsey had observed briefly at the party, everyone believed the man to be the real vice president.

Kelsey knew without a shadow of a doubt that the man

posing as Engstrom was the same man he had operated on
at the clinic. But his father was a problem. If, as Marion
had suggested, the man posing as Engstrom had indeed managed to fool his father, someone who intimately knew his
father's dealings with Engstrom must have been in on the
training.

He turned that thought over for a moment. Locke, whoever he really was, could not have done this alone. Which
meant there must have been some kind of an organization.
A very effective group, probably based here in Washington,
but with tendrils everywhere.

Engstrom must have been the target long ago. His rise in
politics must have been watched, perhaps even aided from
time to time, and when he got into a position of power, the
switch was made.

Another cold thought crossed Kelsey's mind, and he re-
flectively glanced over at Marion, who smiled uncertainly
at him. She looked frightened.

If Engstrom's wife had been alive, they never could have
pulled this off. Acting as an imposter, a very capable and
highly trained person might fool acquaintances, and some
friends, but not a wife.

Engstrom's wife's death, therefore, had been no coincidence. She had been murdered so that Locke could take
over.

He sat back, sighed deeply, and ran the fingers of his right
hand through his hair, and Marion snuggled a little closer
to him.

But none of that fit. There were too many coincidences.
Too many happenstance occurrences. If there was an organization, and if it had watched Engstrom's rise and had murdered his wife so that a switch could be made, it would be
a precise group that would not have left anything to chance.
Every step would have been carefully planned, every con-
tingency expected. From the beginning everyone having

contact with Engstrom's imposter would have been planned for. Which included Kelsey.

He closed his eyes for a moment and allowed his mind to drift, not really focusing on any one thought, until suddenly a glimmering of the entire plan, his part in it included, crystallized in his brain. He snapped forward, sweat suddenly popping out on his forehead.

It was sick. Impossible. Monstrous. For several wild seconds he felt like a cornered animal as he tried to reason himself away from the wall he had pushed himself against.

But it fit. Goddammit, it all fit, including the fact that his father's secretary, Rupert Livermore, knew he was in Washington and would be attending the party.

Engstrom had been the target all along for a number of reasons, among them that he was a fast-rising star on the political scene, and yet he was a loner. No close friends, no brothers or sisters, only a few cousins living, parents both dead. Only a wife to stand in the way. Locke then, had been selected because he was a close physical match to the vice president. He had been trained, which left only his face and fingerprints. The fingerprints were plausibly taken care of in the accident, and Kelsey had given him a new face.

With a sickness building inside of him, Kelsey saw it all. He had been selected as the plastic surgeon to do the work first of all because he was good. And secondly because he could be controlled by his father, who had to be one of the planners.

The problem was to get him to go into clinical work so that the imposter could be sent to him as a matter of routine. But he and Colleen had had plans to go on together in research. Nothing or no one could shake that bond. So Colleen's death had been ordered and carried out.

Tears came to his eyes, and Marion looked at him, growing alarm in her expression.

"What is it, Richard?"

He could only shake his head.

"For God's sake, Richard, what's the matter?"

With Colleen out of the way, it was a fairly easy matter for his father to convince him to operate the clinic in Lake Geneva. Once the place was in operation and well established, his father sent Locke, the engineer who supposedly worked for Farley Chemicals, to him.

That one point had nagged at the back of Kelsey's mind. His father had told him at the time that Locke worked for an old friend. But when Kelsey had telephoned Farley, the man had not recognized the name.

Stan Lowe was in on it as well. Kelsey was certain of that too because the very day they had driven up to Lake Geneva to pull Locke's records, Lowe had the jacket removed.

He let his mind go back to Minneapolis and his wife. If he had gone with her that night, nothing would have happened. They would not have killed him because they needed him, and she would still be alive.

But they would have done it another time. They would have waited until she was alone, and they would have done it.

The expression of grief on his father's face at the cemetery during the funeral came into his mind's eye. It had been a sham. His supporting words, his tears, it all had been make-believe. But why?

He focused again on Marion, staring wide-eyed and frightened at him. Dear sweet Marion. Would she be next?

"They killed her," he said, barely able to form the words.

"What?" Marion asked.

"Whoever was responsible for making the switch with Engstrom, killed Colleen."

Marion's complexion turned a pasty white. "What are you saying, Richard?"

"They murdered her," he said, raising his voice. "They needed me in clinical work so that I could fix Locke's face.

But with Colleen alive I would never have taken the clinic. So they killed her.''

"That means your father knew about it all along," she said, aghast.

Kelsey nodded. "Yes, my father is in on it. As well as Stan Lowe."

"My poor darling," Marion said.

His father had always been the Rock of Gibraltar for him, and now he felt terribly alone. Engstrom's imposter, Stan Lowe, and his own father were in on the fantastic scheme. There were probably others. Many others. Which left him alone as the only one who knew what was really happening.

"Why did they do it?" Marion asked.

"I told you, they needed me in Lake Geneva to work on Locke," he said, his mind still drifting.

"No, I mean why is Locke impersonating Engstrom?" Kelsey focused on her.

"Why the *vice* president?" she asked. "He has no power. Why not impersonate the President?"

"Because Barnes is married and has children—an imposter would never get away with it," Kelsey started to say, but he stopped in midsentence. Marion was correct. A vice president's power stemmed *only* from the fact that he was available should the president die or become incapacitated. He had little or no other power. With Locke firmly established as the vice president, however, Barnes could be assassinated, and control of the most powerful nation in the world, its nuclear arsenal and all, would fall into the hands of a desperate group. Which meant that as of this moment, President Barnes was in mortal danger.

Kelsey sat forward and looked out the window. The Potomac River was to their right, which meant they had not crossed over into Arlington yet, but he did not recognize exactly where they were.

"Driver, I've changed my mind, I want to go back downtown."

"Sir?" the man said over his shoulder.

Kelsey turned in his seat and looked out the rear window. Behind them he could see the Jefferson Memorial beyond the interstate highway bridges.

"You missed the bridge to Arlington," he said, turning back.

"Sir?" the driver said again.

"What the hell is going on?" Kelsey shouted. The driver braked hard and pulled off to the side of the road.

When the cab stopped, the driver turned around and pointed a large pistol with a silencer screwed on the end of the barrel at them. There was no expression on his face, but he blinked his eyes once and pulled back on the hammer.

Kelsey struck out blindly, knocking the pistol aside as it went off, the shot shattering the window a few inches from Marion's head.

The driver tried to push Kelsey back with his other hand, but he could not get his body far enough around in the front seat to put any force into the blow.

Kelsey threw his right arm around the man's neck and jerked backward as hard as he could. There was a sickening crunch as the man's neck broke.

Kelsey loosened his grip, and the driver's body slumped to the left, his head bumping against the doorframe at an unnatural angle.

Several cars passed, none of them stopping or even slowing down, and Kelsey turned to his wife, whose eyes were wide.

"You killed him, Richard," she said. "My God, he's dead!"

She started to scream, and Kelsey slapped her hard across the face, and she went limp, the tears beginning to flow.

When he was sure she would be all right, he got out of the car and eased open the front door, careful not to let the driver's body fall out onto the road.

He pushed the inert form to the other side of the seat, got

behind the wheel, and pulled away from the side of the road, doing a U-turn and heading back toward the city.

"Where are we going?" Marion asked from the backseat.

"The FBI. Locke's impersonation of Engstrom is only the first step. President Barnes will be next."

Marion fell silent, and a moment later the enormity of what he had just done came crashing down on him and he began to shake. He had killed a man. He was a medical doctor, a scientist, a man whose very existence was dedicated to saving lives; but he had killed a man.

He glanced over at the body and shuddered. What in God's name had he done? What if he was wrong? What if his father had been telling the truth and all of this was just a product of an overworked imagination?

He shook his head. Cab drivers did not go around trying to kill people, nor did they carry guns with silencers.

Locke knew that Kelsey had identified him, so at this moment the organization that had murdered Colleen, had killed Engstrom and had placed Locke in his stead, was now out to kill him and his wife.

He glanced at Marion in the rearview mirror. She sat erect, her hands folded in her lap, staring straight ahead. Her face was still a sickly white, and her eyes were red-rimmed, her hair disheveled.

The problem was, would the FBI believe his story? As a medical doctor, he had a certain credibility as a dispassionate observer. But that was countered by the fact that everyone seemed to be accepting Locke as the real vice president.

They crossed over the Washington Canal on U.S. 1, passed the Capitol Mall, then turned right on Constitution Avenue. It was a few minutes before eleven and traffic was light, but he drove slowly, and very carefully. Before he started answering questions about the cabby's murder, he wanted to present his story to someone with the authority and ability to do some checking. If he was stopped now by a District police officer and the body was discovered, his story would sound like nothing more than the ravings of a lunatic. It could take days or even weeks to straighten everything out. And by then it might be too late.

The light was green at Ninth Street by the Justice Department, and he turned left. The huge building that housed the Federal Bureau of Investigation was a couple of blocks away across Pennsylvania Avenue on Ninth and E Streets, and he started to shake again.

Was he certain? he asked himself again. Was he absolutely certain that the man they had met this evening was an imposter?

Yes, he told himself firmly. And he could prove it if the vice president would submit to a physical examination.

They crossed Pennsylvania Avenue and Kelsey drove slowly past the gigantic FBI building, mostly dark at this hour of the night, then turned left on E Street where one of the entrances was lit up. He parked across the street, shut out the headlights, turned off the engine, and swiveled around to face Marion.

"Do you want to wait here, take a cab back to the motel, or come in with me?" he asked.

It took several moments for what he had said to apparently sink in, but when it did she sprang forward and grabbed his arm. "I'm coming with you. I don't want to be alone."

"All right," Kelsey said.

They headed across the street together to the one entrance with a light over the door.

Just inside, a black janitor was waxing the tiled corridor floor, and he looked up indifferently as Kelsey and Marion came through the entrance.

"You people looking for something?" he asked in a southern drawl. He leaned on his mop handle.

"Is there an agent on duty this time of night?" Kelsey asked, the request sounding foolish and somewhat melodramatic to him.

The janitor smiled and nodded. "Yessir," he said, nod-ding over his shoulder. "Down the hall to the right. You can't miss it."

"Thank you," Kelsey said, and he and Marion passed the janitor and hurried down the corridor, their footfalls sound-ing hollow.

Around the corner, a wide door opened into a large room filled with several dozen desks. It looked like a newsroom of a large city newspaper. Near the rear of the room two men were engaged in conversation, one of them seated be-hind a desk, the other perched on the edge of the desk. As Kelsey and Marion threaded their way past the rows of desks, both men turned their way.

Kelsey's heart was pounding, and he could feel Marion shivering as she clung tightly to his arm.

"Can I help you folks with something?" the man seated behind the desk asked. He was young, probably not over thirty, had short hair, was clean-shaven, and wore a dark suit. His tie was loose, and the top button of his shirt was undone. The man seated on the desktop looked and dressed similarly. They could have been brothers.

"I want to report a plot on the President's life, and three or maybe more murders," Kelsey said, the words half catch-ing in his throat.

For a long moment both men sat totally immobile, the expressions of idle curiosity frozen on their faces. Kelsey was certain they could hear his heart beating wildly.

Then the man seated on the desk slowly got to his feet and, never taking his eyes off Marion or Kelsey, pulled a couple of chairs around for them to sit down. The other man reflexively straightened his tie and beckoned for them to sit down.

Kelsey was dressed in a tuxedo, and Marion in an obvi-ously expensive cocktail dress. They did not look like wild-eyed radicals, which, Kelsey hoped, would help lend credence to what he was about to tell them. At least it might at first.

"You better start out by telling me who you are," the man behind the desk said slowly once Kelsey and Marion were seated. The other man stood to one side staring at them.

"I'm Dr. Richard Kelsey, and this is my wife, Marion. We're from Chicago."

"You're a medical doctor?"

"A plastic surgeon," Kelsey said, and he glanced at the other man, who had picked up a telephone on the next desk over and was talking to someone. Kelsey heard his own name being mentioned.

"Who is going to assassinate President Barnes, and when?" the man behind the desk asked.

"I don't know who and I don't know when," Kelsey said. "But it's some organization that has already kidnapped or assassinated Vice President Engstrom in Alaska and has replaced him with an imposter. A man whose face I fixed to look like Engstrom's more than a year ago."

The man behind the desk whistled and sat back in his chair. He looked over at the other man, who hung up the phone.

"You've gained a little weight over the past six months, Dr. Kelsey," the agent said. He turned to the seated agent and nodded. "This would appear to be Dr. Richard Kelsey. Used to run a clinic in Lake Geneva, Wisconsin. Now is director of a research institute in Chicago. Kelsey Institute. He's considered to be one of the top men in his field in this country. They had an up-to-date photo on him downstairs. Descriptions match."

The agent seated seemed to digest this for a moment. "Better alert Secret Service just in case," he said. "And have them send Kelsey's file up here right away." He turned back to Kelsey. "I'd like to take your fingerprints in a little while to verify you actually are who you say you are."

Kelsey nodded, and the other agent was back on the phone.

"And now," the man behind the desk said, pulling a cassette tape recorder from a drawer and setting it up. "I'd like you to tell me everything. From the beginning. Leaving nothing out, and being as specific as you possibly can about dates, times, names, places, and all that."

Kelsey sat forward. "President Barnes is in danger right this moment, and Engstrom is an imposter."

"President Barnes is out of the country at the moment, and both he and Vice President Engstrom have Secret Service agents assigned to them. We are alerting those agents at this moment. Right now I need all the information you can give me."

"Parked across E Street is a cab. The driver is dead in the front seat. He tried to kill us about a half hour ago."

At this the other agent turned around and looked at Kelsey, and once again the enormity and absolute implausibility of what he was telling them came crashing in on him, leaving him with a feeling of almost total helplessness. He wished his father were there to help straighten this out.

22

There was a one-hour delay in Mexico City before Goldmann's Pan American 747 flight to Buenos Aires was due for departure, and it came as no surprise to him when his name was paged over the terminal's public address system to report to the information counter of Pan Am.

Yesodat had sent one of his flunkies to Lod Airport in Tel Aviv to retrieve Goldmann's diplomatic passport, but he had stalled the young man. By the time the hapless lad had been able to phone Yesodat for further instructions, Goldmann's flight had already left.

Yesodat had known, or had at least suspected all along, that Goldmann would never give up the fight. Benjamin Karel, Abraham Silverstein, and finally Levi Asheim all had either disappeared or had been murdered in Buenos Aires. The Odessa plot had first been uncovered there. And Kurt Stoeffel, the former SS *Oberst* and probable present head of the organization, maintained his jungle fortress, Aerie, near there. It was only natural that Yesodat would put two and two together and realize Goldmann would head to Buenos Aires.

"The problem is," Goldmann could almost hear Yesodat's carefully prepared explanation, "that as a civilian, you are certainly free to do whatever you want, providing you are willing to accept the consequences. But as a diplomat—as an Israeli officer carrying a diplomatic passport—your actions reflect directly on our government. And our government does not want you mucking around Buenos Aires."

Goldmann had been a pragmatist all of his life, and although he tended to agree with Yesodat's concern that officially the Israeli government could not go around killing people, he needed his diplomatic passport until he cleared customs in Buenos Aires.

With a civilian passport his luggage would be searched. But with his diplomatic credentials, that necessity would be waived. For the first time in a long time, he was carrying weapons in his luggage, a fact he did not want the Buenos Aires authorities to discover.

He left the Pan Am departure gate area and unhurriedly strolled down the wide corridor to the main concourse where the various airline ticket and information counters were arranged along the wall opposite the main doors.

An elderly man wearing a black hat stood alone at the Pan Am information counter, and Goldmann had to smile to himself as he approached from across the concourse.

If Yesodat had wanted to make serious trouble for him, he would have sent a couple of operatives from the Mexico City embassy to arrest him at the Pan Am arrival departure gate the moment his plane landed.

He had sent instead an innocuous embassy staffer who would no doubt try to persuade him to turn over his diplomatic passport in exchange for a civilian document.

Yesodat knew what was going on, and by this action tacitly approved, yet he had to go through the motions.

"You are looking for me?" Goldmann said as he came up to the counter.

The embassy man looked up with a start. "Colonel Goldmann?" he asked, his voice somewhat timorous. "David Goldmann?"

Goldmann nodded. "My plane leaves in less than an hour. You wanted to speak to me about something?"

The embassy man looked around. "Is there somewhere we can talk?"

Goldmann shrugged. "This is your city, I've never been here."

"It's about your passport, Colonel," the man said in a low voice.

"What about it?"

"I have a civilian passport that I have been instructed to give to you in exchange for your diplomatic credentials."

Goldmann's eyes narrowed. "Who sent you?" he said sharply. The embassy man flinched.

"We were telexed this morning from Tel Aviv. A Colonel Yesodat, I believe."

"Send a message back to Yesodat that I will exchange passports in Buenos Aires. Not before." Goldmann said, and he turned to walk away.

"Sir," the embassy man said, raising his voice. Goldmann turned back.

"Are you going to make a scene?"

"No, sir," the man said, and suddenly gone was his apprehensive expression and demeanor. "Colonel Yesodat also telephoned this morning. Told me to pass a message on to you in strictest confidence if you refused to surrender your diplomatic credentials to me."

Goldmann was interested. "You know Colonel Yesodat personally?"

The embassy man smiled. "Joseph and I are old friends," he said, dropping into Yiddish.

"So?"

"He sends his regards and asked that you take care in what you are doing. He also wishes you much luck. There will be a man in Buenos Aires, outside customs, who will present you with your new credentials."

Goldmann looked at his watch. "I have about fifty minutes before my plane is scheduled to leave. Don't return to the embassy until then, please."

The embassy staffer smiled broadly and took Goldmann by the arm. "I have no intention of leaving the airport until after I've bought you a drink and seen you safely on your way," he said. "Besides, when I return to the embassy, the story of how you and I argued fiercely for a full hour will interest and amuse everyone."

Goldmann was bone-weary, grimy, and somewhat in a daze from the long flight halfway around the world as he left customs at Ezezia Airport outside Buenos Aires. As promised, an operative was waiting for him just on the other side of the gates. The grim-lipped man introduced himself and pulled Goldmann aside, away from the press of the crowd.

It was eleven o'clock in the morning here, but Goldmann was still on Tel Aviv time, and everything around him seemed to be happening in a blur.

The man handed him a manila envelope, and Goldmann handed over his diplomatic passport.

"You have hotel reservations at the Sheraton downtown under the name Walter Heller, an automotive administration specialist from Detroit in the United States," the operative said, his voice low. He looked deeply into Goldmann's eyes. "Your new papers identify you as him."

Goldmann started to ask about Yesodat, but the operative shook his head. "*Shalom*, Mr. Heller," he said, and then he turned and walked away, quickly merging with the hundreds of people in the huge terminal.

"*Shalom,*" Goldmann said softly after the retreating figure. He took a deep breath and, carrying his single suitcase and attaché case, headed toward the taxi stands at the front of the large building.

23

It was nine in the morning before Kelsey was taken from the tiny, soundproofed interrogation room where he had spent a sleepless night. He and Marion had been separated from each other at about two in the morning, and he had not seen her since.

All through the morning the questions had been incessant. Besides the two men he and Marion had first approached last night, at least a half-dozen other interrogators had pulled Kelsey's story apart a hundred times. At one point when one of his questioners had asked him the spelling of his own name, he could not give an answer. His brain was too muddled, his thoughts too confused.

Marion, he supposed, had gone through the same treatment, but instead of making him angry, it had confused and frightened him.

"After all, Dr. Kelsey," as one of his interrogators put it bluntly sometime during the early morning hours, "you are a self-admitted murderer and a coconspirator in some insane plot to take over our government.''

The one name he had not been able to bring himself to mention all through his questioning was his father's. Before he told them that part of the plot, he wanted to confront the old man himself. Of necessity, therefore, he had not told them his suspicion that Colleen had been murdered.

Around seven o'clock someone brought in sandwiches and coffee, and Kelsey had been given a respite for half an hour. But then the questioning had begun anew, this time with a harsher note in the interrogators' tactics.

"It is a federal offense, Dr. Kelsey, to plot against the life of a president or vice president," a tall, husky man with thick, dark eyebrows said, leaning over the tiny table.

Kelsey looked up at him through red-rimmed eyes, and shook his head. "I'm not plotting against anyone. I've told you a hundred times, it is some organization."

"An organization whose name you do not know."

"That's right."

"Or where they are located."

Kelsey nodded without bothering to answer.

"Then why did you do the work on this Locke character? Why'd you fix him to look like the vice president?"

"Like I told you, I didn't put it all together until a couple of days ago. When I was working on Locke I was doing the surgery bit by bit, not realizing who he would look like."

"Goddammit, Kelsey, you're a liar," the large agent shouted, thumping his right fist on the tabletop. "What'd you hope to gain by trying to assassinate President Barnes?"

Kelsey wanted to shout at the stupid man, but he did not have the strength. Instead his voice came out slow and soft. "If I was in on the plot, why did I come here last night and tell you my story?"

The large man stared at him. "That one has me stumped, Kelsey. I've got to admit it. Maybe you had a falling out with your coconspirators. Maybe there isn't a plot, and you're just a nut. I don't know." The man leaned closer. "But mark my words, Doctor, I'll find out what is going on in there." He pointed a blunt finger at Kelsey's head.

Fifteen minutes ago the two agents had been called out of the room, and a few minutes later a well-dressed young man Kelsey had not seen before came for him.

"Where are we going?" Kelsey asked as they rode up in an elevator.

The man turned and looked at Kelsey, a mildly condescending expression on his face, a slight smirk at the corners of his mouth. "There are some papers upstairs we'd like you to sign. Your wife is waiting for you there."

"Papers?" Kelsey said dumbly.

"Yes," the man said. "You're being released. The forms we'd like you to sign merely state that we did not use torture, drugs, or any other form of coercion during your interrogation. Standard, actually."

Kelsey managed a slight smile. "Then they believed me. The president is being protected."

The man said nothing, and the elevator came to a stop, the doors sliding open.

"What about the cab driver? Has he been identified?" Kelsey asked as he followed the man off the elevator and down a long, busy corridor. The people they passed glanced curiously at Kelsey dressed in his tuxedo, the bow tie undone, his collar open.

"What cab driver?" the man said.

"The one across the street. The one I killed last night."

They stopped at a door marked Wilson S. Grant, Assistant Director, Special Investigative Division, but before they went in, the man turned toward Kelsey.

"There was no taxi parked across E Street last night. Nor was there any parked car, truck, or bus anywhere near here with a body in it. You must have been dreaming, Doctor, unless the man you say you killed suddenly revived himself and drove away.''

The man reached for the doorknob, but Kelsey pulled him away.

''What about the vice president? Engstrom? Did you call his doctor and ask the man to look for the postop blepharoplastic scars?''

The man sighed. ''Yes, as a matter of fact, we did, Dr. Kelsey. But the vice president's personal physician said he was in attendance at Bethesda when Engstrom was brought in from Alaska. And he said there was no doubt—absolutely no doubt—that the man is Engstrom.'' He looked deeply into Kelsey's eyes for several long moments. ''You know, Doctor,'' he said finally, ''you have caused us a great deal of trouble. The Secret Service is hopping mad. Half the staff at Bethesda Naval Hospital is jumping up and down. And Vice President Engstrom himself was peeved, to put it mildly, when at four o'clock in the morning we had his press secretary wake him up and talk to one of our people.''

Kelsey was stunned into speechlessness.

''I sincerely hope for your sake, Doctor, that this will all end here and now. Take a vacation from your work. I think you are probably in need of a rest.''

With that the man opened the door, and Kelsey followed him into a large reception office where a pretty young woman sat behind a desk. She looked up and smiled. ''They're waiting for you inside, Mr. Pearson,'' she said pleasantly. ''You're to go right in.'' Her eyes shifted to Kelsey, and for just a moment he was certain he could detect a note of amusement in them, but then the woman went back to her work, and Kelsey followed Pearson into Assistant Director Grant's office.

A tall, distinguished-looking gray-haired man, dressed impeccably in a dark blue three-piece suit, was seated behind a desk nearly the size of a football field. He looked up as they came in.

Seated in front of the desk was Marion, and next to her, Kelsey's father. They too looked up, and a second later Marion jumped up and came to her husband.

"Are you all right?" she asked, her voice nearly normal, but Kelsey could see she was still frightened.

"I'm fine," he said. "How about you?"

"Confused," she said softly.

Kelsey looked over her shoulder at his father. Their eyes met and for a moment he had the distinct impression he was gazing into the face of a total stranger. A man cold, hard, calculating, and certainly ruthless. But the feeling passed as his father's face contorted into a grin, and he stood up.

"You gave us quite a start, Richard," he said warmly.

"Sorry, Father," Kelsey said, and like Marion, he too was confused. One train of thought led him to the conclusion that his father was some kind of a malevolent force. And yet here and now he could not believe that.

Wilson Grant got to his feet. "I'm sorry, Dr. Kelsey, that we had to meet under these circumstances."

Kelsey turned to the man and managed a slight smile. "I didn't mean to cause so much trouble, Mr. Grant."

The administrator waved it off. "August tells me that you have been working yourself too hard lately. But with rather impressive results, I might add. He's been telling me about the warm reception your work and the Institute has had in the various medical journals. Impressive indeed."

"My father tends to exaggerate somewhat when it comes to credits for his only son," Kelsey said, and he could not believe he was saying anything so banal.

Grant chuckled, the sound coming from deep within his chest. "Well, if you will just see my secretary about signing your release forms, you may go. And if you will permit an aging policeman to offer a doctor a bit of doctor's advice— take a vacation, Dr. Kelsey. I think you have earned it." He came around from behind his desk and offered his hand.

Kelsey shook it. "Thank you, Mr. Grant, for at least giving me the benefit of the doubt and checking my story. Perhaps you are correct; perhaps I do need a vacation.''

''Well, good luck to you, Doctor,'' Grant said, and Kelsey, Marion, and Kelsey's father left the office, stopping briefly at the secretary's desk so that Marion and Kelsey could sign their release forms.

Outside, a chauffeured limousine was waiting for them and they all got into the backseat. As the driver pulled away from the curb, the elder Kelsey turned to his son.

''I had your luggage picked up from your hotel and brought out to the house. You can stay there and rest until tomorrow.''

Kelsey started to speak, but his father held him off.

''I took the liberty of informing your office that you would not be back for thirty days. Tom Woodmansee will take over for you. And Dr. Carlson at the AMA is willing to forgive and forget, as is Stew Engstrom. They both were sympathetic, despite your behavior, once they learned the strain you were under.''

Again Kelsey started to speak, and again his father held him off.

''I have a lot to tell you, Richard, but this is neither the time nor the place. I have a number of things I must attend to this afternoon. I want you and Marion to get a few hours sleep. We'll have dinner, and afterward the three of us will have a long talk. Everything will be clear to you then, and you'll see what a terrible mistake you made.''

Kelsey was dead tired, his father's words soothing. Marion lay against his shoulder, already half-asleep, and he finally nodded his acceptance.

''Trust me, son,'' the elder Kelsey said. ''That's all I ask.''

The Kelsey residence in College Park, Maryland, was a surprisingly modest two-story colonial that was actually on University of Maryland property. The elder Kelsey had been allowed to purchase the house several years ago because in 1959 he had been granted the honorary degree of Doctor of Economics from the school.

By 9:30 P.M. Kelsey and Marion had bathed, slept for seven hours, dressed in fresh clothes, eaten dinner in the relatively small but tastefully furnished dining room, and retired to the study for after-dinner drinks and the promised discussion.

Kelsey and Marion sat together on a leather couch, while the elder Kelsey sat with his brandy in a wing-backed chair opposite a low, hand-tooled table across from them. A fire crackled in the fireplace, and only one small lamp in a corner was lit, lending a comforting, secure feeling to the room.

During the meal Kelsey's father had directed the conversation to trivial matters, his mood light and almost gay. But now in his study a look of weariness had come over him, and Kelsey felt a real compassion for his father despite his earlier convictions.

Another part of Kelsey's mind dwelled on Marion. Since their overnight ordeal, she had been silent, as if she had been a spectator to all the events of the past twenty-four hours and not a participant.

Kelsey finally turned to his father. "You told me I had made a terrible mistake," he said. "You promised to explain everything to me."

"So I did, Richard," the old man said. He leaned forward and placed his brandy snifter on the table. He seemed to ponder what he was about to say before he started. "I have kept you insulated from this from the beginning, so it is going to be somewhat difficult in one evening to bring you up to date on a lifetime of work."

Something dark welled up from deep within Kelsey. It was as if some kind of beast that had existed inside of him suddenly were coming to the surface. "Did you have Colleen murdered, Father?" he heard himself asking, but it was as if someone else were speaking. Marion stiffened.

The expression froze on his father's face. His complexion turned a pasty, sickly color.

"My wife, Father. Was it an accident? Was the car crash really an accident?"

"My real name is August Kellner," the old man said.

Kelsey got to his feet and took a step toward his father. "You murdered her, didn't you?" he said, the words coming from behind clenched teeth. "My God, Father, you ordered her killed. All this time your sympathy, your condolences, it was all acting. Jesus . . ."

"Sit down, Richard," his father said.

Kelsey half turned toward Marion. "Is she going to be next? Are you going to have her killed too?" His voice was getting louder. "For God's sake, Father, tell me it isn't true."

"Sit down, Richard, and I'll tell you everything, as I promised I would. Sit down."

Kelsey looked at his father for a long time, then turned to look down at Marion, who sat rigid, her eyes closed, and then he sat down, a numb feeling spreading throughout his body.

"During the war I was not a civilian electrical engineer as I led the Americans to believe. I was a *Schutzstaffel Oberst* working as liaison between the High Command in Berlin and our field research institutes at Peenemünde, Bleicherode, and Nordhausen."

Kelsey felt deflated. All their lives they had lived a lie. He had been proud of the fact that his heritage was German. And doubly proud of the fact that during the war his father had been a civilian, remaining out of the military because of a trumped-up heart condition.

"There was nothing wrong with my heart, of course," his father had explained once. "But I convinced the enlistment office that I was a sick man, unfit for military duty, and they passed me by. I didn't believe in the war, and I didn't want to fight in it, or even be a part of its planning."

"You have formed some kind of an organization," Kelsey said. "There are others."

The old man inclined his head slightly. "Yes, there are others. But no, I did not form the organization although I am a part of it. We are a group of former *Schutzstaffel* men and officers. Worldwide."

"Everything I told the FBI was true." This was unreal.

"To an extent, yes, Richard. But you do not know the entire story, which is why you made such a terrible mistake."

Kelsey was trying to digest this. His father, a man he had looked up to, trusted, respected all of his life, had just informed him he had been and still was a Nazi.

"If you are so proud of what you are doing, why didn't you tell me from the beginning? Why wasn't I a part of this?"

"Because of the environment we lived in. At first, when you were a young boy, we were too close to the war, and the knowledge would have been an impossible burden for you to bear. And later when you had made your decision to become a medical doctor, I was busy with my own work. You were, and still are, a very idealistic young man. I saw very early that you had fully accepted the entire American-capitalist concept. It would have taken much effort and perhaps a terrible shock to your system in order to convince you that what I was doing was not only correct, but was being done in order to save the world."

Kelsey's face screwed up in disgust, and his father sat forward.

"Yes, Richard, what we are doing is designed to save the world."

"How?" Kelsey asked. "By murdering helpless women? By ordering the death of the vice president of the United States, and before long the death of the President himself? By ordering the murder of your own son?"

The old man's face turned ashen. "What did you say?"

"I said how do you intend saving the world with the murders of innocent women?"

"I mean about you," the elder Kelsey snapped. "Who tried to kill you?"

"The cab driver last night," Kelsey snapped back. "You ordered it."

His father was shaking his head. "No, I did not order such a thing."

"And you did not order Colleen's death?"

"This is all wrong, Richard," the old man pleaded.

"You're goddamned right it's all wrong, Father. Jesus Christ, millions of people during the war, and the killing is still going on?" Kelsey's voice had risen in pitch and volume, and he finally took a deep breath and slumped back on the couch. Marion gripped his arm. "Why, Father? Can't you tell me that?"

The elder Kelsey got slowly to his feet. "Unification," he said. "That has always been the plan. And now more than ever it is imperative that the world—the entire world—be governed by one ruling body, with one intent."

"What intent?" Kelsey spat out the words. "Murder?"

His father shook his head. "Survival," he said. He turned and went to his desk, picked up the telephone, and dialed a number. After a short time someone answered.

"Good evening, Wilson, this is August Kelsey."

Kelsey looked at his father, who had his back to him. Wilson Grant? The FBI?

"Just fine, thank you," his father was saying. "But we definitely have a problem with my son."

Kelsey could not believe what he was hearing, and he got to his feet, pulling Marion up with him.

"I'm with him now at my home, and as painful as it is for me to tell you this, I am now convinced that my son has planned and is prepared to carry out the assassination of Vice President Engstrom."

"Father." The single word choked from Kelsey's constricted throat, and he took a step forward.

"Yes, I am certain," the elder Kelsey was saying into the phone. He turned to look at his son. "Yes, Wilson, I will hold him here until your people arrive."

Kelsey stared into his father's expressionless eyes. Even now he could not believe this was happening.

"Hurry, please," his father said. "I'm afraid he may become violent."

"I'll tell the FBI everything. All the names, dates, places—including Farley Chemicals," Kelsey said.

His father broke the connection and dialed a single number.

"We can get an ambulance records. We have the records at the clinic. The sketches. All of it. Your imposter will never hold up as Engstrom under that kind of scrutiny."

"Rupert, it is time," his father said into the phone, and then he hung it up.

Instantly Kelsey realized how foolish he was being. They had killed Colleen and God knew how many others, including the real Engstrom. At this point they would have to kill him. The FBI considered his story insane. But if he was arrested, and if he was brought to trial, records and witnesses could be subpoenaed. They would not let it happen. Livermore would murder him and Marion.

"They tried to escape, and there was nothing else we could do," Livermore would tell the FBI. And the sad case of Dr. Richard Kelsey and wife would end.

Kelsey spun around, disengaging his arm from Marion's tight grasp, and pushed her aside just as the door swung open. In three quick strides he was across the room, slamming into the half-open door with all of his weight.

Livermore screamed, his left arm and leg caught in the door. Kelsey regained his balance, yanked the door open, and pulled his father's dazed secretary into the study, sending him sprawling on the floor.

elder Kelsey picked up the telephone and hurriedly
d as Livermore struggled to his knees while reaching
inside his coat.

Kelsey kicked the man in the face, flipping him over on
his back and knocking him unconscious, blood gushing from
his mouth and nose.

Marion screamed, but Kelsey was barely aware of it as
he pulled the pistol from a shoulder holster beneath the
man's coat.

He turned toward his father, whose eyes went wide. The
telephone slipped from the old man's hand and clattered on
the desktop, then fell to the floor.

Marion fell silent. For an instant the only sound Kelsey
could hear was his own labored breathing. But then he could
hear someone coming down the corridor toward the study.
He swiveled, bringing the pistol up, and a moment later a
large man wearing a chauffeur's uniform burst into the
room, a shotgun in his hands.

The man tried to bring the gun up, but Kelsey fired first,
hitting the man in the chest, knocking him back out into the
corridor, the noise shockingly loud in the small confines of
the room.

It seemed as if he were in a dream and was floating to
his feet, grabbing Marion and heading in slow motion toward the door.

Kelsey turned and looked back at his father; a sad expression was on the old man's face. Then, with Marion in
tow, he stepped over the chauffeur's body and left the house
by the front door, never having noticed the pistol in his
father's hand.

24

David Goldmann had been in Buenos Aires for three days, sleeping during the daylight hours and keeping vigil at the docks on the South Canal by darkness, with no luck until the fourth night when the *Raphael* finally pulled into her berth. She was a sleek forty-foot pleasure boat owned by Manuel and Eugenio Santini. The last word Goldmann had had from Silverstein more than a year ago was that the Santinis had been hired to take him across the La Plata to Montevideo. Goldmann asked Silverstein to wait for Asheim and take him along.

The Santinis denied meeting Silverstein when questioned by Israeli operatives. But Goldmann knew what had happened that night, and he was here now to atone for at least those two deaths.

Within seconds after the boat had eased into its slip, the running lights were doused, a small deck light came on, and two men scrambled down from the flying bridge to secure the boat to the dock.

Goldmann sat in his parked rental car about fifteen meters from the boat, and waited. He wanted to make sure that the Santinis were alone, that no one was coming to meet them and that they were expecting no trouble.

Benjamin Karel had been a hapless little man who had agreed to work down here because his country needed him. Silverstein on the other hand had been a professional who enjoyed this business. And Asheim was a man of much experience who in the beginning had not wanted this assignment, but once he had committed himself, was determined to see it through to the end despite all the obstacles. They had all failed with the worst possible results.

Goldmann had done a lot of thinking about those three men during his nightlong vigils. And he had come to the conclusion that they had failed against a superior enemy not because of a lack of ability. They had failed because they were men with tunnel vision.

Benjamin was basically a paper shuffler who believed he had been sent to Buenos Aires to do nothing more than watch the comings and goings of people. When Goldmann ordered him to the Missiones Province Hospital to question Spannau, Benjamin had gone in over his head, inadequately prepared for possible violence. As a result he lost his life.

Silverstein had always been a man marked for an early death, however. He had once told Goldmann that life was a loaded gun, and the only way to have fun with it was to play Russian roulette. He had, and he had finally lost.

And Asheim had the most fatal flaw of them all. He was a driven man who never stopped to look left or right in his headlong rush. He had been destined either to succeed brilliantly, or fail miserably. He had failed.

Goldmann looked toward the boat, which was now tied up. The two brothers were talking to each other, but then one of them turned and went belowdecks while the other scrambled over the rail and headed up the boardwalk toward the street.

Goldmann stiffened for an instant as he realized that the man would pass by his car as he had hoped, then withdrew the flat 9mm Beretta automatic from his shoulder holster and put the safety off.

He reminded himself for the hundredth time that the man coming his way, and his brother, had killed or were at least responsible for the deaths of Silverstein and Asheim. Therefore the two of them were in the Odessa's employ.

He slid down in the seat so that he could just see over the dash and waited as the Santini brother came closer.

The windows in both doors of the rental car were down, admitting the smells and sounds of the waterfront: the strong sea smell of salt, wet mud, and rotting wood and rope; the distant sounds of water slapping against hulls; the squeak of rubber tire fenders between the boats and the docks; and somewhere across the canal, the powerful throb of a large diesel engine.

Over that Goldmann could hear the approaching Argentinian humming some tuneless song as he mounted two steps up from the boardwalk and stepped into the street just a meter from the car.

A moment later the man passed the open window on the driver's side and Goldmann sat up. "Santini," he said softly.

The brother stopped in midstride and swiveled around, his eyes widening at the sight of Goldmann with a gun in his hand.

"Do not move. Do not make a sound or I will kill you instantly," Goldmann said, keeping his voice soft and even.

The color left Santini's face, but he made no move, nor did he utter a sound as Goldmann carefully opened the car door and got out.

"Put your hands in your trousers pockets, turn around, and go back to your boat. I will be right behind you."

Santini started to speak, but Goldmann shook his head, and the words died on the man's lips. A moment later he stuffed his hands deeply into the pockets of his baggy trousers and headed back toward the boardwalk.

There were hundreds of boats tied up along these docks, yet the place had a deserted air this time of night. There were few lights at this end of the street and no one in sight. Had the conditions been different, Goldmann had been prepared to work out an alternate plan for getting to the brothers. Whatever the risk, whatever the contingencies, he had made the decision that the Santinis would pay the moment he had received the report about Asheim's death.

They worked their way along the narrow boardwalk until at last they came alongside the *Raphael*. Santini stopped and half turned toward Goldmann.

"Is there anyone on board besides your brother?"

A look of cunning came into the man's eyes. Goldmann raised his gun slightly.

"Any lie, any lie no matter how slight, will result in your instant death."

"There is no one else," the man said, the gleam dying in his eyes, and his voice equally as soft as Goldmann's.

"Call your brother topside."

Santini nodded. Goldmann took a step closer. "Do not make a mistake. I will put a bullet in your spine."

"Manuel," he called. "Manuel, I am back."

"Eugenio!" the brother shouted from belowdecks. "You stupid motherfucker!"

Goldmann tensed as the cabin door flung open and Manuel Santini emerged from the hatchway.

"What the fuck is wrong now . . ." the man started to shout, but the words died on his lips as he saw Goldmann.

"Your brother is a dead man if you say another word or make the slightest move," Goldmann said.

For several seconds a play of emotions crossed and recrossed the man's face as he looked from his brother to Goldmann and back to his brother again. But then he sighed and very slowly raised his hands above his head.

"On board," Goldmann said to Eugenio, and the man clambered over the rail to stand next to his brother.

Goldmann remained where he was, the automatic pointed toward the brothers. "My name is David Goldmann—Israeli secret service. You murdered my two friends, Abraham Silverstein and Levi Asheim. I want to know by whose orders you killed them. Do not lie to me."

"My God," Manuel breathed.

"Quickly," Goldmann snapped, raising the gun.

"We did not kill them, señor, I promise you," Manuel said. He was shaking.

"Who killed them?" Goldmann barked.

"Señor Stoeffel's soldiers killed Abraham and took the other man with them."

"Where did this happen?"

"On the Paraná at Señor Stoeffel's place," Manuel said, pleading. "You must believe me."

"I do," Goldmann said, and he shot Manuel in the chest, sending the man crashing backward through the open hatchway down the stairs into the cabin. Eugenio turned and started toward the back of the boat, but Goldmann's second and third shots caught him in the right shoulder and the back of the neck, blowing most of his left cheek away as one of the bullets exited.

He turned and walked briskly back up the boardwalk to his car. Someone surely had heard the shots and was at this moment calling the police. But by the time the authorities arrived, Goldmann would be out of the city and on the highway to Campana, only one item left to take care of.

Back at his car he holstered the Beretta, got behind the wheel, and drove away from the South Canal Marina, north through the city toward the Libertador Highway. Traffic was light at this time of night, and in twenty minutes he made it across town and speed toward the Paraná River town of Campana, forty miles to the northwest.

Although Asheim's daughters, Deborah and Sandra, had

wanted him to drop this entire affair and would be horrified by what he was doing, they would understand. And that was enough for him. He didn't expect any hero's badge for this evening's work, but he did not want what he was doing to go unnoticed, or worse, be misunderstood.

There would be those who would say his motive for killing the Santinis was revenge. Others would label the action salve for his guilty conscience. (After all, he sent poor Benjamin to Buenos Aires in the first place.) And still others, especially Colonel Yesodat, believed that Goldmann was here to finish a job he had started with the capture of Adolf Eichmann. But not Asheim's daughters. Somehow Goldmann was sure they understood that he was motivated by fear of what the Nazis had done during the war, and what the Odessa was still capable of doing.

As he drove, that thought kept crossing and recrossing his mind. It had been so long since Benjamin had taped Spannau's jibberings. Even now his actions might be coming too late. It was possible, even likely, that the Odessa operation had already been implemented. Whatever he was doing now might mean nothing. But he had to try.

In the early seventies the man operating the travel bureau in Buenos Aires had managed to fly an airplane over Stoeffel's estate and take several photographs. Over the years Goldmann often found himself taking the eight-by-ten glossies out of his files and studying them for hours at a time.

Aerie, as Stoeffel called the place, of course, had been named after Hitler's Eagles Nest near Berhchtesgaden. But it had become a cross between the Eagles Nest and the Reichschancelry in Berlin in importance to the Odessa. At least that was Goldmann's belief, despite Yesodat's skepticism. Goldmann passed the CAMPANA—3KM sign and came to the dirt road leading to the right toward the river, access to Stoeffel's stronghold.

He doused the headlights as he turned onto the dirt road.

He drove about a quarter of a mile, then pulled over to the side and shut off the engine.

He sat in the dark car, the engine ticking as it cooled, listening to the night sounds of the jungle. The access gate was a mile farther down the road, the house a half-mile beyond that. Now that he'd come this far, he was impatient to get on with it, to finally confront *Oberst* Kurt Stoeffel. But he held himself in check. He could not make a mistake. Not now that he was this close.

A full five minutes after he had parked at the side of the road, Goldmann pulled the heavy attaché case from the back and opened it on the seat next to him.

Fitted into cutouts on a thick foam rubber pad were the parts for a 30-caliber automatic rifle, a long, heavy silencer, and a bulky infrared scope. Another row of slots held three magazines of ammunition for the rifle, with thirty rounds in each magazine. A final pair of cutouts had held the Beretta and three magazines of 9mm ammunition. Two full magazines were left.

He reloaded the Beretta first, a live round in the chamber, then reholstered it.

Next he fitted the wire rifle stock of the automatic to the firing mechanism, screwed the barrel in place, and added the heavy silencer. The infrared scope clipped into keyed slots forward of the ejector slide. And finally the leather strap clipped to the end of the wire stock and the forward end of the firing housing.

Goldmann had fired hundreds of rounds from this weapon on the range at night, but he never used it on a live target. His hands shook slightly as he rammed a magazine of ammunition into the receiver, then pulled the ejector slide back, jacking a round into the chamber.

Lifting the foam pad, he withdrew a pair of heavy-duty wire clippers from the case, then snapped the lid shut.

The night hung thick, the air rich and damp. Goldmann

was sweating heavily as he got out of the car and carefully closed the door.

He slung the rifle over his shoulder and, carrying the wire clippers in his left hand, started down the dirt road toward the gate.

Each night of his vigil at the South Canal Marina, he had dressed in soft-soled shoes, dark trousers, a dark shirt, and a dark blue jacket. Tonight was no different. There were no silver eyelets on his shoes, no metal belt buckle, nor did his jacket have metal buttons or snaps. The rifle and wire clippers were painted flat black, so there would be no chance reflection to give him away. He was nearly invisible.

The road curved widely to the left, and two hundred meters from the gate Goldmann could hear the low murmur of voices. Two men, laughing and talking.

He did not slow his pace until he caught a glimpse of a soft red light no more than a hundred meters away.

Goldmann set the clippers down, unslung his rifle, got down on one knee, and aimed toward the gate. Two men, one of them smoking a cigarette, came into sharp perspective, although their features were somewhat blurred because of the effect of the infrared viewer.

Goldmann set the crosshairs of the scope in the middle of one man's chest and squeezed off a shot that sounded like nothing more than a low *whump*. As the first man fell backward and the other man dropped into a defensive crouch, Goldmann fired another round, this one blowing the top off the second guard's head.

Goldmann remained on one knee, the rifle's strap wound around his left arm, as he studied the gate area and beyond it the road leading to the house through the infrared scope. But he could detect no activity.

The two guards he had murdered had been alone on duty, and their deaths had come so swiftly, so unexpectedly, that they had no time to sound an alarm.

He got slowly to his feet and unwound the leather strap

from his arm, a sharp pang of conscience stabbing at his gut. This evening he had murdered four men. Without warning. Without mercy or compunction.

But they were Odessa. Nazis. They and their kind had killed millions of people during the war and probably untold thousands since then. When would the killing stop? he asked himself. It was the same question he'd asked himself since Auschwitz in 1945. His answer tonight was the same as it had always been: when the very concept of Nazism and its perpetrators were wiped from the face of the earth, and not before.

Goldmann hid the rifle in the brush alongside the road, picked up the wire clippers, and headed down the road.

The gate, like the perimeter fence that disappeared into the jungle, was ten feet tall and topped with razor wire, but did not appear to be electrified. It opened and closed with an electrical motor, the control for which was in the small guardhouse.

The two men Goldmann had killed lay on their backs, the one's head blown half away, and the other's legs crumpled under him at an odd angle. They wore a light gray uniform, but it was difficult to tell if they had any insignia of rank on their sleeves or collar tabs in the one dim red light over the guardhouse.

Goldmann glanced at the dead men, then pushed into the jungle, working his way about fifteen meters along the fence until he was sure this spot could not be seen from the road. He cut a large hole in the wire fence, pulled back the square of mesh, and crawled through.

Back at the road Goldmann dragged the two bodies to the guardhouse and laid them inside on the floor, closing the door behind him.

Next he scuffled over the blood on the dirt road so that a casual observer might think the blotches were nothing more than oil spots. He pulled the Beretta from his shoulder holster and headed up the road toward the house, only one objective left to complete. Stoeffel.

Goldmann had spent his youth and early manhood in Saarbrücken, near the French border, as a soft-spoken, gentle person for whom violence was something you read about in novels or saw in Wagnerian operas, not something that was real.

He had learned violence, however, the hard, painful way: through its perpetration on himself and his family. Dachau first, and later Auschwitz, hardened his heart, as did the murders of his parents, two brothers, one sister, and his wife.

His education was rounded out in the late forties and early fifties during the fierce struggle for Israel's independence so that such tasks as the kidnapping of Adolf Eichmann, his trial and execution, as well as the manhunt and assassinations of other former Nazis, did not faze him.

But as much as he wanted to deny the soft inner core of his soul, this evening he could not. Despite everything, he still felt miserable because of what he had done and what he was about to do.

"Murder," an old Yeshiva Jew had told him during the fight for Jerusalem, "is the most heinous of all acts, no matter the motivation or reason. Life is sacred, my son, and when you take it you are a blasphemer of God's work."

The words haunted Goldmann through the years, and as he rounded a bend in the road and the jungle opened up to a vast lawn across which Stoeffel's mansion sat huge and formidable, they came back to him: "You are a blasphemer of God's work." But this night, despite the words, his purpose would not be denied.

Hesitating a moment to make sure there were no guards on duty near the house, Goldmann worked his way along the edge of the jungle, keeping to the shadows, until he came to the rear of the mansion. To the left was a service door, probably leading to the kitchen. At the center of the house were large glass doors opening onto a huge patio. And to the right was one set of French doors that opened onto a small rose garden.

From where Goldmann stood, about fifty meters from the back of the house, he could see that the place had been built on a hill. In the distance to the southeast, he could make out the lights of Buenos Aires brightening the night horizon. The view from the upstairs rooms of the mansion had to be spectacular.

Clicking the Beretta's safety off, Goldmann ran across the open lawn to the rose garden, where he worked his way through the bushes to the French doors, one of which stood wide open.

The room was dark, but from Goldmann's position he could see a crack of light showing beneath a door across from the French doors.

He stepped slowly into the room. Suddenly a light came on, momentarily blinding him.

"Welcome to Aerie, Goldmann," a man said.

Goldmann snapped around, his finger on the trigger, but when he saw who it was, his heart nearly leaped out of his chest. "Asheim," he said breathlessly.

Asheim grinned maniacally, as if he was drunk or on drugs. Goldmann lowered his gun and took a step forward as a loud report sounded and something hot and terribly strong slammed into his chest, pushing him backward almost off his feet.

Asheim held a gun in his hand. He fired again and Goldmann identified it as a standard-issue Nazi officer's Luger, then everything seemed to rush away from him, the words "blasphemer of God's work" racing through his dying brain.

The Conclusion

25

August Kellner's ancient heart thumped painfully in his chest as he hurried as fast as his spindly legs would carry him to the back door of the house. He was in time to see his son and daughter-in-law disappear across the backyard into a thick stand of trees that led a quarter of a mile away to the university's maintenance garages.

There was so little time left now. It had come to the point he feared it might. To the point at which his son would stand in the way of the project.

He had known what would have to be done. He had discussed it at length with *Oberst* Stoeffel more than two years ago. But now that the decision was upon him, he found it no less distasteful and painful than he had two years ago in Buenos Aires.

He turned away from the door, forcing his mind to blank out the deep pain and fear he felt, and willing his legs to carry him back into his study.

Ignoring the pool of blood in which his chauffeur's body

lay, and his secretary, Livermore, who was beginning to come around, the old man picked the telephone off the floor, got a dial tone, and dialed a number that was answered on the first ring.

"Yes," a man's voice came over the line.

"Dies ist August," Kellner said. "Listen to me carefully."

"Yes, sir."

"It is time now. The plan must be implemented immediately without delay."

"Jawohl, mein Herr," the man snapped. "Do you have the authorization code?"

"This is on my authorization. There is no time to contact Aerie. This is an emergency."

"Mein Herr—" the man started, but Kellner savagely cut him off.

"You will obey instantly!"

"Yes, sir," the man snapped. "As you say."

Kellner slammed the phone down as Livermore sat up. The man's jaw was broken, and blood seeped from his mouth. He was in pain.

Again the old man got a dial tone, and dialed another number. This one was answered on the third ring.

"Seven-three-one-one," a woman answered with the extension number.

"I'd like to speak with the vice president, please," Kellner said, forcing his voice to sound calm and pleasant.

"The vice president is en route at the moment, sir. If you would like to leave a message—"

"Thank you," Kellner interrupted. "I'll try him later. It's nothing that can't wait."

"As you wish," the vice president's secretary said, and Kellner pressed the phone button down as he heard the sounds of sirens in the distance.

There was so little time. If his son telephoned the FBI within the next half hour, or was captured alive, everything would be ruined. The carefully constructed plan, the myriad of details, the three years of work, would all be for naught.

He got the Washington mobile operator on the line and gave her the number he wanted as the sirens got closer.

Oberst Stoeffel would not accept failure. This plan was to be the salvation of the organization and the implementation of their ideals. One world under one flag. Peace for all time.

It was shortly after ten in the evening when the telephone in the vice president's limousine buzzed and the husky man, dressed in a tuxedo in the backseat, leaned forward and answered it.

"Mr. Vice President," a voice the man recognized came over the line.

"August," he said. "I'm on my way home. What can I do for you?"

"I'm glad I caught you, Mr. Vice President. I'm sending over a book for you to read. Called *Eagles Fly*."

Something sharp snapped inside the vice president's head, and a warm, pleasant feeling spread throughout his body. It was almost sexual in nature, but not so localized. "Yes," he said, and he smiled.

"I want you to read chapter five tonight. I think you'll enjoy it."

"Chapter five," the vice president said, his heart quickening. "I'll do that. Thanks for calling, August."

The phone went dead and a moment later the vice president got the mobile operator on the line and had her ring President Barnes' private number in the White House family quarters. He had no real idea why he was calling the President, he just knew that it was something he should be doing at this moment.

The phone was answered on the first ring by Barnes himself. "What is it?" the President said gruffly.

In the background the vice president could hear music.

"Good evening, Mr. President, this is Stew Engstrom," he said pleasantly.

Over the past few days the President's attitude toward Engstrom had changed. The President had become cold and distant, and Engstrom could not understand what he had done to deserve such treatment. Tonight he wanted to make amends.

Although the past seemed blurred in Engstrom's memory, a phenomenon he could not understand, he knew that his relationship with Barnes all during their campaign against Jimmy Carter and into the early days of the administration had been a warm one. Only lately, since he had returned from the Alaskan trip, had the President been acting differently.

"I'd like to talk to you, Mr. President, about a matter of some urgency."

"First thing in the morning," Barnes said. "I'll inform my appointments secretary."

Engstrom's purpose this night was becoming sharper in his mind now, and it was nothing more than to clear the air between himself and the President, to strengthen their relationship, to bring it back to what it had been at the beginning. But it was imperative that this be done immediately.

"Tonight," he said firmly. "I'm about six blocks away. I could be there in a few minutes."

"Goddammit, Stewart, can't this wait until tomorrow?"

Engstrom wanted to say, *yes, of course it can wait*, but something inside of him was forcing him to act, compelling him to do whatever was necessary to meet with the president this evening in the Oval Office, or better yet, outside in the Rose Garden.

"I would have made a routine appointment for tomorrow if I thought the matter could wait. I'd like to meet you in the Oval Office. Alone."

"What is this all about?" Barnes asked, curiosity in his voice.

"I can't say over the phone."

"All right," Barnes said after a moment's hesitation.

It was 10:25 P.M. by the time the thin, well-dressed man parked his nondescript van with Illinois plates in the nearly deserted parking lot behind the Corcoran Gallery of Art on 17th and E Streets.

The weather was clear and the evening pleasantly warm, but the man was sweating lightly as if he was under a strain. The call from Kellner had come unexpectedly. The timetable had called for the operation to be carried out sometime during the next thirty days, not so soon. And at Aerie the man had been told specifically that he would first be given an authorization code that would indicate specifically which escape route had been put into motion for him.

None of that had happened, and the man was frankly worried. Yet he was professional enough to realize that even the best-laid plans could go awry for the most insignificant of reasons, reasons that were humanly impossible to predict.

He sat in the dark van alternately watching the traffic to his right passing along E Street, and the rear service entrance to the art gallery.

Fourteen days ago he had left Buenos Aires, arriving seventy-two hours later in Miami via Mexico City. He had spent that day and the following evening in a luxury hotel, and on the second day put out to sea as the pilot and lone passenger of a thirty-five-foot pleasure boat. Although he had told the people at his hotel and the marina operator that he would return by nightfall, he had no intention of doing that. Instead he scuttled the boat that night off a deserted intra-coastal waterway beach near Key Largo, where he swam ashore and picked up a waiting car parked just off Highway 905 north of the town.

From there he drove back to Miami and took a flight to Chicago under an assumed name. In a downtown parking ramp he picked up a waiting van and identification, and drove directly to Washington, D.C., arriving six days ago at an apartment in Alexandria that had been rented for him a month earlier.

Instead of luxuriating in idleness for the first week or so, as he might have, the man had completed his preparations for this mission within the first few days of his arrival and then had settled back to wait for the call.

He was ready now, his escape from the city the only thing causing him any concern. But even that, he had worked out in his mind in the half hour since Kellner had called.

"If your true identity is discovered, or if your escape is not made good, the entire mission will have failed," *Oberst* Stoeffel had warned.

And *Oberst* Stoeffel was a man to be believed, trusted, and obeyed without question.

The man pushed back his leather glove and looked at his wristwatch, which showed it was exactly 10:30, then got out of the van, went around to the back, and opened the double doors. From within he pulled out a heavy wooden case with brass handles, closed the van doors, and walked across the parking lot to the art gallery service entrance.

Three cars that belonged to the night security guards were parked in the back lot, as the man expected they would be.

One of the vehicles belonged to an older man by the name of Robert Bjorkland, who worked the night shift watching the rear entrances on the ground floor.

The man set the wooden case down and rang the service bell at the door, then pulled out his wallet and opened it to his identification card.

A moment later Bjorkland came to the door and peered out the thick window. "Can I help you, sir?" Bjorkland's voice came over a tiny loudspeaker set in the wall next to the door.

The man held up his wallet so that Bjorkland could see his identification card and smiled. "My father sent me over with a piece that he didn't want to keep at home. Asked if

I would drop it by and give it to you personally. You are Bob Bjorkland, aren't you?''

The guard smiled and nodded his head. A moment later the door swung open. "I've heard a lot about you, Dr. Kelsey," he said, ushering the man inside.

"All bad, I suppose," the man said, lugging the heavy wooden case inside and setting it down on the floor. They were in a small room off the back stairs. Half a dozen television screens monitored several rooms of the gallery.

Bjorkland laughed. "No, sir, your father brags about you all the time," he said. He went around behind his desk. "We'll put the case in the night depository. I'll sign you in first."

As Bjorkland turned his back, leaned over the desk, and began writing, the man withdrew a length of piano wire from his coat pocket, formed it into a wide loop, stepped forward, dropped the loop over Bjorkland's head, and yanked hard.

Bjorkland snapped upright as he tried to turn around, his fingers clawing futilely at the wire, his eyes bulging out of their sockets, his tongue protruding from his mouth, and his face turning a deep purple, but there was nothing he could do against the wire.

Within three minutes the guard was unconscious, his windpipe crushed, his brain dying from lack of oxygen, and his bowels involuntarily voiding with a rush.

Calmly the man removed the piano wire loop and placed the guard in his chair, his back toward the door, his head resting in his arms.

Anyone coming to the door and looking in would only see the figure of Bjorkland apparently fast asleep.

As if this were nothing more than an ordinary, everyday occurrence, the Odessa agent calmly pocketed the wire loop, picked up the heavy wooden case, and trudged up the stairs past the top floor to the roof access door. He produced a key from his pocket, unlocked the door, and stepped out onto the roof.

Looking at his watch again, he saw it was now 10:40. He walked across the huge roof to the northeast edge of the building, and without looking over the side, unlatched the case. From within he pulled out the component parts of a .50-caliber rifle and high-powered scope that until very recently had belonged to August Kellner, alias August Kelsey, one of the directors of the gallery, and put them together.

When he had loaded the sniper rifle with three shells, each of them more than five inches long, the man looked over the parapet across 17th Street. He had a perfect view of the White House, the Oval Office, and the area of the Rose Garden some 350 meters away as the bullet flies.

Phyllis Sherwood, President Barnes' personal secretary, waited for the vice president in the north entrance foyer. She flashed him a bright smile when he came in. She had always liked Engstrom, and since his return from the nearly fatal Alaskan trip, she had become even more enamored of him.

Engstrom returned her smile, then turned to the two Secret Service agents who had come in with him. "I might be a while, so you two can relax a bit," he said.

"Yes, sir," they said, and Engstrom followed Ms. Sherwood through the receptionist's lobby, then down the corridor past the Roosevelt Room to the Oval Office.

"If I can be so bold, Mr. Vice President," Ms. Sherwood said, "I might warn you that he is in a very foul mood tonight."

Engstrom laughed out loud. "Not to worry, Phyllis—what I have to say to him will cheer him up."

"Good," she said, glancing at Engstrom. "He had a pretty rough go of it at the summit conference. He can use all the cheering up you can give him."

At the Oval Office door they paused a moment. "He's

expecting you, so go right in,'' Ms. Sherwood said. "Will you be needing anything tonight?"

Engstrom shook his head. "Thanks, no, Phyllis," he said. "You might just as well go home unless he's got something for you."

"I'll stick around for a while," she said, and then she nodded toward the door. "Good luck," she said, then she turned and went back down the corridor.

Engstrom watched her go, trying to place her in his mind. It was strange; he knew her, and yet he didn't. That is, he had no real memory of her.

He shook his head, knocked once on the door, and entered the Oval Office, a grin on his face, ready to do whatever was necessary to patch up the apparent rift that had come between them. The time was 10:40 P.M.

The Odessa agent on the roof of the Corcoran Gallery of Art had watched the arrival of the vice president's limousine a few minutes before he had driven around to the gallery parking lot. When he had arrived on the roof, he had seen that the lights were on in the Oval Office.

Once he had the rifle set up, he had risked bringing it up to the parapet, resting the stock on the brickwork and looking through the powerful scope. The French doors opening toward the Rose Garden from the Oval Office came into sharp focus. He studied the doors for a moment, then pulled the rifle back.

Soon, he told himself. And his heart began to accelerate.

The sounds of traffic below on 17th Street, the smell of exhaust fumes, and some other odor, probably the river, seemed to the man to be a part of another world; far away and unreal from where he was at this moment. For him here and now the only realities were the powerful rifle he held expertly, and a spot some 350 meters distant.

He looked over the parapet toward the White House. Again he brought the rifle up and looked through the scope.

President Barnes, Vice President Engstrom, and two other men, probably Secret Service, stood talking just outside the French doors. One of the Secret Service men moved in front of Barnes as the Odessa agent pulled the bolt back and rammed it forward, bringing a shell into the firing chamber. He clicked the safety off and lightly held his finger against the trigger.

The two Secret Service agents moved off, looking around nervously, and a moment later Engstrom moved away from the President as if he was going back into the Oval Office.

At that instant President Barnes was facing directly toward the art gallery, his shirt collar open, his hands stuffed deeply into the pockets of his smoking jacket.

The Odessa agent centered the crosshairs on the President's chest, held his breath, and squeezed the trigger.

A tremendous roar filled the man's ears, the recoil from the massive rifle knocking him nearly off balance, but an instant later he rammed a new round into the firing chamber and trained the scope on the same spot.

The two Secret Service men raced toward the French doors. Vice President Engstrom was down on one knee. And President Barnes, most of his chest missing, lay spread-eagle over a low bush.

Lying the rifle down on the roof, the Odessa agent hurried back to the door, went down the stairs, past Bjorkland's body, and left by the same door by which he had entered the building. Within three minutes he had climbed into his van and had headed west on E Street toward Virginia Avenue, which would take him to the Whitehurst Freeway leading out of town. No sirens sounded until he was nearly six blocks from the gallery.

26

About twenty miles outside of Washington, Highway 50 went from a divided highway to a two-lane road that rose and fell through the hilly Virginia countryside. Another thirty-mile stretch of divided highway around Winchester finally gave way again to a winding two-lane road near the West Virginia border, and by the time the University of Maryland Maintenance Division pickup truck, painted yellow, crossed the state line, Marion was almost crazy with fear and Kelsey was numb.

The events of the past few days, especially the all-night interrogation by the FBI and the incredible things that had happened at his father's house, had finally caught up with them both.

From the moment he entertained the suspicion that Engstrom was an imposter, a part of him was convinced that Marion was correct, that he was on a wild-goose chase, because the alternative was to believe that his father was a part of some insane plot to take over the world.

But this evening when his father had revealed to them that he had been and still was a Nazi and one of the planners of the vice president's assassination, Kelsey's brain had gone numb. Only the certainty that at any moment he and his wife were to become victims of the plot had jerked him back to reality long enough to defend himself. From that point on, his actions had been nothing more than reflexive motions.

He had half dragged, half carried Marion out of the house, across the large, well-tended backyard, into the wide band of trees and brush that separated his father's property from the university grounds.

With no other thought than to put as much distance as possible between themselves and the sirens beginning to sound in the distance, Kelsey managed to push a way through the stand of trees to the University Maintenance Division garages.

To the right were large piles of sand and gravel used in various university construction projects. Parked along the far edge of the lot were about thirty cars and trucks ranging from pickups to several large dump trucks all of them yellow with the University of Maryland insignia painted on the door.

The sirens finally stopped and Kelsey supposed the authorities were already beginning to search the woods behind his father's house. If they were overtaken now, there was a possibility they would be shot and killed. His father's chauffeur was dead, and Livermore was seriously hurt. Kelsey was a dangerous man: a murderer who had talked about a plot on the president's life, and was now armed.

He stuffed the gun in his belt and, guiding Marion by the arm, hurried toward the parked vehicles.

Their first step would be to getaway from here, putting as much distance as possible between themselves and not only the FBI agents now looking for them but his father's men. Once they had done that, they would decide what their next move would be.

Kelsey left Marion behind one of the large trucks as he looked inside the cars and smaller vehicles, racing as fast as he could from one to the other.

Near the end of the second row he found what he was looking for. Someone had been careless and had left the keys in the ignition of a pickup truck.

He hurried back to Marion, brought her to the truck, and within a couple of minutes they pulled out of the Maintenance Division parking lot and headed southwest. Later they had crossed the Potomac near Bethesda and had swung west on Highway 50 where it crossed Interstate 66.

That had been several hours ago, and during that time Marion had said nothing. But each time a car or truck overtook and passed them, she jerked upright in the seat for an instant and then pushed down into the corner against the passenger door, shivering.

Kelsey was a deeply frightened man. All his life he'd been a nonviolent, even-tempered person who was slow to anger and quick to cool down. But in the last twenty-four hours or so he had murdered a cab driver and his father's chauffeur, and had seriously injured Rupert Livermore, a man he had known and liked most of his life.

Despite all that, however, he had accomplished nothing.

He turned and glanced at Marion. She was hunched up against the door, her cheek against the window.

"We're going to stop soon," he said. At the sound of his voice, she looked at him. There was a wild expression in her eyes, as if she were some poor concerned animal, no fight left, only fear and resignation.

He gently touched her arm. "It's going to work out, darling," he said softly. "I promise you."

"How?" she asked, her voice low.

"I don't know," he said. "I thought if we could get far enough away from Washington, I could call the FBI and explain everything to them. Before they could get us, they would have to listen.''

"It didn't work before, and Wilson Grant is your father's friend,'' Marion said.

"Then I'll call the Secret Service with my story,'' Kelsey countered.

"They're loyal to the President and vice president.''

"The real vice president, not an imposter.''

"God . . . Richard,'' Marion cried, and Kelsey again took his eyes away from the road to glance at his wife. She had buried her face in her hands and was shaking.

"Don't cry, darling,'' he said, feeling utterly helpless.

"There's nothing we can do. They had us beat before we started.'' Tears stream down her cheeks. "Your father will make sure that we never live to tell the FBI or Secret Service anything.''

Kelsey instinctively looked in the rearview mirror. He could see nothing behind them other than a large truck in the distance.

"We'll stop at a phone, and I'll call the Secret Service. All they have to do is give Engstrom a physical examination.''

She laughed, but the sound was humorless. "On whose say-so? Yours? A murderer's?''

The words cut deeply. "It's the only thing we can do.''

They passed a sign that read AUGUSTA—3 MILES, and a few hundred yards later, around a wide curve, came to a small motel with the vacancy sign lit. It was shortly after midnight, and Kelsey figured they had come at least a hundred miles from Washington. It would have to be far enough.

He pulled off the highway into the motel's parking lot, shutting off the headlights and killing the engine in front of the motel office. Inside it was dark, but a single lightbulb illuminated a button for the night buzzer.

His call would be traced, but even then it would take an

hour for them to get here by helicopter. He doubted they would send a local cop to pick him up, although roadblocks would probably be set up.

Marion stared at him, and he looked into her eyes. In one hour on the telephone he would have to convince a highly skeptical person or persons to at least believe in enough of what he was saying to make a couple of checks. Even if they would not agree to a physical examination of the vice president, they could at least check with Farley Chemicals in London. That, combined with the flight and ambulance records on Locke, would tell them that one part of his story was true. From there it would be up to them.

"We've got to try," he said finally.

Marion said nothing.

"President Barnes is in danger. If he's killed, Engstrom will take over the country, and men like my father will control everything." The words hurt even as he said them.

Still Marion made no reply, and after a long time Kelsey got out of the truck and went to the motel office door and pressed the buzzer. Before dinner at his father's house he and Marion had dressed in slacks and light sweaters, and despite the fact it was a fairly warm evening, he shivered.

The truck that had been behind them passed on the highway, followed a moment later by a car and two more semis. Kelsey rang the buzzer again.

He could hear someone coming, and then the door opened. An old man, completely bald, wearing a checkered bathrobe and no slippers on his bare feet, stood there looking at Kelsey.

"Well?" the old man croaked after a moment. "Do you want a room?"

Kelsey nodded. "Yes, we . . . my wife and I . . . would like a room for the night."

"All right then," the old man said, and he turned and went back inside, leaving the door open for Kelsey to follow.

The motel office was nothing more than a tiny cubicle with a narrow counter, a television set on a shelf bracket near the ceiling, and a Pepsi machine in one corner.

The old man went around the counter and pushed forward a registration card and pen. "Sign your name and address here. I'll get your license number in the morning," he said. "Eighteen dollars for the night, in advance."

Kelsey filled out the card using his real name without thinking, and then handed the man a twenty-dollar bill from his wallet.

"Cash drawer is locked this time of night, so I can't make change till morning," he croaked. He sounded asthmatic.

"That's fine," Kelsey said, and the old man pulled a key attached to a large wooden disk down from a Peg-Board and handed it across.

"Television in the room, but if you're going to play it tonight, keep it low. Don't want you disturbing the other guests."

"Of course," Kelsey said. "Is there a phone in the room?"

The old man eyed him for a moment. "Sure is, but all calls have to go through me here, and I sure as hell don't want to stay up any longer tonight. I'm tired."

"How about if I pay you now for the call? You can check with the operator in the morning to find out the exact cost."

"Where you calling to?" the old man asked.

"Washington," Kelsey said.

"Going to talk long?"

Kelsey nodded. "Probably."

"Be twenty dollars then. I'll give you your change, if you got any coming, in the morning."

"Thanks," Kelsey said, and he handed the man another twenty from his wallet.

"Keep the TV down," the old man said, and he followed Kelsey to the door, locking it behind him. A second later the light in the office went out, and Kelsey got behind the wheel of the truck, started it, pulled around to the end of the long, single-story motel, and parked in the back so that the truck would not be visible from the highway.

For several minutes they sat in the darkened truck staring out the windshield at the back of the building, but not really seeing anything.

Marion finally broke the silence. "There's nothing else we can do, is there?"

He looked at her. "We have one alternative," he said. It was something that had been playing at the back of his mind. But it was like contemplating a covenant with the devil.

She looked over, but said nothing, waiting for him to explain.

He chose his words carefully, not believing them himself. "What my father said to us . . . back at the house. It makes a strange sort of sense. Unity. World peace."

Marion slapped him in the face, the blow as sharp to his mind as it was to his body.

"Don't ever say that," she snarled. "Don't ever think it! Your father and men like him killed your wife! Your own father ordered *your* execution! Your father and his henchmen killed the vice president!" She looked at him, an expression of amazement slowly growing on her face. "My God . . . don't tell me that it's your German heritage. Wagner. Valkyrie. Honoring the fallen hero. My God, tell me it isn't true."

"I don't want to hurt you, Marion. Not like Colleen. I love you more than you can ever know."

"Oh . . . my darling," she cried, and they were in each other's arms, tears streaming down Marion's cheeks and Kelsey choking back his own tears.

The possibility of convincing anyone was negligible. He was a murderer. No one would believe him. They were fighting a worldwide organization that was too big, too well run, too well financed. But they would have to try it. If only they could convince one person in the right position to ask just one question, it would be a beginning. But Kelsey knew that he was afraid not only for his wife's safety, he was afraid for himself. He did not want to die.

After a while they parted, got out of the truck, and went around to the front of the motel where they let themselves into their room, which was surprisingly large and modern.

A big double bed was centered on one wall. A bathroom led off the room, and beyond the foot of the bed was a chest of drawers and mirror, beside it a large-screen portable color television set on a roll-about stand. The telephone was on one of the night tables that stood on either side of the head of the bed.

Kelsey locked the door, turned on the television set without turning up the sound, and went over to the phone as Marion went into the bathroom.

When he had the operator on the line, he asked for Washington, D.C., information, and the Washington operator came on.

"Information, what city please?" a pleasing woman's voice said.

"Washington," Kelsey said. "I need the number for the Secret Service."

"That is the Treasury Department, sir," the operator said without hesitation, and she gave him the night operator's number at the Treasury Department.

Marion came out of the bathroom as he dialed the number, and the Treasury Department operator came on the line.

"United States Treasury Department, may I help you?"

"I need to speak with someone in the Secret Service," Kelsey said, his voice shaky.

"That number is nine-six-four eight-three-five-one, sir. You may direct-dial it."

"Thanks," Kelsey mumbled, and he pressed the button down. When he got the dial tone again, he started to dial, but a muffled gasp from Marion caused him to snap around.

She stood in front of the television set, her eyes wide, her color white, and her entire body shaking.

He looked from her to the television set and his heart skipped a beat. On the screen was an artist's rendering of a scene outside the Oval Office of the White House. A man was hustling another man, obviously Engstrom, back into the office, while another large man was crouched next to what obviously was the body of President Barnes.

Kelsey slowly put the telephone back on its cradle, got up from where he had been sitting on the edge of the bed, went to the television, and turned the sound up. A somber-toned announcer was speaking.

". . . rifle belonging to August Kelsey, president of Kelsey Electronics, Ltd., was found on the roof of the Corcoran Gallery of Art."

The sketch flashed off and was replaced with another hastily drawn diagram of the view of the White House seen through a telescope from the roof of the art gallery.

"The night guard at the gallery, Robert Bjorkland, was found dead at his desk. The assassin apparently killed the guard, went up the back stairs of the building around ten-thirty-five P.M., and from there assassinated the President as he stood talking with Vice President Stewart Engstrom outside the Oval Office."

Kelsey looked at Marion, who held her hands over her mouth, stifling her sobs.

He turned back to the television, and this time the shock nearly made his legs collapse under him. His photograph, one taken several years ago, filled the television screen, as the announcer continued.

"Before the FBI cut off further communications with the Kelsey residence, August Kelsey told CBS that his son, this man, Dr. Richard Kelsey, of the Kelsey Institute in Chicago, murdered the Kelsey chauffeur and stole a handgun as well as the high-powered rifle and ammunition that was used to assassinate the President. This happened about ten o'clock in the evening.

"The elder Kelsey managed to tell our reporter that his son had been under a heavy strain recently, and for the past several days had spoken of a plot against Vice President Engstrom as well as President Barnes.

"Unconfirmed reports indicate that Dr. Kelsey, driving a blue Ford van with Illinois license plates, was indeed at the Corcoran Gallery of Art at the same time the night security guard was murdered . . . apparently to gain access to the building's roof."

"It's happening," Kelsey said, awed. "It's actually happening."

27

It was three o'clock in the morning, and word had just been received by the Speaker of the House that President Barnes had been officially pronounced dead.

The aging, white-haired representative from Arkansas had taken the call in the President's press secretary's office down the corridor from the Roosevelt Room, where everyone had been hastily assembled.

There was very little talk in the large room that was just across from the Oval Office, but when the speaker returned, all eyes turned toward him, and a hush fell over everyone.

He walked up to Engstrom, who stood at a podium taken from the press briefing room earlier, and in a loud, very clear voice that nevertheless was cracked with emotion, said: "Mr. President, it is my sad and very painful duty to inform you that the fortieth President of the United States, Philip P. Barnes, was officially pronounced dead by a medical team at Bethesda Naval Hospital at two twenty-four A.M. Under the Presidential Succession Act, the powers, duties, and responsibilities of the President fall on your shoulders. And may God guide your actions.''

There was an awed silence in the room that was filled with two dozen reporters, including three television crews, many of President Barnes' staff and cabinet members, two of the Joint Chiefs, and the directors of the Central Intelligence Agency and Federal Bureau of Investigation, as well as the Chief Justice of the Supreme Court, who stepped forward, a Bible in his hand.

The speaker shook hands with Engstrom, then moved aside for the Chief Justice.

''Mr. President, are you ready to take the oath of office?'' the man asked.

''Yes, I am,'' Engstrom said. He was still dazed from the events of the past few hours. But beneath that, deeper in his mind, nearer the levels of his subconscious, were a torrent of mixed emotions: fear of the awesome responsibility he was about to take on himself; shock that some madman had assassinated the best President this nation had seen in the past four decades; and oddly, just a wisp of triumph.

The Chief Justice handed the Bible to the speaker, who held it out for Engstrom, who placed his left hand on it and raised his right.

Flashbulbs flicked through the room, and the television video cameras came on as the Chief Justice spoke.

''Repeat after me,'' he said, and after a pause he began the oath. ''I do solemnly swear that I will faithfully execute the office of President of the United States . . .''

Engstrom repeated the first part of the oath, the feeling of triumph building inside of him, but not yet overriding the solemnity of the occasion.

The Chief Justice continued: ''. . . and will, to the best of my ability, preserve, protect, and defend the Constitution of the United States, so help me God.''

Although the last four words of the oath of office were not set down in the Constitution, they were a tradition that had begun with George Washington. Every President except for Hoover had continued the tradition, as did Engstrom this morning.

When it was done, the Chief Justice lowered his right hand and shook Engstrom's. "Congratulations, Mr. President, and may I share the sentiment with you that you make your awesome decisions in the coming months from good counsel and your own conscience with God's help."

"Thank you, Mr. Chief Justice," President Engstrom said, and then he turned to the assembled gathering, coughed once, and self-consciously pulled at his open collar. There had been no time to change out of his tuxedo, and somehow his bow tie had gotten lost in the shuffle.

"I will hold a briefing for the ladies and gentlemen of the various news media in the press room at two o'clock this afternoon, which will give me a little time to catch up with some of what I'm going to need to know. Thank you."

President Barnes' appointments secretary, Robert Pleasance, tears in his eyes, came up to Engstrom and suggested that he meet immediately with the Chairman of the Joint Chiefs and the Director of the CIA for his briefings, after which, at the President's discretion, he could meet individually with President Barnes' cabinet members.

"I know you have been through a terrible ordeal tonight, Mr. President, but I feel this is absolutely necessary."

Engstrom nodded.

"Afterward there will be time for you to get some sleep. I imagine you're exhausted."

Engstrom cut him off. "I'm fine," he said. "I've been getting along on a lot less sleep lately." He thought a moment. "Despite the inconvenience it may cause, I'll want to meet with President Barnes' staff, including you, after the cabinet meeting. I think one at a time will be best. I'll let you arrange it."

"Yes, Mr. President," the appointments secretary said, obviously impressed with Engstrom's instant organization.

"Also, I want to see the chief of protocol as soon as I'm finished with those items to discuss the proper articles of national mourning and President Barnes' funeral arrangements."

Engstrom started to turn away, but then thought of something else. "The President's wife and family, where are they now?"

"Upstairs, Mr. President, in the Oval Sitting Room. They just arrived."

"I'm going there now. Have the military and the CIA wait for me in the Oval Office," Engstrom said, and he turned on his heel, left the Roosevelt Room, and strode down the corridor to the elevator, Secret Service men seemingly everywhere.

Upstairs he crossed Center Hall, knocked once on the Oval Sitting Room door, and went inside to offer his condolences to President Barnes' family. It was his intention to bunk in the Blair House behind the White House for as long as the family wanted to remain here. Although he could not accurately remember his feelings of grief at the death of his wife almost two years ago, he knew that it had been a terrible blow to him from which it had taken many months to recover. The first few days especially were a traumatic time, and he wanted to put President Barnes' wife and children through as little strain as possible.

One thing was certain, though, and it was a feeling that was growing stronger and stronger in his mind: His administration would be run differently from Barnes'. Barnes had been a great President, but he had never really had a strong grasp of foreign policy. International goodwill and cooperation were the key concepts toward a goal of peace; *harmony between nations* and *worldwide unity* would be his bywords.

28

"Stewart Wordsworth Engstrom became the forty-first President of the United States in a brief swearing-in ceremony just moments ago in the Roosevelt Room across the corridor from the Oval Office," the television announcer said as the picture flashed away from the White House back to the studio in New York.

Kelsey and Marion sat side by side on the end of the bed, where they watched the news bulletins and the ceremony in stunned disbelief, neither of them trusting themselves to speak.

"In a brief announcement following the administration of the oath of office by Chief Justice Warren Burger, President Engstrom informed the press corps that he would hold his first news conference at two o'clock this afternoon, eastern standard time."

Beyond the first mention of Kelsey's name, which they had caught a few minutes after they had entered their motel room, nothing else had been said about him, although the details of the assassination that had been made available to the television networks had been rehashed at least a dozen times in the hours they had been watching the screen in the darkened room.

"President Barnes had been kept technically alive for the first three hours after his transportation to Bethesda Naval Hospital, but at two twenty-four A.M. the team of specialists who had been laboring to save his life announced that the President was dead.

"The brief announcement said that as of two twenty-four A.M. eastern standard time, no evidence of brain wave activity could be detected from electrodes placed on the President's skull.

"President Barnes was the first President to be assassinated since John F. Kennedy was killed November twenty-second, 1963, in Dallas, Texas, and the first President to be murdered while on White House grounds."

Kelsey suddenly got up and went to the window that faced the highway, pushed back one edge of the heavy drapes, and looked out. The motel vacancy sign illuminated the edge of the parking lot, its red light spilling out onto the empty highway.

Most of the country was sleeping at this moment, and yet in Washington and elsewhere, men were awake, beginning the search for him. The FBI, certainly, and the Secret Service would be taking up the search. But even more significantly, his father's men would be looking for him.

He turned that thought over in his mind, his back toward Marion, who still sat on the edge of the bed. He could feel her eyes on him.

The FBI or the Secret Service would listen to him. If he turned himself in and could be protected long enough, they could check his story and would find the inconsistencies. Sooner or later they would force Engstrom to submit to a physical examination, and the plot would be uncovered.

But the key was to be protected long enough for all of that to happen.

If his father's men got to them first, they would be as good as dead. His father's people could not afford to leave him alive. At this very moment the organization would be fanning out across the countryside in ever-widening circles from Washington.

"Kill them on sight," the orders would be.

The papers would report the incident in the morning editions, comparing their deaths to Lee Harvey Oswald's death at the hands of Jack Ruby.

Investigations would be ordered, another Warren Commission would be convened, and the conspiracy theories would blossom and race across the country as they had after 1963.

But like that time, nothing would come of it. The commission would report that Dr. Richard Kelsey, working alone, had assassinated President Barnes. Unbalanced, would be the cause given. He cracked under the strain of his work.

He turned away from the window and looked at Marion. And then what would happen? What was happening in the White House at this very moment with Locke, whoever he really was, as the President of the United States?

The Army officer with the black attaché case containing the war authorization codes would be sitting outside the door of a man who was in reality in the employ of a group of desperate, ruthless men. The Director of the Central Intelligence Agency would be briefing an imposter on the innermost secrets of the nation. President Barnes' cabinet members, in a scramble to save their own positions, would be giving the new President their best counsel, trying to befriend the man, their eyes blinded by the power of the office.

The man sits in the Oval Office; he *must* be the President of the United States. Thinking otherwise is insanity.

"What are we going to do, Richard?" Marion asked.

Pursuit. Someone should have come after them by now. They had no car, nor had they taken one of his father's from the driveway.

It had to be obvious in which direction they had gone on foot. Within minutes after they had left the house, the sirens had sounded close. At that point his father should have been telling the authorities about the woods behind the house, and beyond that, the university's maintenance garages.

Someone should have checked with the university and discovered that a pickup truck was missing. The description and license number should have been radioed in all directions, and roadblocks should have been set up.

But none of that had happened. And something else was forcing its way into his consciousness. Something the newsman on television had said earlier.

Before the FBI had cut off communications with his father, he had told newsmen that his son had spoken about a plot against the President and vice president. He had told them that his son had killed his chauffeur. And that his son had taken a handgun from his private secretary and the elephant gun and shells from his collection.

Someone had found the rifle on the roof of the Corcoran Gallery of Art, where the assassin had also killed the night security guard. The assassin was Dr. Richard Kelsey.

He tried to think.

The assassin was Dr. Richard Kelsey. Unconfirmed reports placed him at the art gallery. Driving a blue Ford van with Illinois plates.

That was it! A blue Ford van. The FBI would have issued an all-points bulletin for a blue Ford van, not a University of Maryland pickup truck.

Which meant his father had deliberately misled the FBI so that his own people could get to his son first.

He leaned his forehead against the cool glass of the window, one hand on the edge of the drape he had pushed aside.

Something was wrong with that thinking, too. It was too loose. Too many things would have to be left to chance.

This was a big country. The only hope of catching Kelsey would be an all-points bulletin with his photograph and a description of the vehicle he was driving. He could have gone in any direction. It would take an army of people looking for him.

But his father had deliberately misled the authorities into believing that he was driving a Ford van. Why?

There was little doubt in Kelsey's mind that the real assassin had indeed been driving the van with Illinois plates. And it is not beyond his father's powers to have the van registered in his son's name.

But where was the real assassin and the van at this instant?

For a moment he let his mind drift around his image of his father, and automatically a wave of love for the old man washed through him.

He had always thought he knew his father pretty well. But last night he had learned differently. How well did his father know him? Enough to know that his son, when in trouble, would run for familiar territory—the Midwest: Chicago, Lake Geneva, Minneapolis?

He straightened up and turned once again toward Marion, letting the heavy drape fall back across the window, but not moving from where he stood in the shadow.

The FBI was looking for him; there was no doubt of that in his mind. They had his photograph, and they had been told by his father that he had taken the rifle that had killed the President. Nor would he be able to convince the FBI any differently, because Wilson Grant, the head of the Bureau's special investigative branch, was evidently either a friend of his father's or a member of his father's organization.

The FBI was out.

The Secret Service worked hand in hand with the FBI,

and their first loyalty was to the President. President Engstrom. The imposter. They would never believe Kelsey.

Both services would be looking for him. But their search would be hampered by the fact they believed he was driving a blue Ford van, which would probably be found within the next few hours in any direction other than west. The real assassin would have abandoned the van in New York or Baltimore. Probably not far from an airport or a train station or a bus depot. And the search would intensify in that direction.

Meanwhile his father would be betting that his son would head toward the Midwest, in a University of Maryland vehicle.

He was getting closer to the truth. He was certain of it.

In the morning the university would report a stolen vehicle, give its license number and description, and the police would be looking for it. But that was another dead end, Kelsey reasoned. His father would have made sure another pickup truck was put in the parking lot to replace the one his son had taken. That was stretching it pretty thin, one part of his brain argued, but another part of him knew that his father's money and organization could do almost anything. It was not beyond possibility.

Marion got up from the edge of the bed, a wild look in her eyes. "They think you killed the President," she said.

"My father set it up," he replied softly.

"You've got to call them and tell them it wasn't you."

"They'd never believe me. And even if they considered it for a moment, my father would prove that I was insane and was making it all up. He'd have us both killed."

"He's going to do that anyway," she cried.

"Yes," Kelsey said half to himself. "Yes, he is."

It didn't really matter who caught them; the FBI, the Secret Service, some local authorities, or his father's men. They would be murdered within hours of their capture.

Meanwhile the President of the United States was an imposter working for the Odessa. Thirty-five years after the war had ended, the Nazis were in control of the most powerful nation in the world.

His thoughts trailed off at that point, and he looked deeply into Marion's eyes. She had no business being involved with this. But it was too late now. Perhaps it was too late for the entire world.

A picture in his mind of jackbooted men in black uniforms goose-stepping down Pennsylvania Avenue in front of the White House, a swastika flying over the nation's capital, flashed through his mind, and he recoiled from the thought.

No, his mind screamed. It could not be allowed to happen.

Engstrom had been assassinated in Alaska. And Barnes had been assassinated just outside the Oval Office. A few steps in either direction from his security detail.

Despite the best efforts of the United States government to protect its top two leaders, they had been murdered.

The protection would continue much the same as before. At least for the time being. The changeover from a democracy with its relatively lax, informal atmosphere to a Nazi dictatorship with its strict controls would not happen overnight. It would take time. Perhaps several years or more.

Meanwhile his father's people would be looking for him, and would continue the search until they found him unless Engstrom was toppled.

Toppled—the word repeated itself in Kelsey's mind. Toppled by word or deed. No one would believe his word, which left only . . .

The door was flung open, and a man in a dark jacket leaped into the room, raised his arm, and fired a pistol twice, the muzzle flashes bright in the dark room, but the noise only a dull plopping sound.

Blindly Kelsey struck out from where he stood, clubbing the man in the back of the head with his fist. Caught completely off guard, the man went down hard, his forehead slamming into the corner of the chest of drawers, and then he crumpled in a heap at the foot of the bed, his right arm outstretched in front of him, the pistol with its fat silencer lying half a foot away from his fingers.

Kelsey shut the door and relocked it, then checked the man's pulse. He was unconscious but still alive. Kelsey, whose heart was pounding nearly out of his chest, sat back on his haunches and breathed a deep sigh of relief.

It had been close. Too damned close.

He looked up. "Marion?" he said. "It's all right now."

There was no answer, and he was about to call out her name again as he got to his feet when the words choked in his throat. The bedspread and the wall behind the bed were splattered with something dark, and caught on the edge of the bed he could see a bare foot.

He took a step around the bed and a haze filled his eyes. *Marion!* his brain screamed, but no sound other than a low gurgling came from his mouth.

He scrambled over the bed and on the floor next to his wife, ripped open her blouse and put his ear to her chest.

Please, his brain screamed. Please let this not be true. Dear God, not Marion!

But there was no sound. Her chest did not rise and fall, nor did the blood pump out of the gaping hole in her chest or the ragged tear in her throat.

Her eyes were open and filled with blood, as were her nose and mouth.

Either bullet would have killed her instantly.

For a long time Kelsey knelt next to the body of his wife, his right hand caressing her still warm cheek as he listened to the occasional car or truck passing outside on the highway.

One of his father's men had found them after all. They had known about the university truck, just as he had reasoned, and his father had probably sent his men fanning westward along all the major highways, checking for the truck. This one had seen it parked behind the motel, silently picked the lock, jumped into the room, and fired at the first thing he saw. Marion.

Kelsey looked down at her. Dear sweet Marion. Her face had already turned a ghostly, unnatural white, and suddenly she wasn't Marion any longer. She was nothing more than a med school cadaver. A stranger. He did not know her.

A noise behind him made him turn around in time to see Marion's killer struggling forward in an attempt to reach the pistol.

Kelsey jumped up, grabbed the pistol, and fired it point-blank into the man's face, which erupted in a spray of bone chips, blood, and white brain matter.

The man's head snapped back and his body flopped over. Kelsey got to his feet and fired the remaining three rounds point-blank into the dead man's face, completely destroying all the features, leaving nothing but jagged bone and flesh.

Then he leaped to the man's side, raised the butt of the pistol over his head and in an insane rage, started to bring it down with all the force he could muster, wanting nothing more than to hurt Marion's killer. To crush him to pulp. To pound him into the floor. Beneath the floor. Deep into the ground, and still hurt him more and more and more . . .

But suddenly Kelsey came to his senses, the pistol raised over his head, and he saw for the first time the destroyed remnants of what once had been a man. He got to his feet, went into the bathroom, and vomited, his mind spinning round and round, two central thoughts in the middle of it all: Marion was dead, and somehow he was going to have to remain alive at all costs, because he was the only one who knew about Engstrom.

29

Stan Lowe had been jumpy all week. Ever since Dr. Kelsey had come snooping around. But finally it had happened, he thought as he finished burning the last of the records tying Locke to President Engstrom, and now they could all breathe a sigh of relief.

It was shortly before 10:00 P.M., a scant twenty-four hours since Barnes had been assassinated by their east coast special operative, and Lowe was tired. He had remained awake through most of last night and this morning as much of the world had, watching the bulletins and news reports on the President's assassination and manhunt for Dr. Kelsey.

Earlier this evening he had managed to nap for a few hours until shortly after nine o'clock when his orders had come in from Aerie via Chicago.

"Destroy the subject records after replacing them with the new package," the voice had come over the phone. "The flags are high." The caller had given the proper authorization code words.

With mounting excitement Lowe had driven from his condominium in Lake Geneva out to the clinic, where he let himself in the back way, pulled Locke's jacket out of his safe where he had kept it since Monday, and replaced Kelsey's sketches and the photographs Locke had brought with him with another set. If the new file was ever checked by the authorities, a possibility now that Kelsey was a marked man, it would show that Locke had indeed come to the clinic for reconstructive surgery. But the sketches would show that his face had been rebuilt to resemble someone other than Engstrom.

Lowe managed to place the new version of the file in the records section without attracting any attention of the staff, especially not that bastard Sharpenberg, and then he had gone downstairs to the furnace room, where he had burned the old sketches and photographs.

The clinic had been in an uproar all day. Even Sharpenberg, the bear of the hospital, had been upset, canceling all but one of the day's scheduled operations.

The opinion among the staff ranged from stunned disbelief to a studied nonchalance.

"A terrible mistake has been made by those bunglers in Washington, but not .to worry, Doc Kelsey's father will straighten it all out."

"Dr. Kelsey assassinating the President? Don't be an ass. Such a thing is totally impossible."

But overall the clinic had been tense through the day, with none of the light banter that normally went on among the staff.

The flames from the open furnace reflected off Lowe's sweaty forehead, and he smiled, bearing his teeth like an animal ready for the kill.

He had taken shit all of his life. The worst assignments, the lousiest jobs; ever since he had been a boy in the German section of Milwaukee, his father had assigned him the dirty work.

As a delivery boy for a number of influential Milwaukee citizens. As a houseboy for the mayor of the city one summer. And finally working nights earning a college degree in business administration.

How he hated business administration, he thought as he watched the flames consume the last of the photos and sketches. All his life he had wanted to be a military leader, or perhaps a medical doctor. Like Kelsey. Looked up to. Respected. Treated with deference. But orders were orders. And he had been ordered into business administration.

Years ago he had been invited down to Aerie, and he had gone expecting to meet with *Der Oberst* himself. A private conference, he had told himself. At long last he would be given a serious assignment.

But it had not happened that way. Lowe had been one of nearly a hundred other men and women from all over the world to arrive at Aerie within a few days of each other for a weeklong indoctrination course. When the course was completed, each of them was supposed to be willing and able to subjugate their lives to the higher principles of international socialism, toward the bright day when a new world order would dawn.

Bitterly disappointed, Lowe had returned to his mundane job in the States as an administrator for the All-America Insurance Corporation in Miami, until three years ago when he had been assigned as administrator of the Lake Geneva clinic.

He had been given his assignment routinely with no hint of its importance. In fact, he had not been informed of what was happening until three days before Locke arrived; when Dr. Kelsey's father, *Oberst* Kellner himself, had personally told him everything.

And now, Lowe thought, his smile deepening as he closed the furnace door and trudged up the stairs to his office, the new world order he had been promised in Aerie years ago was finally dawning. Now he would finally become an important man. Looked up to. Respected.

In his office he pulled on his coat, put on his hat, and went out the back way to where his car was parked.

A light snow had begun to fall, and he shivered as he slid in behind the wheel and put the key in the ignition. He paused a moment before he turned the key to think about Dr. Kelsey out there somewhere on the run. They would get him. It was only a matter of time. A very short time.

Lowe turned the ignition key and the car exploded, the blast blowing out many of the clinic's downstairs windows and several on the second floor, sending bits of steel, upholstery, and human bone as far as two hundred feet.

At that moment it was eleven o'clock in Washington, where Charles Anderson, the former head of Vice President Stewart Engstrom's Secret Service detail, lay in a coma in the Walter Reed Army Medical Center.

Twenty-four hours after the helicopter crash in Alaska's Mt. McKinley Park, Anderson's condition had stabilized from critical to serious. But during the days since, he had regained consciousness only once to ask about the safety of Engstrom.

Extensive head injuries in the crash had caused pressure on the brain, which kept Anderson unconscious and would eventually kill him. The operation to cure that damage by relieving the pressure and eventually leading to his recovery was scheduled for six tomorrow morning.

A young, white-coated doctor who was doing a special internship from Georgetown University entered Anderson's room, wheeling a stainless steel cart in front of him.

Anderson was scheduled to be given muscle relaxants and a preliminary anesthetic about this time preparatory to the deep anesthetic he would be given in the morning, so the night duty nurse thought nothing of the young doctor's appearance at this hour.

Inside the darkened room the man moved to the respirator automatically controlling Anderson's breathing and turned it off.

For a few seconds Anderson's breathing continued, although somewhat raggedly, and then it stopped.

The intern went about his business administering the shots, and noting the times on the medical chart as if nothing had happened, spending a full six minutes with the dying man.

Finally, just before he left to complete his rounds, he turned the respirator back on and air once again began pumping into Anderson's lungs, only now the machine was connected to a dead man.

Some eighteen hundred miles to the east, Robert Farley, president of Farley Chemicals, Ltd., was awakened from a deep sleep by his telephone.

He struggled awake, flipped on the table light next to his bed, and glanced at the clock as he picked up the phone. It was just four o'clock.

"Yes," Farley said sleepily. "What is it?"

His wife had awakened as well, and she sat up to look past her husband at the clock.

"Mr. Farley . . . oh God . . . this is George at the plant!" an excited, barely understandable man's voice came over the line. There was a great deal of noise in the background that sounded to Farley like sirens. He was instantly wide-awake.

"George?" he said. "George Newell?"

"Yes, sir . . . oh, Mr. Farley, you must come quick, sir. There has been a terrible accident."

Farley's heart raced as he pushed the covers aside and swung his legs off the bed. "What is it, George? What has happened, man?"

"An explosion, sir. A terrible explosion. Mrs. Grance, Mrs. Stanhope, and some of the other ladies were here . . .

oh, God, sir—I don't know why . . . but they were burned.
It's horrible, Mr. Farley . . . horrible . . . You must come
quickly.''

"Yes, of course, I'm on my way," Farley said. Newell,
who was the night plant engineer, rang off, leaving Farley
holding a dead telephone.

"What is it, Robert?" his wife asked.

"George Newell at the plant," Farley said. "There's been
an accident. Dotty and Margaret were there for some un-
godly reason, and they were apparently hurt."

"Oh, my God," Mrs. Farley said. She pushed back the
covers and jumped out of the bed. "I'm coming with you,
Robert."

"Yes," Farley said dully. He was in something of a daze.
He turned back to the phone and tried to get a dial tone. He
wanted to call his day shift plant engineer and have the man
round up his crew to meet him there, but something was
wrong with the telephone, and he gave up after a moment.

Within five minutes Farley and his wife had dressed and,
without rousing their chauffeur, got the Mercedes out of the
parking garage and headed west out of London past New-
ham, where the plant was located.

There was little traffic on the road this evening, and once
out of the city, Farley speeded up well past the posted limits.

What he could not fathom was what the wives of two of
his senior vice presidents were doing at the plant at this
strange hour of the morning. It made no sense.

He turned to his wife and was about to ask her just that
question when she looked over his shoulder out the window
on the driver's side and screamed.

Farley turned in time to glimpse a large, dark shape out
of the corner of his right eye, and then a terrific crash
slammed in the side of the car, crushing his right arm and
shoulder, sending him across the front seat nearly out the
opposite door with his wife.

The car spun around, then hit something hard, and Farley,

before he and his wife both died, was only vaguely aware
that they were airborne, flipping end over end, and then
there was nothing.

It was dawn in the eastern Mediterranean, and this day
promised to be as warm as yesterday in Tel Aviv. A small
group of military men crouched behind a sandbag bunker in
a deserted section of the military side of Lod Airport, waiting breathlessly as the army bomb disposal squad opened
the large aluminum coffin two hundred yards away.

Among the men crouched behind the bunker was Colonel
Joseph Yesodat, in charge of the Israeli Secret Service Operations Branch, to whom the coffin-sized metal case had
been delivered this morning.

Sometime during the night a canvas-covered truck parked
a half block from the front gate of Government House. A
patrolling civil police radio car team had investigated the
deserted truck, which contained the coffin with an address
label to Yesodat.

The colonel had been informed, the box had been removed by the army bomb squad to Lod, and was being
opened now.

A terrorist bomb, everyone was convinced, and twenty
minutes after they began, the bomb squad team confirmed
the suspicion by walkie-talkie.

"It's a bomb, all right, Colonel," the walkie-talkie Yesodat held blared.

He keyed the microphone and held the instrument to his
lips. "Is it disarmed?"

"Yes sir, but . . ."

"But what, Sergeant?" Yesodat snapped.

"That isn't all that's in this box."

Yesodat got to his feet and looked over the bunker across
the field where the heavily padded figures of the two volunteers stood next to the open box. One of them waved.

"You better come look at this yourself, Colonel," the walkie-talkie blared.

Yesodat, along with the other officers crouched behind the bunker, strode across the field.

As they got closer, Yesodat could see that both of the volunteers had taken off their face shields, and both of them were as white as ghosts.

"What the hell is going on . . . ," Yesodat said, but the words choked in his throat.

Lev Asheim and David Goldmann lay face-to-face in the coffin, nude, their bodies horribly torn up with high-caliber bullet wounds.

"My God," Yesodat breathed, coming closer to the side of the open coffin. His stomach churned. Sweat popped out on his forehead and upper lip.

At the foot of the coffin was a large lump of what Yesodat recognized as plastique explosive. He turned questioningly to the bomb disposal volunteers.

"It's disarmed, sir," one of them said. "Simple contact switch on the lid."

Yesodat stepped to the side of the coffin and reached inside.

"I wouldn't do that, sir . . . ," one of the bomb squad men said, moving toward him.

But Yesodat had seen what appeared to be a slip of paper with writing on it, tied around Goldmann's wrist. He gingerly took it as the bomb disposal volunteer screamed no, and suddenly the entire world went white for Yesodat and the others, the explosion from the plastique-filled corpses breaking windows in the airport terminal building nearly a mile away.

30

August Kellner's Lincoln limousine sped down Pennsylvania Avenue toward the White House. The driver had said nothing since they left the house in College Park, and Kellner had been lost in his thoughts during the drive.

It was with some trepidation that he was keeping his appointment with Engstrom on this the fourth day after Barnes' assassination. Nothing serious had gone wrong with the operation yet, but a number of minor anomalies had begun to appear in the carefully laid plans.

Stoeffel had called yesterday and ordered Kellner to get everything straightened out and on track within the week. The final phase of the operation was to begin immediately.

The work that had been done by the Odessa leadership over the last year in every major capital in the world was completed, merely awaiting the signal from Washington. The signal that Kellner would put into motion.

He was nervous about it. Besides the fact it was coming

too close after Barnes' assassination, there was still the un-resolved problem of his son.

As of nine o'clock this morning when Kellner received his briefing from his field operatives, Richard was still at large.

The FBI had been beating a dead horse ever since they had found the van registered in Richard's name at the Rich-mond, Virginia, airport, and had subsequently traced the man identifying himself as Kelsey to the New Orleans area, where he had disappeared at sea aboard a forty-foot cabin cruiser.

Already talk was beginning about a Cuban plot, although as yet no one had been able to find a satisfactory connection between his son and the Cubans.

Kellner's operatives, on the other hand, had found the Uni-versity of Maryland truck parked behind a motel in a small West Virginia town shortly before seven o'clock that first morning after the man who was supposed to be checking that section of Highway 50 west had failed to radio in.

Inside the motel room they had found the bodies of Kel-sey's wife and their operative.

The two men who discovered the bodies managed to get them out of the motel room, clean up the mess, get rid of the pickup truck, and make sure no other traces had been left behind before the motel operator asked too many ques-tions. They bribed the man into handing over Richard's reg-istration card, and incredibly they found that Richard had used his real name.

That had been a dangerously close call, Kellner thought now as his limousine approached the White House. If it had come out that his son had checked in at a motel in West Virginia that night, it would have blown their decoy's trail sky high. Too many questions would have to be asked, and the entire operation would have fallen like a house of cards in a strong wind.

Now Richard was armed, was driving an inconspicuous tan Ford LTD with New York license plates, and had eluded detection for three days.

The Institute in Chicago was being watched and its telephones and staff monitored, as was the Lake Geneva clinic and his son's old haunts in Minneapolis and St. Paul.

For a moment Kellner put himself in his son's shoes. His wife was dead, he was wanted for the assassination of President Barnes, and he knew that his own father had ordered his death. He was on the run. Frightened, certainly, confused, and grief-stricken that his wife was dead.

Kellner looked up as the limousine came to White House gate. The driver rolled down the window and spoke with the guards, who were checking appointments on a clipboard list.

His son was angry—or more accurately, enraged—and yet he was a desperate man. What would he do next? What would he be planning?

General Stoeffel and the others had, from the beginning, underestimated his son's resourcefulness. And for a time it seemed as if they were more correct in their assessment than he was. But now Kellner was worried. They had not heard the last of Richard. He was sure of it, and although he would not consciously admit it, even to himself, his concern was tinged with fatherly pride.

The limousine moved through the gate to the east portico, and his thoughts turned to another perplexing anomaly in their carefully laid plans: Engstrom.

Over the past four days the man had changed. Subtly, but the change was there. It was the pressure of the job, Kellner supposed, and Stoeffel had agreed, ordering the next phase of the operation to begin before Engstrom became too locked into some other course of action.

"We have come this far, August. We cannot afford to falter now. We must keep one step ahead of our man, leading him along, instead of allowing him to handle the reins himself.''

"It's too soon. The announcement will be too dramatic. We're not ready. The world is not ready.''

"It is in readiness," Stoeffel, who had taken the rank of general, insisted.

"We could lose everything, Kurt.''

"We will lose nothing!" Stoeffel shouted, enraged. "You will do as you are ordered, *Herr Oberst!*''

"Of course, *Herr General*," Kellner had capitulated.

The chauffeur pulled up at the east portico and let Kellner out of the car. Just inside the foyer he was electronically checked for weapons by two Secret Service men, and then was taken into the receptionist's lobby, where Barnes' appointments secretary, who had remained on the presidential staff, met him.

"Mr. Kelsey, if you will follow me, sir, the President will see you now.''

"Thank you," Kellner said, and he followed Pleasance around the corner from the Roosevelt Room and down the corridor to the Oval Office.

The offices and corridors were busy, Secret Service men everywhere. Many of the people glanced curiously at Kellner and did double takes. He was the father of the man who was wanted for the assassination of Barnes. And Kellner, who had always been a very private man, felt uncomfortable in his new notoriety.

As they approached the Oval Office, the door opened and Wilson Grant emerged along with another man Kellner did not recognize. When they saw him, Grant's animated expression dropped.

"August," he said, shaking hands with Kellner. "I'd like you to meet Albert Sousa, my chief investigator.''

Kellner nodded and shook hands with the man, and he had the uncomfortable feeling that the FBI agent was looking directly through him.

Grant's voice lowered. "I haven't had the chance to tell you how sorry I am about all of this. I know you tried to help, and I know what you must be going through now."

Kellner nodded. They were talking about his son, and despite his loyalty to the organization, it still hurt. Deeply.

"Are you free for lunch today?" Grant asked.

"I think so, Wilson," Kellner said. "Why don't you let me call you when I'm finished here." He nodded toward the Oval Office door.

"Of course," Grant said.

"I wasn't aware that you were a friend of the President's, Mr. Kelsey," Sousa said.

Kellner turned toward him. "We go back years together," he said. Again he had the uncomfortable feeling the man was looking right through him.

"Call me," Grant said again, and he and the agent headed down the corridor as Pleasance showed Kellner into the Oval Office and closed the door after him.

Engstrom was seated behind the large desk, and when Kellner came in he smiled, got to his feet, and came around the desk, extending his hand.

"August, I'm happy you could come," he said, and Kellner shook his hand.

It was uncanny, but Kellner could almost believe that the man standing in front of him really was Engstrom. His son's work, along with that of the psychiatrists in Aerie, was magnificent. He had known this man as Hempel, and Locke, and a dozen other names. An efficient, dedicated, and totally ruthless operative. But this man now was Engstrom, his boyish grin subdued apparently only by the pressures of the office.

"I want to offer you my condolences about your son," Engstrom was saying, and Kellner focused on him. "And you have my assurances that when he is finally apprehended, he'll be given the best treatment."

"Mr. President?" Kellner asked, somewhat confused.

Engstrom shook his head. "I'm sure that Richard was unbalanced. The strain of his profession became too much for him. I also understand that his first wife was killed in a car accident a few years ago, which probably contributed somewhat to his condition." Engstrom again shook his head. "Richard will get the best care this country can give him, I promise you that."

"Thank you, Mr. President," Kellner said, and Engstrom led him across the office to a leather couch, where they sat down.

Engstrom lit a cigarette, then looked into Kellner's eyes. "And now August, I hate to rush you, but I've got one hell of a schedule for the rest of the day. What is it you wanted to see me about?"

It took a moment for Kellner to remember exactly what he had come here for, and when he did, he realized with a start that he had fallen under the spell of the office: If the man sits in the Oval Office, he *must* be the President. It was powerful.

Kellner took a deep breath. "It's about that book I wanted you to read a few days ago."

Engstrom's eyes narrowed in disbelief. "What?"

"You remember, Mr. President," Kellner said, his heart beginning to pound.

"What the hell, August—" Engstrom started to say, but Kellner cut him off.

"It was called *Eagles Fly,* Mr. President."

Engstrom's eyes went glassy for a moment, the surprised look fading from his face, being replaced slowly with a different, dreamy expression.

"*Eagles Fly,* Mr. President," Kellner repeated, awed himself by the effect the two words had on the man.

"Yes, August, what can I do for you?" Engstrom said, his voice without emotion.

It was actually working. He could taste the victory. At long last. The triumph would be sweet.

"Over the next weeks you will appoint an international commission to study plans for your new World Peace Proposal."

"Yes," Engstrom said. His right hand held the cigarette motionless over the ashtray, his eyes locked into Kellner's.

"You know about the World Peace Proposal. It is chapter six in the book. *Eagles Fly*."

"Yes," Engstrom said, flinching at the two words.

Kellner sat forward and lowered his voice. "The men you will appoint to this commission will include me, representing the United States; Kurt Stoeffel of the Bank of Buenos Aires, representing South America; Herman Mueller of Bonn and Otto Bergholtz of Paris representing the European nations; Walter Deering of Cairo, representing the Middle Eastern countries; and Alois Hartmann of London, who will represent the British Isles."

"Yes," Engstrom said, his voice still devoid of emotion.

"Do you have all of that?"

"Yes," Engstrom said.

Kellner stared into the man's vacant eyes for a long time, and then got to his feet. "Have a pleasant day, Mr. President; it was a pleasure talking with you."

Engstrom seemed to slide slowly out of his daze, and then he blinked, looked up, stubbed out his cigarette, and stood up.

"It was good of you to come this morning, August," he said in his Engstrom personality. "And I want to thank you for agreeing to serve on my World Peace Commission. But don't say anything about it yet, please. I'll make the formal announcement within the next couple of weeks."

"Of course, Mr. President," Kellner said, smiling. "I'm honored to serve in your administration."

31

President Engstrom would have to be assassinated. It was a conclusion Kelsey had come to after Marion had been murdered. And it was a conviction that had grown to an obsession with him three days later as he approached Lake Geneva from the west through Janesville, Wisconsin.

He had discovered the tan Ford LTD parked behind the motel. He had exchanged clothes and identification with the dead man, and had taken the car west, keeping to Highway 50. The next day near Indianapolis he had turned north along minor highways and county roads.

At first his decision was nothing more than something vague in the back of his mind. He knew it was the only thing that could be done, and yet he had not at that point consciously planned its details.

With Engstrom in the Oval Office, no one would believe his story. And despite everything that had happened to him, he had difficulty believing it himself.

Yet Marion was dead. Dear sweet Marion, who had never

hurt anyone in her life, who had, as far as Kelsey knew, never even said a bad word about anyone, was dead.

And it was because of him. Had he said nothing, had he done nothing other than continue his work at the Institute, Marion would be alive.

At times, driving along some stretch of highway, Kelsey would cry tears of sadness and frustration for his wife. But at other times the rage would build so strongly that it was all he could do to keep from turning around in the middle of the road and heading directly for Washington.

For an entire day he had driven southwest, toward St. Louis, as he tried to review his life, beginning with his earliest remembrances of Berlin before the war.

He could remember the linden trees, and the Wannsee with its sailboats, and he could remember a summer spent in the mountains, probably south of Munich. He could vaguely remember the soldiers, the endlessly marching soldiers, and then the bombings, and finally the mountains and peace of Switzerland.

But each time he tried to focus on some particular scene from his childhood, his mind would wander back to three faces that would come in and out of focus; the first was Colleen with her short, dark hair, intense brown eyes, and smiling, off-center laugh; the second was Marion, much softer and rounder and in some ways a warmer person than Colleen; and finally he could see his father that night in Berlin, the bombs still falling, crying because his wife, Kelsey's mother, was dead. Killed by Allied bombs. Buried under tons of rubble that had once been their apartment building.

But each time his thoughts turned to his father, they would lead him to a kaleidoscope of feelings and impressions, invariably ending with Engstrom, a malevolent grin on his face, sitting at a large desk in the Oval Office, a swastika on the wall behind him.

In the early morning of the third day, after he had spent

a few hours of restless sleep at a small motel outside of Springfield, Missouri, he had headed north toward Wisconsin and whatever fate awaited him. He knew, at long last, what he would have to do. He knew the dangers, and he knew how long it would take. But he was a committed man.

From Janesville, about twenty-five miles from the town of Lake Geneva on the northeastern end of the lake, Kelsey headed south along the lake until he was at a point opposite the clinic. At this time of the year the area was deserted, locked up for the winter.

It was nearly midnight when Kelsey doused the lights of the car, pulled down a narrow dirt road that led to the lake, and parked behind a cabin.

A light snow was falling when he got out of the car, zippered up the dark jacket he had taken from the dead man, and hurried around to the front of the cabin, which faced the lake. The boat dock had been pulled up for the winter and was stacked neatly under the front porch. Next to it was an aluminum canoe covered with a tarp.

Kelsey walked across the yard, the snow about an inch deep on the still green grass, and stood at the edge of the lake. To the east, across the water, he could see the lights of the town in the distance. He let his eyes wander along the shore until he could make out the one light over the pavilion below the clinic.

It was a mile and a half across the water, but it was the only way there for him. Kelsey knew that the clinic would be watched. There would be someone on the highway and probably a monitor on the phone. But they would not be expecting him to come across the water. At least he hoped they would not be thinking that clearly.

During the last three days he had listened to the radio news broadcasts, which reported that a man identified as Dr. Richard Kelsey had been traced from Richmond to the New Orleans area, where he had disappeared at sea aboard a cabin crusier. There were rumors that Kelsey had been given aid by the Cubans, and already Castro had angrily denied the allegations.

It told Kelsey that his father's people would be the only ones watching the clinic, which meant that if he was caught, he would be killed on the spot.

But it was the only way, he told himself.

He pulled the canoe from beneath the porch and carried it down to the water's edge, then returned to search for a paddle.

Beneath the tarp was a tangle of old life jackets, several bamboo fishing poles, and the remnants of a large landing net, but nothing more, so Kelsey went up the three stairs to the screened-in porch and peered in the door.

At one end of the porch he could just see a couple of canoe paddles beneath a pile of fishing gear and a half-dozen new life jackets. He pushed his fist through the screen, reached inside, and unlatched the door.

He went across the porch, grabbed one of the paddles, and a moment later was back at the canoe, shoving it into the water.

Before he climbed into the boat, he checked the pistol and silencer that he had taken from Marion's killer, and stuffed it back in his belt beneath his jacket. He had found spare ammunition beneath the front seat and had loaded the gun on his first night away from the motel at Augusta.

Finally he pushed off from the shore and began paddling across the lake, his motions smooth, regular, and as quiet as he could possibly make them.

It was cold on the lake, but a few minutes from shore he was sweating from the exertion looking back, it seemed like the cabin he had just left was as far away as the clinic light was in the opposite direction. He felt alone on the lake, and for a moment he lost his conviction and almost turned back.

The sheer audacity of what he planned to do amazed him. He was the suspected assassin of one President, had killed three men, had been the indirect cause of the deaths of both

Colleen and Marion, and was now planning the assassination of another President.

It was outside the realm of reality. It was the stuff of movies, not of the real world. Yet he continued, the mental picture of Engstrom with the swastika behind him strong in his mind.

About a third of the way across the lake he looked back again toward the cabin to get his bearings on a pair of tall pine trees for the return trip. It would do him no good to get what he needed at the clinic and then not be able to find his way back to the car.

He would have to ditch the car and then take a bus or a train into Chicago, where he planned on renting a room in a flophouse, probably in Cicero. He would need two undisturbed weeks before he would be able to move around, and then three months before he would be ready to head back east to Engstrom.

Beyond that point he had no clear idea how he was going to accomplish his goal, he just knew that he was somehow going to do it.

Over the past days, whenever he could take his mind off Marion, he was able to think rationally, and he would review his options. But each time, his thinking led him to a dead end. There was no way anyone would believe him. By now, he knew, his father's people would have probably destroyed Locke's records at the clinic, and had almost certainly covered their tracks everywhere else. Even if the authorities did agree to listen to his story with an open mind, and even if they agreed to investigate, they would find nothing.

Either Engstrom had to be forced into submitting to a physical examination, in which case he would be discovered as an imposter, or he had to be killed. And there was no way that Kelsey could force anyone into making Engstrom undergo such an examination. It would be simply unthinkable to subject the President of the United States to such an indignity on the say-so of a murderer.

Which left him only one option.

About a hundred yards from the clinic's pavilion, boathouse, and sauna, which were right onshore, Kelsey stopped paddling and watched any signs of life.

Above the shore, through the trees, he could just make out a few of the lights of the clinic, but he could hear no sounds other than the waves lapping against the boathouse foundation, and could detect no activity.

After a few minutes he resumed paddling, careful now to make no noise, his gut tightening, until the bottom of the canoe grated on the sandy bottom and the prow pushed up on the beach.

Kelsey scrambled ashore and pulled the canoe farther up onto the beach, then hurried up the path toward the clinic, away from the boathouse light, in a crouching run as he pulled the gun from his belt.

The wide, asphalt path led up the hill, crossed the entrance road, and then led across the open area of the front lawn to the main clinic entrance.

Just before the path emerged from the woods, Kelsey stopped in the shadows. Parked in front of the clinic entrance was a black Cadillac limousine. He could see the glow of what apparently was a lit cigarette arc from the window of the car.

They were here, waiting for him to show up, just as he thought they would be, and he was suddenly frightened. Across the lawn was a man, perhaps two, waiting to kill him. It was a strange feeling.

He stepped off the path and, working his way through the woods as silently as possible, made his way to the back of the clinic. The maintenance garage and generator building were between him and the back service entrance. Several of the windows of the clinic were boarded up, and the garage and generator building were scorched as if there had been a fire. But Kelsey paid little attention to those details.

Besides the car in front, there was probably another on

the highway, but they would not be able to see the back entrance, and Kelsey could detect no one on this side of the clinic.

He took a deep breath and then rushed out of the woods, around the garage, and across the narrow driveway to the back entrance, where he huddled in the doorway, his grip tightening on the pistol, waiting for the sounds of an alarm. But everything remained quiet, and after several long seconds he opened the door and stepped inside the dark corridor.

He held his watch up, the luminous dials glowing strongly in the dark. It was nearly two o'clock. It had taken him almost two hours to paddle across the lake.

Shivering from the chill, the exertion, and his fright, Kelsey moved on the balls of his feet to the door that led out to the reception area. He opened it a crack.

The large room was lit up, but no one was seated behind the desk. The only on-duty staff would be upstairs at the ward station at this hour of the morning, and Kelsey had contemplated running into no one unless his father had posted people inside.

He opened the door and stepped into the reception hall, pistol at the ready, hurried across the open area, and ducked down the corridor that led to the operating theater, tensing for a gunshot or a shouted command.

But the clinic was silent as he slipped into the prep room, crossed it, and pushed open the swinging doors into the operating theater. The room was dark except for a single dim light behind the large plate glass window in the observation room above. Kelsey's eyes automatically strayed up there and he froze. Sam Sharpenberg was seated looking down at him, his eyes wide, his mouth open.

For a seeming eternity Kelsey could no nothing more than stare, the instant stopped in time. Then he started to turn, but Sharpenberg had jumped to his feet and was gesturing for him to wait.

Kelsey hesitated a moment not knowing what to do, and Sharpenberg disappeared through the observation room door.

Tightening his grip on the pistol, Kelsey waited in the doorway until Sharpenberg came into the prep room from the corridor, closing the door softly behind him.

"Richard," he said.

Kelsey held his silence.

"If it will help, I don't believe you killed President Barnes," Sharpenberg said, his voice low but urgent.

"I didn't," Kelsey said.

"I knew it before, but I was a hundred percent convinced when I saw you in the operating theater," Sharpenberg said. "You're supposed to be in Cuba, or somewhere in the Gulf. You could not have gotten here."

"The assassin is an imposter posing as me."

"Who is he?"

"I don't know," Kelsey said. "But he works for my father."

Sharpenberg took a step forward, and Kelsey raised the gun.

"Don't come any closer, Sam, please."

"Where's Marion?" Sharpenberg asked.

"Dead," Kelsey said bitterly. "On my father's orders. He tried to kill me, too."

"My God" Sharpenberg said. "How? Where?"

"Three nights ago in a little motel in West Virginia. One of my father's henchmen came looking for us and shot her to death. I killed him."

It took Sharpenberg several seconds to digest all of that, and he took another step forward.

"Please, Sam, no closer; I don't want to hurt you," Kelsey said. He was even more frightened now than before.

"Jesus Christ Richard, I believe your story. I'm on your side. But what the hell are you doing here? Why haven't you gone to the FBI? Your father's people are out front and up on the highway watching this place. They told me they were here for our protection because of Stan Lowe.''

''What about Lowe?'' Kelsey asked.

''He was killed a couple of nights ago. His car exploded.''

For a moment Kelsey was confused. Why had Lowe been killed? He had worked for the organization. Then it came clear. It was because of Locke's records. Lowe was probably the one who doctored them, and when he was finished he had to be eliminated. He knew too much.

He focused again on Sharpenberg, who was watching him. How far could he trust the man? Sharpenberg was a friend, a fellow doctor, but he was also a law-and-order citizen. Despite his assurances to the contrary, might he just be stalling for time, trying to get Kelsey off guard?

''Why haven't you turned yourself in?'' Sharpenberg said.

Kelsey didn't answer, his mind a jumble of contradictory thoughts and feelings. If he could not trust Sharpenberg, he would have to kill him. It was as simple as that.

After a long while Kelsey sighed finally and stuffed the pistol in his belt. ''I've got a lot of incredible stuff to tell you, Sam, and I'm going to need your help tonight.''

''Do you want to stay here for a while?'' Sharpenberg asked, obviously relieved.

Kelsey shook his head. ''I can't, Sam. Besides the fact this place is being watched, I don't want to involve you in this any more than I have to.''

Sharpenberg nodded. ''Let's go into my office and talk. You look as though you could see a drink.''

''Yeah,'' Kelsey said, and he followed Sharpenberg to his old office.

When Sharpenberg had the door locked and made sure the drapes were tightly closed, he turned on the desk lamp, poured Kelsey and himself a stiff shot of brandy, and they sat down in easy chairs on either side of the cold fireplace.

Kelsey sipped his drink and then looked into Sharpenberg's eyes. "What were you doing here so late, Sam? And why were you up in the observation room?"

Sharpenberg smiled wanly. "I do a lot of my heavy thinking up there. Always have. This morning your father called and said we would be accepting no new patients. As soon as we discharge the ones with us now, the clinic will be closed. I'm out of a job."

"The clinic has served its purpose," Kelsey said, and Sharpenberg looked at him questioningly.

Kelsey took another drink, the brandy warming his insides and straightening out the flutter in his gut, then he put the glass down on a low coffee table and began telling Sharpenberg everything he knew about the Odessa plot to take over the world, beginning with Colleen's murder in Minneapolis, what seemed like a century ago.

Several times through the telling Kelsey had to backtrack in his story to fill Sam in on various details, and twice Sharpenberg asked penetrating questions.

A half hour passed before he was finally finished, and he sat back in his chair, drink in hand, and closed his eyes.

"So what happens now?" Sharpenberg asked, his voice subdued. He was troubled by what Kelsey had told him.

"I'm going to assassinate President Engstrom," Kelsey said simply. It was the first time he had voiced his intention out loud, and the words sounded foreign to his own ears.

"I thought so," Sharpenberg said. "But why did you come here? What do you want?"

Kelsey opened his eyes. "I need a medical kit."

Sharpenberg's eyes narrowed. "What for . . ." he started to say, but stopped in midsentence, a look of incredulity coming over his features. "Your photograph has been plastered over every newspaper and on every television station since Barnes was assassinated. The only reason you got this far was because they're looking the other way, and because you haven't shaved, you're wearing a hat, and you stopped to get gas, eat, or check into a motel only at night.''

Sharpenberg waited for a confirmation of what he was saying, but Kelsey remained silent.

"You'd never make it back to Washington, and even if you did, you'd never make it close enough to Engstrom to kill him. At least not looking like you do now.''

Still Kelsey held his silence.

"Jesus, Richard, you can't do this—it's impossible!''

"It's the only way,'' Kelsey finally said.

Sharpenberg was shaking his head. "Not alone, Richard. You'd never be able to do it. I'll help. You can stay here; we'll manage to hide you somehow.''

"It won't work, Sam. I left the car nearby. They'll find it, put two and two together, and turn this place upside down looking for me. And when they found out that you were involved, they'd kill you. Probably kill the entire staff.''

"I don't care,'' Sharpenberg exploded, and Kelsey got to his feet.

"I'm in this alone. I know I can do it, but if I don't get out of here and away before daylight, we're both dead men.''

Sharpenberg slumped back. "You'd have to work very slowly. With only local anesthetics. Maybe take months, perhaps even a year. There'd be a lot of bruising that would be impossible to cover with makeup.''

"Dye,'' Kelsey said. "From black walnuts.''

"I see,'' Sharpenberg said. "I can't talk you out of this?''

Kelsey shook his head.

"Then I've got the perfect place for you to stay,'' he said. "Last summer I bought a cabin in Door County. It's on Lake Michigan between Sister Bay and Northport.''

"It's a tourist area, crawling with people.''

"Not much happens this time of year, and besides, the cabin is off the beaten path. I've got about ten acres. Cost me a fortune.''

"What about my father's men? They must know about it."

"I don't think so. Even Loraine doesn't know about it. It's my little retreat."

"Food?"

"There's enough there for an army to winter over. LP gas for the stove and hot water heater, and plenty of wood for the fireplace. You should be able to stay there for at least two months or more without detection. Don't use the fireplace during the day, and no one will see the smoke at night."

Kelsey looked into Sharpenberg's eyes. "If they find out, they'll kill you."

Sharpenberg just smiled.

"Why?" Kelsey asked. "Why are you helping me?"

"Because I believe you, Richard," he said simply.

Within twenty minutes they had put together a complete medical kit for Kelsey, stuffing the supplies into a soiled clothing bag from the prep room, they had said their good-byes, and Kelsey was once again paddling his way across Lake Geneva. A couple of dozen black walnuts he had picked up behind the clinic that he would use to make a powerful skin dye were in the bag as well, and Sam's last warning still in his ears.

"A thousand things can and probably will go wrong. Shock. An infection your antibiotics won't be able to handle. A bleeder that could get away from you. Unconsciousness at the wrong moment. And on top of all that, you'll have to work from a mirror, and every move you make will be backward. It can't work."

THROUGH EARLY
1983

Door County is a peninsula in east central Wisconsin that juts out more than seventy miles into Lake Michigan, sep-arated from the state of Michigan by the fifteen-mile-wide Green Bay.

In the summer the area is ripe with tourists who golf, swim, sail, fish, backpack, and camp.

During the winter a few hardy vacationers come to Door County for ice fishing, snowmobiling, and skiing, but for the most part these people keep to very limited areas of the peninsula, far away from Sharpenberg's cabin.

For the first week Kelsey did little other than give himself massive doses of vitamin complexes to rapidly build up his strength and resistance to infection and shock, and wait to see if this place was truly deserted and therefore safe.

During the first week Kelsey readjusted his sleeping and working schedule so that he became a night person whose waking hours began at dusk and ended at dawn.

Sharpenberg's ten acres consisted of a rugged strip of rocky shoreline, pounded by waves that sometimes came within a few yards of the cabin steps. And it was accessible only by a narrow, sandy road that would be closed once a first hard winter storm arrived.

During the first week Kelsey spent most of his waking hours listening to the large all-band radio set up on a win-dow ledge overlooking stormy Lake Michigan. The news broadcasts were filled with President Engstrom's World Peace Proposal. Very little was broadcast about the assas-sination once Barnes' funeral had been held; the general opinion was that although Castro was telling the truth and Cuba had not been involved in the plot, Kelsey had probably headed there anyway, and went down in a storm in the Gulf.

Finally, near dusk on a Sunday, Kelsey felt that he was

as ready as he would ever be, and after a brief walk on the deserted, ice-encrusted beach, he came back to the cabin and began setting up his medical kit on the large kitchen table.

He had unscrewed the clips that held the bathroom mirror to the wall and propped it up on the kitchen table after he had shaved his face and the sides of his head twice, disinfecting the entire area with alcohol.

The first day he began on his nose, watching his face and hands reflected in the mirror as he injected Novocain into the nasal tissues and around the bridge of his nose beneath each eye.

Within a few minutes he could no longer feel his nose, and within ten minutes he could not feel exploratory pricks with a sterile pin, and he was ready.

He held the scalpel up in his rubber-gloved right hand, took a deep breath, and leaning close to the mirror, began his first incision inside the right nasal passage, separating the upper tissue from the cartilage.

Blood spurted down on his hand, splattering the table, and some of it ran down the back of his throat, causing him to momentarily choke.

His head was spinning as he put the scalpel down, swabbed out the area of the incision with cotton, and, with shaking hands, clamped off the two major bleeders.

He could not do this. Sharpenberg had been correct. A doctor, no matter how good he was, simply could not operate on himself.

But he stared at his reflection in the mirror for a long time, blood down his chin and in his mouth, the clamps hanging obscenely from his mutilated nostril, and again he took a deep breath. He had run out of options. This was the only way. And after a while he continued, slowly, carefully, cutting tissue away from cartilage, and finally removing an entire section of both the left and right nostrils, leaving large, empty cavities high beneath the bridge.

The Novocain began to wear off within the hour after the first incision, and the pain came at him in waves, until he gave himself more injections.

During the second hour of the operation his eyes began to swell shut, and he had to stop long enough to inject the area with mild muscle relaxant, so that he could see to continue.

In the third hour his stomach began acting up, the bile rising up his throat to gag him.

And in the fourth and final hour he began losing control of his hands, his work becoming less and less precise, his vision going double.

He had begun at 5:00, and at 10:00 P.M. he had inserted the last of the silicone implants, had taken the last of the stitches, and had fallen off the chair in a faint. He lay unconscious on the cabin floor until seven o'clock the next morning, his face swollen and on fire.

In two weeks the swelling in all but his nose had subsided, although his eyes and cheeks would remain deeply bruised for at least another month. Most of the major pain had passed, and he had again built up his system to begin on his lips, this operation easier and less painful.

During those two weeks he had monitored the progress of the President's World Peace Proposal, marveling at the fact that not one voice had been raised in question about Engstrom's extraordinary commission. The names of the men sounded to Kelsey like a litany of his father's old cronies. Most of the names he had heard his father mention at one time or another over the years. But what was most incredible to Kelsey was that his own father had been appointed to the commission to represent the United States. The father of the man who supposedly assassinated President Barnes was serving on such a commission? It was unbelievable, except it was happening.

For ten days after he had inserted the silicone implants

in both his upper and lower lips, Kelsey was unable to eat anything but lukewarm soup, and on the first day he tried eating solid foods, he vomited. But when his stomach had calmed down he had tried again, keeping a little of the macaroni and cheese inside of him.

From that moment until he began on his cheeks, his recovery went fast.

At times during the long winter mornings and the days when he was supposed to be sleeping, Kelsey sat huddled in his bed, listening to the radio, too deeply in pain to sleep even with pills. The loneliness during these times was crushing, and the pain deep inside his soul at the loss of Marion was even worse than the terrible physical pain. He would rock himself back and forth like a small child with a toothache, the motion somehow soothing, and listen mindlessly to the music and news broadcasts, waiting out the hours until it was time to take another of his severely limited supply of painkillers. Waiting for the time when the operations would be completed, and he would not have to feel the constant pain, the constant headaches, the constant nausea.

The United Nations General Assembly was called into special session on February 15, a little more than two months after Barnes had been assassinated, and the first evening on which Kelsey had been able to skip a painkiller.

The operations were completed, most of the swelling had gone down, and his hair had grown back over his ears, hiding the angry red postop scars.

He felt like he had been run over by a truck, but the impossible part was over now, and each day he could feel his strength coming back, and each day he had to avoid thinking about the future.

This night, however, his future came crashing down on him with the first news on the UN meeting that had been called by the World Peace Commission on behalf of President Engstrom.

"World peace is finally and at long last within the grasp

of mankind." Engstrom spoke from the United Nations. The broadcast was coming live from the General Assembly, and Kelsey sat in front of the bay windows, which looked over a completely ice-locked Lake Michigan, and listened.

"I am inviting the leaders of all the world governments and their representatives to meet here one month from this day on March fifteenth, to sign a World Peace Government Charter.

"I am telling the peoples of the world on this day that I and members of my World Peace Commission have worked these months toward a goal that mankind has striven for since the dawn of time.

"I am telling the peoples of the world on this day that I have personally spoken with most of the world's leaders, who have agreed in principle to this concept of everlasting peace.

"And I am telling the peoples of the world on this day that I will call for the creation of a legislative world governing body composed of the kings and queens, the prime ministers and presidents, from the world over. One government, under one flag, unified under one legislature for world unity and everlasting peace."

It was happening, Kelsey thought, just as his father had wanted it to. Incredibly, awesomely, it was happening, and he had thirty days to stop it. One man against an entire world.

He wondered briefly what threats Engstrom and his World Peace Commission—which was nothing more than a new name for the Odessa—had made worldwide in order to insure success for their insane plan.

Instant annihilation? Nuclear holocaust? Biological war?

Whatever it was, Kelsey knew in his soul that it would work, that the world's leaders would indeed meet at the United Nations in one month's time. The entire world would be there or watching, and so would Kelsey. Only he would be there for a different purpose.

32

It was the evening of March 11, and the snow that had fallen most of the day had finally stopped, but the wind still howled around the corners of the cabin, rattling the windows and shrieking off the rocky lakeshore.

Kelsey had gotten up four hours ago to begin his final preparations, and now he came out of the bathroom, nude, padded across the main room to the bedroom alcove, and looked at himself in the full-length mirror on the closet door.

His hair was a black, kinky mass from the hair coloring and perm kits he had purchased at an all-night drugstore near Madison, Wisconsin, three months ago.

His eyebrow line was thick, giving his entire forehead a flattened look. His cheeks were high and sharply arched. His nose was broad and flat, flaring widely at the nostrils. And his lips were heavy, jutting away from his mouth.

The dye that he had concocted from the back walnuts and the leftover hair coloring had stained his entire body a rich chocolate brown, and stepping closer to the mirror so that he could study his face, he was satisfied that the dye had completely blended the remaining bruises around his eyes and nose with his skin color.

He smiled at his reflection, his teeth gleaming white in sharp contrast to his skin.

"Salese Kotura." Kelsey spoke his new name aloud, inflecting his voice with a British accent as best he could. "From the independent African state of Botswana, at your service, sir."

He stepped back again from the mirror and began to shiver. It was insane. What he was doing was totally insane. Even if he was able to make it to New York by the fifteenth, there would be tens of thousands of people jammed everywhere in and around the UN building. On the one hand, the crowds would provide him with a cover. Who would pay any more than scant attention to another African black man? But on the other hand, the crowds would effectively insulate President Engstrom.

He turned away from the bedroom alcove and went back to the kitchen table, where he had left his clothes.

Over the past three months, during the terrible pain he had endured, Kelsey's convictions had begun to diminish. At times he wanted to give it all up. What would it matter if his father and men like him finally won?

But on the night of the first UN broadcast, Kelsey's convictions had been renewed. Once the world charter went into effect, it would perhaps mean world peace, but it would also mark the beginning of world enslavement, the end, perhaps forever, of any kind of freedom.

Over the past three months he had thought about Colleen and Marion constantly. In his mind they had combined into one woman, one love, and one deep ache inside of him. His father had killed them both. His father and men like him would continue the killing until the world was as they wanted it.

Perhaps the final solution of the Jews would begin again.

Or maybe the black man would be eliminated.

Kelsey looked at his own hands and could feel rage building inside of him.

He had come this far, and he was not going to quit. Somehow he would not only make it to New York within the next four days, he would get close enough to Engstrom so that if there was no other way, he would strangle the man with his bare hands.

Kelsey reached for his underwear when a high-pitched whining sound rose over the noise of the wind and then faded. He held his breath, straining to listen for the sound, his right hand on the edge of the table, his heart pounding. And the sound came again, this time louder, apparently much closer.

A snowmobile, he realized. For a moment he lost the sound again, but then it was back, much louder, and he could hear that there were at least two of them.

He raced around the table to the kitchen cabinet where the loaded pistol had lain for three months, grabbed it, and then flipped off the lights in the main room and bathroom before he went to the back door and peered cautiously out the window.

At first he could see nothing in the darkness except for the swirling, blowing snow curling around the long drifts down the driveway that led to the main highway. But then he saw two single headlights bobbing and weaving down the road, and the wind blew the whining noise of the machines his way.

His brain raced as fast as his heart. Somehow they had found out he was here. Probably from Sharpenberg. And another stab of fear hit his gut.

Sam would never have told them a thing unless he had somehow been forced into it. And the force it would have taken to move Sharpenberg into doing anything he did not want to do would have been harsh.

There were two men, one on each machine, both of them

dressed in dark snowmobile suits, heavy boots and thick mittens, and dark helmets. They stopped about twenty yards from the back of the cabin, shut off the headlights and engines, and headed on foot toward the cabin, one of them swinging around toward the front.

If he remained here, he might take one of them out, he knew, but not both.

He turned away from the back window and hurried into the bathroom, sweat suddenly rolling down his chest. Setting the gun down on the toilet seat, he unlatched the bathroom window and pulled it, but it was stuck.

One of the men came up on the back porch, and then there was silence as Kelsey renewed his efforts to open the small window.

Suddenly it came free and swung inward, banging against the bathroom wall. Kelsey froze.

There was a noise at the front porch, and he could hear someone trying to open the front door.

Grabbing the pistol, Kelsey climbed up on the tiny bathroom sink and pushed his way out the narrow window, falling out into a snowbank, scraping his shins, and nearly screaming with the shock of the cold snow and wind on his bare body.

A moment later he scrambled to his feet and hurried around to the corner of the cabin, not worried about making any noise now over the shrieking of the wind.

He cocked the pistol and peeked around the corner of the cabin in time to see a man getting ready to ram the back door with his shoulder. He stepped around the corner, raised the gun, and fired twice, the silenced pistol making almost no noise. The heavily dressed man spun around and fell backward down the steps.

Kelsey raced to where the man was sprawled in a heap in a snowbank at the foot of the stairs, and rolled him over. His eyes were open and glassy, and Kelsey was about to reach inside the collar of the man's suit to check for a pulse when something slammed into his left arm, knocking him on his back in the snow.

He looked up in time to see the second man barging out the back door, firing his gun, and something hot grazed Kelsey's side, causing him to cry out in pain.

Blindly he raised his own pistol and began firing as fast as he could pull the trigger. The man jerked once to the right and tried to raise his own gun, but then was flung backward through the screen door, and still Kelsey fired up at the house, until the hammer fell with a click on an empty chamber.

The pistol slipped from Kelsey's hand and he fell back in the snow, his body screaming in pain from his wounds as well as the freezing cold.

They had come for him. They knew he was here, and they had come to kill him. They had probably already killed Sharpenberg and perhaps everyone else at the clinic for helping him. Which meant that they knew what he was up to. They knew about the medical supplies and they probably knew about his operations.

He screamed into the night, his voice drowned out by the wind, and he felt himself going faint, drifting away.

If he remained here, he would die. It would be as simple as that. His father would have won.

He forced his battered body up, staggered to his feet, and lurched drunkenly up the steps, falling over the body of the man half in the cabin and half out.

Crawling on his hands and knees Kelsey managed to drag the dead man's body inside so that he could close the door. He went to his medical kit in the bathroom, where he fumbled out a hypodermic syringe that he filled with a stimulant. He plunged the needle into his hip and forced the drug into his bloodstream, then waited, counting by thousands to ten when suddenly his head began to clear in waves, almost like taking a cold shower on a hot day.

His left arm was numb and hung uselessly at his side. A

quick examination told Kelsey that the bullet had gone completely through the flesh, missing most of the major muscles and completely missing the bones.

The wound in his side was nothing more than a graze, although he would be sore for a week.

He shivered violently from the cold and the delayed reaction of shock by the time he finished bandaging his side and his left arm, in which the feeling was beginning to return.

The pain was excruciating, although it was nothing in comparison to the pain he had endured during his operations, and he decided against any painkillers.

They knew he was there now, and when these two did not report back, others would come looking. He got dressed, being careful not to bump his side or his wounded arm.

When he was ready he went back outside and dragged the body of the man by the back porch into the house and searched his pockets, coming up with a couple of hundred dollars and several credit cards under the name of Felsen Holding, Inc., which was a subsidiary of his father's electronics firm.

The other dead man's pockets contained less than a hundred dollars and only one credit card under the name of Felsen Holding, but Kelsey found a set of car keys.

The stimulant was doing its work, and although he was in pain and he felt light-headed, he was thinking clearly.

Their car was probably up on the highway from where they had taken the snowmobiles the final mile down the snow-blocked driveway. He would make his escape the same way they had come for him.

Kelsey dressed in one of the snowmobile suits after he had packed his remaining medical supplies, the dark jacket he had worn when he first came here, and one of the guns he had taken from the dead man. The other gun he stuck in his belt beneath the bulky suit.

He had nearly five hundred dollars in cash plus several

credit cards, so getting to New York and making his final preparations would not be difficult.

Before he turned off the cabin lights, Kelsey took a quick look around to make sure there would be nothing here to give away his purpose, forgetting completely about the first volume of the desk encyclopedia he had found in the bedroom alcove. The book was lying open on the floor next to the bed, at the heading *Botswana*.

Outside, he trudged across the yard to where the snowmobiles were parked and climbed on one of them, wedging the cloth sack in front of him.

The machine started instantly, and Kelsey headed as fast as he dared back up the driveway toward the highway. Parked on the side of the road was a dark, medium-sized, nondescript Buick sedan with a double-wide snowmobile trailer hooked to a bumper hitch.

Kelsey left the machine below the road, out of sight in the ditch, and carrying the bag with his things, scrambled up to the road and threw it on the front seat. He struggled out of the snowmobile suit before he slid in behind the wheel.

He started the car and got the heater going, then stuffed the snowmobile suit in the backseat, pulled the jacket out of the bag, and struggled it on, having trouble for just a moment with his wounded arm.

With shaking hands, Kelsey put the car in gear, made a careful U-turn on the highway, and headed southwest back down the peninsula.

33

Kelsey had originally planned driving directly to Green Bay, sixty-five miles southwest of Sharpenberg's cabin, and there abandoning the car and taking a flight to New York City. But it was past one in the morning by the time he arrived in Green Bay, and the airport was deserted, not even the coffee shop open, so he had pushed on, heading toward Milwaukee, another hundred miles or so south.

A few miles below Green Bay, Kelsey stopped long enough to give himself another shot of stimulant from his nearly exhausted supply. He unhooked the snowmobile trailer in a closed wayside park on the shore of Lake Michigan.

The wind had finally died down, and there was a lot less snow on the ground by the time Kelsey finally pulled into Milwaukee. It was five in the morning, and he was exhausted and hungry when he parked behind an all-night diner on the north side of the city.

He sat down at the booth and ordered breakfast from a black waitress who flashed him a smile.

"Where you from anyway, good-lookin'?" the young woman asked.

Kelsey looked wearily up at her, confused. "Pardon me?" he said.

The woman looked at him strangely for a moment, then went away. He went into the bathroom to splash cold water on his face. A black man stared back at him in the mirror, and Kelsey almost turned around to see who was standing behind him when he realized that *he* was the black man, which explained the waitress's friendliness.

Back at his booth he waited until the waitress came with his food and then he managed a smile, and remembered his British accent. "Sorry, love, I'm just a bit tired."

"Sure," the woman said, setting his plates down in front of him, and then she left.

He was going to have to watch himself carefully. Once he got to New York, he was going to have to remember who he was now. He was no longer Dr. Richard Kelsey, white, well-to-do plastic surgeon. He was a black man. An African.

After he had eaten his breakfast he felt somewhat better, although he was deeply tired, and before he left the diner, he called North Central Airlines and found out that the first flight direct to New York left Milwaukee's Mitchell Field at 7:00 A.M. He made reservations in the name of Robert Smith, the best he could do in his condition.

Downtown, Kelsey found a parking ramp where he left his car on the top level, hiding the guns and his remaining medical supplies in the trunk after giving himself the last of the stimulant. Then he threw the keys in a trash bin on the first level, walked four blocks until he found a cab waiting in front of a hotel, and ordered the driver to take him out to the airport.

The remainder of that day, the twelfth, seemed unreal to

Kelsey, fighting off the effects of his operations, his gunshot wounds, his lack of sleep, and the cumulative effects of the stimulant on his overworked heart.

He slept fitfully off and on during the flight to New York, then made his way to the cab stands at the front of the terminal.

The midday sun was bright although the weather was cool, and he was nearly on the verge of collapse when he slipped into the backseat of the first cab.

"Where to, buddy?" the driver said, half-turned in his seat.

"I need a hotel," Kelsey mumbled. He tried to make his brain work. Tried to think out what his moves would be over the next few days. There were several items he needed, and he would have to have security. "Harlem," he told the driver. "I need an inexpensive hotel in Harlem."

"Out, nigger," the driver said.

Kelsey just looked at the man, in a daze.

"I said get the fuck outta my cab, nigger. I don't do Harlem."

Kelsey started to protest, and the cabby raised his voice.

"You want me to call a cop and I will. You've gotta be on something, so I don't think you want trouble. You want to get to Harlem, get yourself a spade driver. Now, get the fuck outta my cab."

He mumbled his apologies, got out of the cab, and four taxis down a long row, found one with a black driver, who agreed to take him into Harlem.

Only vaguely did he understand what was happening to him when the driver helped him into a lobby, took some money from him, and an old man helped him into an elevator and then into a bed. And then he dreamed.

He was running through the snow naked, but for some strange reason, he was burning up. Far ahead of him he could see a woman being beaten up by two large men. They were hitting her over the head with large clubs. But no matter how fast Kelsey ran, he could not seem to get any closer. He was sure that he knew the woman, but he could not see her face in the distance, and yet he was frightened because he knew that the two men would kill her before he could come to her rescue.

He was also aware, from time to time, of a flashing orange light, and twice there seemed to be someone standing over him, asking him questions, and feeding him, but he was never sure if that was part of the dream or of reality.

And then he awoke, the sun streaming in the window, and the first thing he was aware of was a large, jagged crack that ran completely across a dirty, plastered ceiling. He sat up in bed with a start, his head spinning and his left arm throbbing.

"You into some pretty heavy shit, my man."

Kelsey snapped around toward the sound of the voice, the motion causing a wave of dizziness and nausea to course through his body. But when his head cleared he could see an old black man, his face vaguely familiar, leaning against the doorframe. The door was open.

"Where am I?" Kelsey said, the words croaking out of his dry throat.

The old man laughed. "Where is he indeed." He laughed again. "My good man, you are in paradise. That is, the Paradise Hotel in the heart of Harlem. Where'd you think you were?"

Kelsey stared at the old man for a long time, until he became aware that he was wearing no clothes. His eyes flicked around the room, and he saw that his trousers and jacket were lying over a chair, and his shirt lay crumpled in a heap atop the bureau.

"You were in powerful bad shape when you showed up on my doorstep, my man. And I suppose you've been up to some kind of no good."

Again Kelsey turned to the old man. "How long have I been here?" he asked. His kidneys ached almost as badly as his left arm, and he felt weak and dragged out.

The old man laughed even louder, "I'd say just about two hundred and eighty-nine dollars and sixty-seven cents worth, that's how long you been here."

Kelsey's eyes flicked to his clothes.

"Yup," the old man said. "Got every last cent of it. But then I don't suppose you'd be turning old Abraham in to the police now, would you? No, don't think that's hardly so."

Kelsey flipped back the covers and carefully got out of bed, the room spinning around for several moments, and then he sat back down. "What day is it?"

"What day indeed," the old man said. "Why, it's the day of reckoning, I suppose. The fifteenth day of March."

For several long seconds what the old man said did not sink in, but when it did the information hit Kelsey hard, and he struggled again to his feet, his knees weak, his stomach flopping over, and his head threatening to burst at the seams.

It was today. This day. He had been unconscious for the better part of three days.

"Hold on now," the old man said, and he came all the way into the room and helped Kelsey sit back down on the bed.

"The World Peace meeting," Kelsey said. "When is it scheduled for?"

The old man looked down at him, his face seemingly at the end of a long tunnel. "What you saying?" he said, his voice far away.

"The big meeting at the UN. When is it?"

"I suppose it's happening right now," the old man said. "It's all honky bullshit anyway."

Kelsey pushed away the old man's hands and once again got to his feet, this time the dizziness and nausea coming at him less strongly. "I've got to get out of here. I need a gun and some clothes." Kelsey tried to make his brain work. What was it they called the robes? Then he had it. "Muslim robes. That's what I need. Black Muslim robes."

The old man stepped back as if he had been slapped, and Kelsey took a step toward him.

"You've got to help me. Please. There'll be money in it for you. Lots of money."

"Money?" the old man said, obvious interest in his eyes.

"Can you get it for me? I need a gun, too."

"You're talking big money, my man. Even if it is for the brotherhood," the old man said.

Kelsey lurched forward and grabbed the man's shirt. "I'm talking five thousand dollars if you can get the stuff there within the hour. Five grand."

The old man licked his lips. "You just a jive turkey. You got no money like that."

Kelsey tried to make his brain work. "Money," he said. "You've got my credit cards. Felsen Holding Company. That's the big time. I work for them. They've got the money."

"You the token nigger?"

"I'm the goddamned owner," Kelsey shouted. "One hour. Five grand."

The old man looked at him.

"Please . . ." Kelsey cried. "God . . . please, you've got to help me before it's too late."

"I believe I will, brother," the old man said, moved. "I do believe I will."

The cold winter wind blew up the East River, whipping the water into whitecaps and blowing the robes of Salese Kotura, one of the emissaries from the African nation of Botswana, as he got out of the cab in front of the UN headquarters building.

Thousands of people jammed the driveways and parking lots, and soldiers and police were everywhere.

"Botswana," Kelsey said to the cordon of police guards around the front entrance as he pushed his way through the crowd. He had no idea what procedures were being used to check in the delegates, nor did he know if what he was doing would work. He just had to try.

A harried cop looked up at Kelsey and shook his head. "Your delegation is already here . . ." he started to say, but then stopped in midsentence. "Botswana?" he asked.

Kelsey nodded, his heart hammering.

"Moment, sir," the guard said, looking through a list. A moment later the man looked up, a smile on his face. "Your delegation is inside, sir. You'll have to go in and get your credentials."

"Of course," Kelsey said.

The crowd was pressed to within a few feet of the security station just outside the main doors, and they were shouting and screaming, some of them watching Kelsey with curiosity.

"Just inside," the guard was saying. "You'll see the credentials desk to the right."

And incredibly Kelsey found himself passing through the doors inside the UN building, and he stopped short. Ten feet inside the front doorway his father and several other men were deep in discussion.

Kelsey moved slowly toward the right, but his father turned and glanced his way, and then looked again. A moment later he said something to the men he was with, broke away, and came over to Kelsey.

For a long moment both men stared into each other's eyes, and then the elder Kelsey motioned for his son to follow him.

It was all over. He had failed. And now he was going to his death. All those thoughts ran tiredly through Kelsey's brain, but he did not care any longer. His father had gestured for him to follow, and he found himself following the old man across the main lobby, down a crowded corridor, and finally into a small office.

The old man closed the door behind them, then turned to

stare at his son. "Ingenious," he said after a long moment. "We knew you'd be coming as a representative of Botswana, but we never dreamed you'd be coming as a black man."

Kelsey stared dully at his father.

"I expected as much from you, Richard," the old man said with fatherly pride in his voice. "Your only mistake was the desk encyclopedia you left open back at Sharpenberg's cabin. It gave us the clue. But you're too late." He glanced at his watch. "In five minutes Engstrom is going to be speaking to the General Assembly, and when he is finished the world will be ours."

"Why?" Kelsey croaked. He was on the verge of collapse, his body on fire.

"World peace," the old man said, but Kelsey was shaking his head.

"Why did you kill Colleen and then Marion? Why, Father?"

A look of pain crossed the old man's features, and he took a step forward and laid his right hand on his son's shoulder.

"I did not want to do that to you, Richard. If it would have been within my power, it would not have happened. None of this would have happened."

"Then stop it," Kelsey said with passion. "Please stop it before it's too late."

The elder Kelsey shook his head. "It's already too late."

Kelsey looked into his father's eyes. "How did you know it was me out there?"

The old man's face contorted into a friendly grin. "You could never hide from me. I'd know you anywhere."

"No!" Kelsey shouted, and he pushed his father's hand away from his shoulder. "Stop this now, Father! I beg you, before it's too late."

"I can't, Richard," the old man said.

Kelsey backed away. "Then I'll stop it," he said. He

reached inside his robe and pulled out the .38 snub-nosed revolver the old man at the hotel had given him.

His father stepped back and reached for the phone on the desk, but Kelsey was on him instantly, shoving him aside.

The old man lost his balance and was flung to the floor, his head bouncing on the bare tiles with a sickening thud. A moment later blood poured over the floor, and Kelsey was beside his father.

"Dad," he cried. "Jesus, what have I done?"

The old man's eyes were half-closed, his breathing shallow. "Richard," he whispered.

Kelsey felt for his father's heartbeat, which was weak and erratic. "I'll get an ambulance," he said, but his father grabbed his son's arm.

"Eagles fly," he whispered, the words half dying in his throat.

"An ambulance," Kelsey said, but his father's head rose up out of the growing puddle of blood.

"Eagles fly," the old man croaked. "The key . . . eagles fly . . ." And then he slumped back to the floor, his grip on Kelsey's arm loosening and falling away, the final breath wheezing out of his body.

"Father?" Kelsey cried. "Father?" But the old man was still.

After a long time Kelsey was aware of Engstrom's voice speaking from overhead, and he looked up. The General Assembly speech was being piped into this room.

He put the pistol back in his robe, and then gently picked his father up, mindless of the hurt in his arm and side. Carrying the old man's frail body, he trudged out of the office and down the corridor toward the huge doors that led into the General Assembly.

Only a few people were left in the corridor, and they shrank away from Kelsey carrying the bloody body of his father. At the doors to the General Assembly, two guards stepped forward and one of them started to speak, but Kelsey cut them off.

"This is the body of August Kelsey, a member of the World Peace Commission. Step aside."

Eagles fly. The two words screamed in Kelsey's brain. He had no idea what they meant, he only knew that his father had given them to him as a dying legacy. A gift for his only son. And he would use them, even if it meant the end for him.

The guards fell back, and one of them opened the doors.

Kelsey strode into the huge hall and carried his father down the wide center aisle until he came out from under the low ceiling that supported the press rooms and gallery above, and then he was in the assembly hall proper.

As he walked it was as if he were moving in a pocket of silence that followed him, like a seashore wave that paused on the beach and then rebuilt to a murmur behind him.

Halfway down the aisle, Engstrom, standing at the podium with the huge UN symbol on the wall behind him, stopped his speech and watched Kelsey coming.

Engstrom turned and said something to a uniformed man seated behind him. A half-dozen guards carrying rifles converged on Kelsey, who stopped about a hundred feet from Engstrom.

Kelsey looked up at the man, and even from this distance he knew that the President was an imposter. He had known the man as James Locke. But he was certain that the man had gone under many different names in the past.

The armed guards nearest Kelsey were raising their guns now, and Kelsey, not knowing what he was doing, only following the last words his father had spoken to him, shouted at the top of his lungs: "Eagles Fly!"

Engstrom stiffened, almost as if he had been slapped, and Kelsey screamed again.

"Eagles Fly!"

"Yes, sir," Engstrom shouted. The guards racing toward

Kelsey stopped in midstride and looked uncertainly back toward the podium.

"Eagles Fly!" Kelsey screamed a third time.

"*Jawohl, mein Herr,*" Engstrom's voice thundered through the General Assembly.

"Who are you?" Kelsey shouted.

"Reinhardt Mueller," Engstrom's voice boomed over the PA system.

"Where were you born?" Kelsey yelled.

"Leipzig, Germany," Engstrom snapped, his body at rigid attention.

"Who do you work for?" Kelsey screamed, his father's body slipping from his arms and falling to the floor.

"*Der Organisation der ehemaligen SS Angehörigen*" Engstrom shouted proudly.

Epilogue

It was late summer and Kelsey, fully recovered now from his reconstructive operations, got out of his car and trudged up the narrow path between the gravestones, finally stopping at two small markers.

He had just come from the grave of his father, and earlier today Sam Sharpenberg's, and now he stood looking down at these two tablets, tears coming freely to his eyes.

One of the stones read:

> Colleen Susan Kelsey
> Née Stewart
> 1952–1979

The other read:

> Marion Elizabeth Kelsey
> Née Bloggs
> 1949–1982   He remained by the graves for a

long time, conscious of nothing other than his own deeply aching heart. For a while he let his mind wander down the corridors of time because finally he had been able to separate his memories of both women.

And for a time he was almost happy in his thoughts of the two women he had loved, but then his remembrances turned to the happenings of the past two months.

All the members of the so-called World Peace Commission, other than his father, had somehow managed to escape. No one as yet knew where they were. Nor, Kelsey thought, was anyone trying very hard to find them. Everyone wanted to forget.

Engstrom, or actually the man named Mueller, had told the entire world the story that day under Kelsey's questionings. The revelation had shaken the U.S. government, but within a few weeks everything had begun to return to normal.

The world, Kelsey thought, looking up finally, was all right after very nearly failing. And despite the accolades that had been heaped on him, he had escaped most of the notoriety by keeping a low profile.

But what he was going to do from this day on, he had no idea.

He turned away from the gravestones, and a dark-skinned, good-looking woman stood a few feet down the path. She had been watching him.

He stared at her for a long time before he moved away from the graves and walked down to her.

"Hello," he said. "Do I know you?"

"I don't think so," the woman said. "But I would like to express my sympathy at your loss." She had an accent Kelsey could not define.

He hung his head. "Thank you," he said. He looked up again at the woman. She had a pretty face.

"My name is Deborah Asheim," the woman said, the name meaning nothing to Kelsey. "I was sent to talk to you. To ask for your help."